Praise for *New York Times* bestselling author
CELESTE BRADLEY
and her previous novels and series

DUKE MOST WANTED

"Passionate and utterly memorable. Witty dialogue and
fantastic imagery round out a novel that is a must-have
for any Celeste Bradley fan."   —*Romance Junkies*

"A marvelous, delightful, emotional conclusion to Bradley's trilogy. Readers have been eagerly waiting to see
what happens next, and they've also been anticipating a
nonstop, beautifully crafted story, which Bradley delivers
in spades."   —*Romantic Times BOOKreviews*

THE DUKE NEXT DOOR

"This spectacular, fast-paced, sexy romance will have you
in laughter and tears. With delightful characters seeking
love and a title, [this] heartfelt romance will make readers sigh with pleasure."

—*Romantic Times BOOKreviews*

"Not only fun and sexy but relentlessly pulls at the heart-
strings. Ms. Bradley has set the bar quite high with this
one!"   —*Romance Readers Connection*

MORE...

DESPERATELY SEEKING A DUKE

"A humorous romp of marriage mayhem that's a love-and-laughter treat, tinged with heated sensuality and tenderness. [A] winning combination."

—*Romantic Times BOOKreviews*

"A tale of lies and treachery where true love overcomes all."

—*Romance Junkies*

SEDUCING THE SPY

"Thrilling up to the last page, titillating from one sexually charged love scene to the next, and captivating from beginning to end, the last of the Royal Four series displays Bradley's ability to tell an involved, sexy story. If you haven't yet read a Bradley novel, let yourself be seduced by the mistress of the genre!"

—*Romantic Times BOOKreviews*

"Have you discovered the bawdy charms of Celeste Bradley? Laced with intrigue and adventure, she has quickly become a staff and reader favorite and with each book we just fall further in love with her characters. This is the final book in the superb Royal Four quartet, with her most dangerous deception yet!"

—*Rendezvous*

THE ROGUE

TO WED A SCANDALOUS SPY

St. Martin's Paperbacks Titles by
CELESTE BRADLEY

THE HEIRESS BRIDES
Desperately Seeking a Duke
The Duke Next Door
The Duke Most Wanted

THE ROYAL FOUR
To Wed a Scandalous Spy
Surrender to a Wicked Spy
One Night with a Spy
Seducing the Spy

THE LIAR'S CLUB
The Pretender
The Impostor
The Spy
The Charmer
The Rogue

DEVIL IN MY BED

Celeste Bradley

St. Martin's Paperbacks

This is a work of fiction. All of the characters, organizations, and events portrayed in this novel are either products of the author's imagination or are used fictitiously.

DEVIL IN MY BED

Copyright © 2009 by Celeste Bradley.
Excerpt from *Rogue in My Arms* copyright © 2009 by Celeste Bradley.

All rights reserved.

For information address St. Martin's Press, 175 Fifth Avenue, New York, NY 10010.

ISBN: 978-0-312-94308-0

Printed in the United States of America

St. Martin's Paperbacks edition / August 2009

St. Martin's Paperbacks are published by St. Martin's Press, 175 Fifth Avenue, New York, NY 10010.

10 9 8 7 6 5 4 3 2 1

In memory of Jack Bird, at whose desk I write.

ACKNOWLEDGMENTS

I could not have drawn Melody so convincingly if not for the help of little Frankie Jean Baca-Lucero and her moms. Frankie, of all the three-year-old big-eyed tornadoes out there, you are the coolest! In addition, I could not have managed the last year without my patient, tolerant and lovingly supportive friends and family: Joanne M., Robyn H., Cynthia T., Darbi G., and Cheryl L. Thank you all for the endless hours on the phone.

Good agents are hard to come by and good friends are even harder. My very special thanks to Irene Goodman, agent and angel.

And always, to my beautiful girls, thank you for the joy you bring me.

PROLOGUE

Did every woman want to vomit on her wedding day? Lady Melody shuddered. Well, perhaps not *that*. Perhaps only to run screeching in tight circles, waving her arms and gibbering madly until someone force-fed her a few stiff brandies and sat upon her for awhile?

The mirror she gazed into had no answer for her. Idiot glass.

The window behind her betrayed only the faintest of dawn's pale beginnings, yet there was no dismissing the fact that her wedding day had most definitely begun. She was still in her dressing gown, her hair still down around her shoulders like a child. Noting the faint trace of freckles that remained across her nose in the mirror, Melody felt as though she wasn't really a woman at all, much less a bride.

In only a few hours she was to be married in the opulent chapel where her ancestors had been wed for centuries. So grand a chapter in a life which had begun so invisibly. She'd been found, she felt, not born. Even she had no real memory of the life before this one. It was as if she'd appeared out of thin air somewhere around her third birthday.

She tried to picture herself walking down that aisle

clad in satin, ready to give herself away forever. Unfortunately, being at home on the family estate only reinforced the impression that she'd never grown up at all.

Nerves made her hands shake until she clasped them together before her.

Her maid was busy by the grand fireplace, pouring great brass pails of steaming water into the hammered copper tub and adding scented herbs for a soothing bath.

Melody closed her eyes, sure that there was not enough hot water in all of England to warm the chill ball of anxiety in her belly. "What if I'm wrong? What if he isn't the right man?"

"You're not a child, my dear." The crisp voice behind her belonged not to her maid but to the man who had created her wedding gown. Her father had insisted upon the best for her, and Lementeur was the very best mantua-maker in all of England. He was also a long-time family friend.

Melody opened her eyes to meet his in the mirror. The world might know him as Lementeur, that arbiter of fashion for England's most elite, but since early childhood she'd always called him simply Button.

He certainly looked the part. He was short and crisply elegant, with the crinkles of years of humorous observation about his eyes and the silver hair to match it.

Despite her anxiety, she could not help smiling at the picture of the very small man swathed in her very long veil. "Sorry about that. Her ladyship insisted that it trail halfway down the aisle."

"Hmph. Well, *your* ladyship ought to have stood your ground. It is your wedding. This—" He hefted it off himself impatiently, his arms extended entirely upward and still not long enough to hold the miles of net off the carpet. "This extravagance almost treads on poor taste." Then he smiled and smoothed the veil gently. "How delicious, that balancing point between luxury and vulgarity. You'll start a whole new fashion. I think I'll invest in a laceworks."

"Another? I thought you owned one already."

"I own two, actually, but one that exclusively produces wedding veils . . ." He trailed off in thoughts of cornering the lace market. Then he finally seemed to notice her malaise. "Mellie, whatever is the matter?"

Melody twisted her clasped hands in anxiety. "Button, I'm not so certain—"

He placed her veil upon its specially constructed stand and came up behind her. His blue eyes held her nearly matching ones in the mirror. "Pet, you are sure. You're mad for the fellow and, of course, he's entirely smitten with you."

She shook her head, unwilling to be so easily reassured. "How can I know? The whole courtship was so complicated. Shouldn't these matters be simple if they're truly meant to be?"

He turned her then to gaze into her eyes, his own crinkled in amusement. He was so dear. She felt her anxiety begin to ease. "Mellie, my darling, don't you realize that you come by your tendency toward complications honestly? You've quite the family history of circuitous romance. From the very beginning, even before your parents met—well, perhaps I ought not to carry tales."

She leaned into his embrace and lay her head on his shoulder, as she had so many times in her life. For a moment she longed to be a little girl again, to live in simpler, easier times. "Carry tales, Button." She closed her eyes. "Tell me a story." Anything to still her wildly contradictory thoughts!

She heard him chuckle, then take a deep breath. "Well, I suppose there's time." He led her to sit on the small settee near the fire and nestled her into his side like a child, though she was a bit taller than he. She let her eyelids close out the view of the wedding preparations. Her chambers were far from the pomp and madness elsewhere in the house. If she shut out all thought and simply listened the crackle of the small fire in the hearth, she could pretend, just for a moment, that this exciting, taxing day was still far, far in her future and that she was just a little girl hearing a favorite tale.

"Once upon a time," Button went on, his voice low and soothing, "there was a man who had everything. He was rich and handsome and wellborn, yet there was something missing in his life."

Melody smiled slightly. "Me."

Button laughed. "No interruptions, now. And no, not you, not quite yet. Now, one day this man was riding in his fine carriage down Bond Street, minding his own matters . . ."

1812, twenty-three years earlier
Her lithe figure caught Aidan's eye first, for he'd never been one to miss something lovely within his sight. He wasn't sure if the appeal lay in the turn of her shoulder or the fragile arch of her neck, but Aidan de Quincy, fifth Earl of Blankenship, found himself captivated by the

slender widow as she strode the opposite way down the walk.

She looked . . . determined, just by the briskness of her walk and the set of her chin beneath the black net veil.

You can tell so much from a quick look at her profile and a rather more lingering stare at her backside?

Aidan sat back in tufted velvet seat of his carriage, wondering if she could possibly be pretty enough to live up to that graceful figure. Probably not—

Furtive movement at the edge of his vision caught his attention and he leaned forward once more to peer through the square window at the teeming street outside. It looked as though he wasn't the only one to be snared by the allure of the lissome widow. Following her now was a man in dark, rough clothes with his cap pulled down over his eyes and a tendency to glance back over his shoulder a little too often.

When he shifted his attention back to the widow, Aidan caught a glimpse of an ivory cheek beneath the fluttering veil as the woman sent a worried glance over her own shoulder. Her renewed hurry indicated that she'd seen the man behind her and that she was alarmed by him. Intent on fleeing, she ducked into the nearest escape—a narrow alleyway between shops. The man followed her.

Damn.

There wasn't time to order the carriage turned about— or even to call it to a complete halt. Aidan simply opened his door, hung there a moment with one foot on the running board, and then flung himself into the busy street.

He kept his footing well enough on the slick cobbles but it was several breathtaking moments before he could dash and dodge his way through the oncoming carts and carriages to the other side of the street.

Aidan ran pell-mell for the mouth of the alley. Should he be calling for the watch? He doubted that the gouty old buzzards who served as watchmen would be any help at all, even if they managed to drag themselves there in time. No, better to appraise the situation himself first.

The situation, he found when he rounded the corner, was quite the classic tableau—a veritable cautionary tale of what became of unescorted ladies in lawless London.

Except that there was something wrong with this depiction. There was the thief, knife in hand—bloody hell, look at that knife!—with other hand held out to take what wasn't rightfully his. There was the lady, cowed and trembling, backing away in the dimness with her hands held up in supplication.

But she wasn't backing away at all. No, this lady was *advancing*—with a brick held threateningly high, no less!

Aidan wasn't the only one nonplussed. The thief had halted his obviously well-practiced routine and now seemed to waver in confusion, his knife hand dropping slightly.

Aidan shook off his own paralysis of wonder and moved forward swiftly. "You there!" he shouted.

The brick sailed through the air at that precise moment, even as the thief whirled toward Aidan's harsh command with his knife at the ready.

Aidan was helpless to stop his own reckless forward momentum. His boot soles slithered on cobbles slimed with years of best-not-dwell-upon-it while his horrified gaze riveted on the vicious gleam of the horrible curved blade pointed directly at his oncoming heart.

The brick missed the thief entirely but hit Aidan square in the shoulder—

Spinning him aside with not a moment to spare. His opposite fist, clenched from sheer terror, followed through on his spin to smash powerfully into the jaw of the startled thief. Aidan caromed off the brick wall of the neighboring building, barely managing to keep his feet.

I am a whirling dervish. How ridiculous I must look.

At the end of his wild spin, he blinked his gaze clear of dizziness to spy, with great surprise, that the thief lay face down in the ooze and the thief's knife lay in the hands of the willowy widow, who stood triumphantly over the fallen knave's body with her veil thrown back and blazing fury in her eyes.

Oh. My. God. She was lovely. Her features were delicate but dramatic, a queen carved in alabaster with huge dark brown eyes and full lips that gleamed richly red against her pale skin. Dark curls of fallen hair traced one perfectly carved cheekbone, gleaming nearly black in the dim alley. Her face more than matched her delicious figure. It surpassed it.

In that single breathless moment, Aidan was swept with a powerful urge he'd never before experienced. He had no thought in his mind except a ringing deep in his primal mind. *Must possess this woman. Must have her for my very own.*

Always.

Which was ridiculous, of course, mad beyond words, complete hogwash, and many other such dismissive phrases—until he'd nearly convinced himself that it was only the close call with danger that spurred such a violent, aching, acquisitive lust.

Then she raised her fiercely gleaming eyes to meet his gaze. "That," she said, satisfaction sizzling in her words, "was bloody brilliant!"

It was no use. He was a complete goner. Widow one, Aidan naught.

Like a fish hooked on a line, he moved toward her. He'd never been known as the sort of fellow to sweep a woman off her feet. Perhaps more the type to unwittingly intimidate—he preferred to think that rather than bore them to somnolence. Still, Aidan couldn't help feeling an absurdly romantic surge of heroic protectiveness as he bowed over the lady's hand.

Her gamine smile, her low, delicious laugh, the feeling of her slight hand lost in his large one—it was a heady combination. He liked the way she looked at him, as if he were nine feet tall and had dragon's blood dripping from his sword. Charming. His title might be envied, his wealth very nearly adored, but he'd never had someone gaze at him—him!—with quite that mix of amusement and admiration.

"St. George, I presume?"

She *was* mocking him, but for once in his life Aidan didn't mind being the butt of a jest, not if it bought him another moment of that husky laughter.

He bowed deeply as if sweeping his aforementioned dripping sword out of the way. "Sacrificial virgin, I presume?" God, had he truly said something so risqué to a respectable woman he'd not even been properly introduced to?

Luckily, his sally was rewarded with another laugh that made his chest expand and his groin tighten. Perhaps it was true that widows were much less likely to be offended than wives or maidens.

She bent to dust off her skirt and his mouth went dry at the grace of her willowy form and the vulnerability of the dainty curls on the back of her neck. She seemed so fragile, so in need of rescue and protection. Yet when she straightened, her eyes were bright and her chin high and proud. "Your assistance is most appreciated, good sir." With a brisk tug at the sleeves of her spencer and a swift maneuver of her fingers that swept her tousled hair neatly back into her bonnet, she removed all traces of her ordeal as if it had never happened.

As if *he* had never happened. She was preparing to walk away, he knew it. He ought to allow it, for he had no idea who or what she was. She was no one from his world, or he would have remembered her instantly. Just an ordinary woman in black, a war-time widow, as common in the city as ravens on the Tower of London. Yet, as she bobbed a quick curtsey and turned away, the words to stop her ripped from his throat through no will of his own.

"You ought never to walk alone." God, he sounded breathless and frantic, even to himself!

She froze in place, as if his ridiculous words meant something in particular to her. Then she turned to send an oddly shy glance over her shoulder. "Perhaps you should always walk with me, then." Her words were flirtatious, but her voice—ah, her voice was every bit as breathless and surprised as his own.

He'd tilted his head, a slow involuntary smile taking him over. "Perhaps I must."

After that, his recollection of the day was a blur. A ride in his carriage through Hyde Park; a dinner in a private dining room of a restaurant; a walk down the Promenade in the dark, hours after everyone else had departed. They spoke of her childhood, of his friends, of her impressions of London, art, literature. They laughed about the antics of the Prince Regent, whom he was personally acquainted with and had very good intelligence on. He never recalled the exact words they said, only the way the syllables rushed off their tongues as if they had years to make up for.

The moment that was most clear was the instant he turned to her in the dark carriage, well past the clock strike of four. "I ought to take you home," he'd murmured regretfully.

Her ready, wanton reply surprised him.

"Yes, indeed. Won't you join me for breakfast?"

His eyes widened and his jaw slacked a bit, but she only waited with a fierce glint in her eyes and her chin raised without shame while he recovered from his shock.

Fortunately, that didn't take long. His brow smoothed and his lips twitched into a shy, boyish smile.

She sat back then, her wrap tight over her crossed arms. "And tell your man not to spare the whip," she commanded archly, only to giggle when he laughed and pulled her close.

The kiss . . . ah, that memory was clear as crystal and just as shimmering. Her mouth was soft beneath his but not dormant. She kissed him back so wholeheartedly, as if she were determined to taste everything life had to offer her.

When he drew back at last, gasping and dizzy with

her, she stayed still in his arms for a long, heated moment, her gaze lowered, her bravado abruptly gone.

He ran the backs of his knuckles down her cheek and nearly lost his breath at the silken heat of her skin. "Are you real?"

She shook her head a little at that, almost a startled tremor. "I'm only . . . only Madeleine."

He tipped her chin up with one finger and gazed down into her face. There was enough light for him to delight in the answering wonder in her eyes. "Correction," he said. "You are only *my* Madeleine."

Mine. Ridiculous, to make such a vow when he'd never seen her before this morning. Yet it was true. She was, from that moment forward, always and forever his.

As often happens to a man who has everything when he is presented with the unattainable, Aidan de Quincy became infatuated.

He could not get enough of her. He could not make it through a single day without her in his arms. It should have appalled him, this hunger, yet it only made him ache for more.

For despite the freely given smiles and the sighs of pleasure, there was something within his Madeleine which he could not touch. He held her in his arms all night long, yet he sensed that he didn't truly have her.

Trying to bring her closer only caused her to hold herself further away. Panicked by her stubborn coolness, one day he proposed. He tore his heart out of his chest and served it up on toast with her tea, offering her everything he had, everything he ever would have, if only she would be forever his. "I *must* have you for my very own!"

The moment the words left his lips, he felt the way her hands shrank within his. His impassioned grip tightened in protest, only a little, yet she gasped and tore herself from him.

As he watched in frozen, shattered rejection, she turned her back for a moment with her arms wrapped tightly about herself. Then she straightened, pushed back a fallen strand of dark hair with the back of one hand, and turned to him with a smile.

It was a false, shallow smile. He couldn't see through to its true meaning, for her façade, brittle and sudden as it was, was complete. Horrified at the disappearance of his warm, lovely Madeline, he tried to persuade her to reconsider.

Her broken, artificial laughter sounded in his ears like shattering glass. "There's no need to be so earnest, darling," she told him with a little toss of her head. "We're only having a bit of harmless fun. There's no need to ruin it with this ridiculous talk of marriage."

Ridiculous. The word, the laughter, the bright spots of color in her white cheeks—the moment seared hotly into his mind and heart forever. She thought his passion was ridiculous.

He should leave. He should gather his shredded dignity about him and walk away.

Instead, in a strangled, helpless voice, he begged. When that moved her not at all, he pulled his grandmother's ruby ring from his pocket and went down upon his knee. "My love, my darling—please! Be mine forever!" Even as the pleading left his lips, he knew it was for naught. The look of appalled wariness in her eyes was all he needed to see.

He didn't remember standing, just the agony in his

chest that slowed his movements as if he moved under-water. He found himself in the entrance hall with his hat in his hand before he could take in enough air to speak to her again.

He turned to gaze at her coldly where she stood in the doorway of the tiny parlor where they had spent so many happy hours.

"In that case, madam, I have had my fill of harmless fun. Good-bye."

CHAPTER 1

A little more than three years and nine months later . . .
Gentlemen weren't supposed to stare at ladies, but Aidan couldn't help but stare at the female gracing the top step of his London club, shifting her bottom restlessly on the cold stone.

She was very pretty and very clean, if one ignored the smudge of city soot on her nose, so he had no objection there. No, the problem—if indeed there was one—was the lady's maturity.

She looked to be no more than a very young three years of age.

Not quite the sight one expected—a tiny female person dwarfed by the imposing Georgian façade of Brown's Club for Distinguished Gentlemen. Even the shuttered windows seemed to look down upon her with dour disapproval, just as the grand portico threatened to make a mouthful of her.

It was not as intimidating as the clubs known as Brooks or Boodles, though, fiercely Palladian structures that they were with their Grecian columns, standing down the more fashionable end of St. James Street. No, Brown's was like an old uncle, stout and brick-shaped and rather too fond of its port to be truly daunting. Brown's hovered here, among the shops that sold fine tobacco and liquor, as if unwilling to trade proximity to its pleasures for a more fashionable address.

The club's elegantly curved semicircle of steps were marble, and though they'd been scuffed into genteel fatigue by generations of "Distinguished Gentlemen," Aidan would have comfortably wagered his grand estate of Blankenship that they had never before been used as a bench by a very small female person.

In general, Aidan avoided females of all sorts. As it was the week before the opening of Parliament, Aidan had with great relief left his mother in queenly solitude at the Blankenship estate. Usually if he took great care, he found that he could claim duty for a great part of the year. He traveled between his various estates and played his part in the House of Lords. He took care to avoid balls and house parties of any kind, for attendance would be construed by Lady Blankenship as consent to look for a bride. That was the very last thing on his mind.

Still, even a house party full of fawning debutantes and social-climbing Society mamas would be preferable to endless weeks of cool, impersonal conversation with the woman who had borne him but with whom he'd spent less than half an hour a day as a child.

Mother, unfortunately, had promised the London house to Aidan's cousins, the Breedloves—whom his friend Jack had once dubbed "the Breed-loads"—for the introduction into Society of the eldest female offspring of that numerous brood.

The idea of such raucous company was nearly as repellent as the thought of spending a single further inert day with Lady Blankenship. For the sake of his own sanity,

Aidan had taken himself off to live at his club for the duration of Parliament. Excellent Brown's, that bastion of male solitude, devoted to life without women.

So here he stood, gazing at what should not have been there. Aidan was no longer one to mind someone else's business for them, not even when that someone was only slightly higher than his knee. After all, children were the province of women, and since Aidan didn't care to complicate his life with one of those, this miniature, painfully neat female person could have nothing to do with him.

Still, he stopped as he came halfway up the stairs and stood there, gazing at the wee creature now at eye level. She gazed evenly back at him with eyes wide and bright blue. She sat primly on a sort of lumpy satchel with her plump little hands clasped about her knees and her feet neatly tucked together. Dark brown ringlets covered her head, bound by a blue ribbon that was a bit frayed at the ends. Her little face was round and pink, and her features rather indistinct in that childish way— not that he looked carefully at many children. Did he even know any children? He thought not.

He could have passed her easily, for her tiny figure didn't block the way, yet he found himself unable to ignore her. He looked about but didn't see any maternal sort of person nearby. At this time of early evening, the gentlemen of London had not yet begun to orbit their brandy bottles, and ladies . . . well, ladies were never a common sight on St. James.

There was no help for it. He was going to have to offer his assistance to a lady. How annoying. He tried so hard to avoid situations like these, for his knight errant days were long over.

He cleared his throat. How did one address such a person? "Er . . . child?" That didn't sound too odd. "Child, where is your mother?"

She didn't change her even, cornflower gaze. "I don't know." She spoke clearly enough, her high voice lilting easily above the clatter of hooves and wheels on the cobbles behind him. St. James was a busy enough street, even this less fashionable end.

"You've lost your mother?"

She considered that for a moment, tilting her head slightly to one side. "I don't have a mother. I have a Nurse Pruitt."

"Did Nurse Pruitt lose you in the crowd?"

The little mite shook her head firmly. "No. She didn't lose me. I held her hand all the way."

Aidan did not allow a fragment of his frustration to show. "All the way to where?"

She drew her brows together again, this time in a way that implied that he wasn't very bright. "To here."

"Here? Brown's Club for Distinguished Gentlemen?"

She looked a bit unsure at the full title of the establishment. "My papa is in there." She pointed over her shoulder at the once-grand, now somewhat-outdated entrance of Brown's. "He's going to take me home and give me a kitten." She plunked her chin down on her clasped hands. "A white kitten," she informed him in a confidential tone.

"Ah." Excellent. No rescue needed. If her father was a servant in the club, the fellow couldn't very well bring his child to work with him. She didn't seem to be in any danger waiting out here on a sunny afternoon and he supposed it was preferable to the alley.

"Then if you'll excuse me, miss." Out of habit, he

bowed, lifting his hat. Catching himself, he straightened. To a child! He really had no idea how to deal with children.

Yet she gurgled a charming laugh in response, making his lips twitch. "You're a funny man," she said.

He grunted. "You are the first and only person to tell me that." Well, there had been one person to laugh at him in the past, but she was long gone. Now the world treated him with distant respect, just the way he preferred. Even so, he could still hear that rising peal of delight, playfully mocking, yet fond. She'd found him so amusing, mostly when he wasn't trying to be.

Old thoughts, old pain. Nothing to do with the present. Nothing at all.

"Really, Blankenship, have the courtesy not to block the steps with your extreme lordliness." The mocking voice was familiar and very unwelcome.

Colin. Bloody hell.

Tall, lean, and as fair as he himself was dark, Sir Colin Lambert was an annoying complication in Aidan's otherwise smooth existence. Unfortunately, Colin came attached to Aidan's close friend, Jack. Since their days at school, Colin had made it his business to needle Aidan as much as possible.

With a barely concealed grimace, Aidan turned to Colin. "I am attempting to assess a delicate situation."

"You? That's like asking a blacksmith to take out a splinter." Colin took a knee on the steps to make himself eye level to the little mite.

Of course, Aidan thought, that's what one does with children. He was both relieved that Colin seemed to know what to do with the creature and annoyed that Colin seemed to be making a better job of it than he.

"Ask her who her father is," Aidan prompted.

The little girl looked up at him with a tilt to her head and a slight frown that clearly said, *I can hear you, you idiot.*

So familiar . . .

Colin gave the child a conspirator's grin. "Himself wants to know who your father is, pet—but why don't you tell me your name first?"

She dimpled at Colin. "Melody."

What a little flirt! Not sure why he did so, Aidan found himself kneeling beside Colin. "What is your surname?"

Melody crinkled her brow. "My name is Melody."

"Yes, but what is the name that comes after Melody?"

Colin elbowed him. "Don't bark at her. She obviously doesn't know."

"How can she not know her own name?"

Colin turned his head to stare at Aidan. "Because she's not yet three years of age. I doubt she can count the fingers on one hand yet."

Aidan scowled at the child as if she'd kept something from him. How did Colin know such things?

Melody began to look wary now. Colin tugged gently on a curl. "Don't worry, lemon drop. He's just a big—"

"My apologies, my lady," Aidan interrupted. He bowed as graciously as he could from one knee. He was not about to allow Colin Lambert to make social excuses for him! "My curiosity has outmatched my manners, I fear."

Melody switched her attention to Aidan, gratifyingly entranced once more. "You're funny."

Colin rolled his eyes and raised his hands in defeat. Aidan felt a little silly then, competing for the smiles of a child. Colin stood and dusted off his knee.

"I'll just leave the two of you—"

"There's a note." Aidan leaned forward. Colin bent down as well. Sure enough, there was a folded note pinned to the rough wool of Melody's tiny coat, half-hidden beneath the lapel.

Aidan gently pulled the pin and removed the note. Melody watched calmly as the two men unfolded it and read with their heads tilted close together.

The mony stopped coming from the mother. I can't keep her no more. The father can take her now. Don't know his name. He's a memmber of Brown's.

Simple became complicated in a heartbeat.

"Oh, damn," Colin breathed. "She's not a lost child—she's a foundling!"

"Indeed," Aidan murmured. They both gazed somberly down at the child who was no longer simply a little girl, but a large and awesome responsibility.

One that Aidan wanted no part of. "We should take her to the local magistrate."

"They'll put her in one of those places."

"An orphanage, yes. Isn't that what's done in these cases until they find her family?"

"Look at the little mite—she'll be eaten alive!" Colin turned to glare at him. "Think, Aidan. Her father is a member of this club, correct?"

"According to a misspelled note."

Colin tilted his head and narrowed his eyes. "She's

probably not quite three years. It's spring now, meaning she would have been conceived perhaps end of summer of four years past."

"I commend your mathematics, but what does that have to do with taking her to an orphanage?"

Colin grabbed his arm and pulled him aside. "Stop saying that word in front of her!" he scolded in a whisper.

Aidan shook him off. "Get to your point then."

Colin glared at him. "Do you think any of the men in that club were out sowing their oats so recently?"

Aidan had to admit Colin had a point there. Most of the members of Brown's were of the geriatric variety. He wasn't entirely sure that the two dotty old fossils permanently installed before the fire playing chess were actually still breathing. Aidan doubted a single game piece had been moved in a decade.

He folded his arms and gazed narrowly at Colin. "What about you? You're a member of Brown's and you're still full of oats."

Colin snorted. "I was keeping my oats to myself right about then, thank you very much." He looked suspicious, however. "What about you? Weren't you mooning over some lovely creature three and a half years ago?"

Aidan stiffened. "A bit more than that, actually. She was already in my past at that point in time." He was quite sure of his own mathematics—if the child were not yet three.

Colin nodded. "My point still stands. If it isn't one of them," he hooked a thumb over his shoulder at the club, "and it isn't one of us—"

"Oh, God," Aidan breathed. "Jack."

Colin nodded. "Precisely. That was just the time he

came home from the war. Remember how grim he'd become?"

Aidan rubbed his hand over his chin. "And then that little Clarke creature jilted him . . . God, what a mess that was!"

Colin grimaced in remembered worry. "There were weeks that summer when we couldn't find him at all, if you'll remember."

"I'm not likely to forget it." Aidan shrugged uncomfortably. Jack's black and disheartened bender had been frightening enough at the time. Now it took on a new significance indeed. "Does she look like Jack?"

As one they turned to gaze intently at her. She gazed solemnly back while chewing the end of her wispy little ribbon. Her features were still too babyish and unformed. Colin shrugged. "She doesn't *not* look like Jack."

Aidan straightened. "Yet that doesn't prove—"

Colin lifted his chin. "I don't care. If there is the slightest possibility that she is Jack's child, then I refuse to expose her to some filthy, crowded orph—institution for even a single moment. You'll have to take her to your house."

"Er—that's a problem." God, the Breedloves would think the child was his, no matter what story was told them. They, in turn, would instantly inform his mother. "Unless you *want* me to bring Lady Blankenship into this matter?"

Colin shrank back slightly. "Crikey, no."

"What of your house?"

Colin shrugged. "Rented out. I hate rattling about in that thing alone. Besides, I wanted to wait for Jack here at Brown's."

They might not have much else in common, but Aidan knew that Colin was just as worried about Jack as he was. "Right then. We'll all wait at Brown's. You, me, and Melody. She can stay in my rooms. There's hardly anyone in residence nearby to hear or see her. It won't be long. Jack is due back from his plantations in Jamaica any day now."

Colin's eyes widened. "Aidan de Quincy, best boy at Eton, break a rule? Should I inform the Prince Regent that the world is at an end?"

Aidan gazed at Colin gravely. "It's for Jack."

Sobering, Colin nodded. "Right then. For Jack."

CHAPTER 2

It was all very well and good to decide to conceal a child in his rooms for the few days until Jack returned, but Brown's wasn't known for its excellent service for nothing. The house man, Wilberforce, chief of staff and general captain of the ship, was not the sort of fellow to let a mouse take up residence in the linen closet, much less allow a female of any size into the male bastion of Brown's Club for Distinguished Gentlemen. No wives, no mothers, not even so much as a girl to scrub the steps.

Wilberforce was tall, with the profile of an eagle and black eyes just as sharp. Add a shock of coal black hair and the elegant blue and gold livery of Brown's and one had the impression of a general very much in control of his troops. The various footmen and chambermen followed his orders to the letter, without chatter or hesitation. It was one of the blessings of Brown's—no cheeky commentary, no grudging service, no miffed feelings because one forgot to notice someone's new hairstyle. Only seamless attendance without a single shrill voice to break the tranquility.

Melody would hardly fit in his pocket. Too bad the weather was too fine for a cloak.

"You go first," Aidan told Colin. "Hold Wilberforce's attention while I get her through the entrance hall."

Colin shook his head. "We'll never get that far. Haven't you noticed the doorman?"

Aidan had forgotten the fellow, quite frankly. He usually simply walked up to the club and through the open door without seeing who opened it for him. "Right."

Colin tapped his fingers on his folded arms while thinking. "The kitchens."

"Aren't they full of cooks and such? It's nearly supper."

"Exactly. They'll be far too busy to notice anything. I'll carry her and you walk between to block their view. If someone gets curious, just give them the Blankenship Glare. That'll stop them in their tracks."

Aidan shook his head. "No, that's my mother."

Colin gave him an unreadable look. "You think so?" Then he shrugged. "All set then. Let's go."

Surprisingly, the mission began much as Colin had suggested. The kitchen staff never even looked twice as they scurried past the steaming kitchens burdened with pots and racks and large, indescribable hunks of meat.

Such luck never lasts long. Footsteps, military-crisp on the tiled hall between the kitchens, rang unmistakeably ahead.

"Damn," Colin whispered. "Wilberforce is on the move!"

Prompted by what self-sacrificing instinct he could not be sure, Aidan handed the tiny child off to Colin. "Take her while I distract him!"

A flare of respect in Colin's usually ironic gaze was all the answer there was time for. Wilberforce rounded the corner just as Colin leapt back into the shadows.

"Ah, there you are, Wilberforce!" Aidan strode forward with his hand raised high, waving energetically and, he realized, foolishly, for there was no possibility of Wilberforce missing his presence.

The man was no fool. No matter how outrageously one of his "charges" behaved, no one had ever seen the fellow lose his serene composure. Not even the time that old Lord Bartles and Sir James had nearly come to blows over a chess move—well, that was perhaps an exaggeration. As the story went, Bartles raised his rheumy gaze from the board long enough to glare at James and denounce his last move. "Balderdash." James had more or less immediately responded with a bang of his cane on the floor and an actually audible "Hmph!" Of course, that had been years ago when both men were much younger and still full of piss and vinegar.

"Yes, my lord? How may I be of service?"

Aidan gazed helplessly at the butler for a long moment. Think! He opened his mouth. "Jack—I mean, Lord John Redgrave—is expected back to town in a few days."

Wilberforce didn't so much as blink. "Yes, my lord. His rooms await him, fully prepared."

"Right. Of course. Er . . . you see . . ." Bloody hell. "It's the . . . it's the . . . it's the monkey." What? What monkey?

Wilberforce didn't move a muscle, not a twitch, but Aidan rather thought the man's sallow complexion faded, just a touch. "The monkey, my lord?"

Aidan nodded a bit too enthusiastically. "Yes. The monkey. It's coming along."

"To Brown's, my lord?" Tendons tightened momentarily in Wilberforce's throat. As far as the inscrutable servitor's reactions went, he might as well have screamed in outrage and despair.

Aidan replied, "Yes. That's right. To Brown's." He

was going to go to hell, that's all there was to the matter. Poor Wilberforce. "So there will be a need for . . . er . . . bananas."

Wilberforce nodded. "I see, my lord." Some color returned to his cheeks. Bananas, it seemed, were a soothing thought. Bananas could be bought at the market for a dear price, but they could be had. Brown's would not fail in its perfect record of perfect service.

Aidan nodded absently, hearing suspiciously girlish sounds from somewhere behind him. "And flannel nappies." Where had that come from? He had babies on the brain.

"Nappies, my lord? For the—" Was that a shudder? "The ape requires *nappies*?"

Taking the considerably deflated manservant by the arm, Aidan managed to turn him back down the hall. "Nappies, Wilberforce. Lots and lots of nappies. A veritable mountain of them. The laundry will never be the same."

Wilberforce began to move down the hall, somewhat shaky and the worse for wear. Just as Aidan hoped he would turn the corner and disappear, the man turned back to him with a faint trace of plaintiveness in his frozen expression. "Do you know, my lord . . ."

Aidan twitched with impatience. There were definite sounds of childish rebellion behind him. "What is it, Wilberforce?"

Wilberforce twitched as well. "My lord, is it . . . is it a very *large* monkey, do you think?"

Aidan's lips shivered slightly, but he kept the grin easily in check. From behind him, he heard Colin's helpless snort of laughter. "It is, I'm afraid to say, a perfectly *enormous* monkey. The very biggest one of all."

Wilberforce nodded and turned somewhat blindly to make his way back down the hall, his crisp tread rather slowed. "Thank you, my lord. That's . . . excellent news. Have a good evening, my lord."

Aidan watched him go out of sight, then swiftly turned back to Colin and the girl. She was bright-eyed and pink-cheeked and had Colin's fine gold pocket watch stuffed in her mouth. She waved at him happily. Aidan blinked. "Is that sanitary?"

"Probably not, but it worked." Colin was gazing at him worriedly. "You're a bit on the evil side, aren't you? The poor bloke might never recover."

Aidan snorted. "Knowing Wilberforce, he'll have prepared the world's finest indoor monkey environment by the time the supper gong sounds."

Colin grimaced. "True."

With that, Colin and Aidan calmly walked their own little monkey up the back stairs to the fourth storey.

Colin complained, of course. "Too many bloody stairs," he gasped.

"Don't be theatrical," Aidan grunted. "You're not carrying anything but that little satchel." He liked the fact that his room was high and isolated. Most of the members had gravitated to the lower floors because of their age. Their preference had defined Aidan's.

"Why your room? Why not mine? It's closer."

"The only man sharing my floor is old Aldrich. He won't hear a thing. In addition, Jack's room is just below mine, so no need to be careful of noise."

Colin only grunted, but ceased his argument nonetheless.

Brown's Club for Distinguished Gentlemen was once

a prime establishment, a grand refuge for the fathers and scions of the finest families in England—a refined place of stately grace, sedate cards, and fine tobacco.

The tobacco was still quite good, but the place itself had slipped somewhat off the fashionable palate. Respectable had become stuffy, refined had become monastic. While still grand in a previous-century manner, with high majestic ceilings and dark-paneled walls, the dining rooms and card rooms were silent with disuse.

Altogether, it was comfortable and masculine and if it was a bit aged about the edges, there were no women present to go on about it, so no one seemed to mind.

The clientele had aged along with the establishment until most members were naught but portraits on the walls of the club room. The few who remained tottered painfully about, then seated themselves in front of the fire while servants very nearly as elderly as they hovered in a leisurely, semi-retired fashion.

Aidan only frequented the club because of Jack. Not highly ranked enough to belong to the best of the clubs, Jack had cheerfully invited Aidan and Colin to join him at Brown's. "We'll have the run of the place," he'd assured them. "Those fossils won't be in our way."

Jack had been correct about that. The three younger men had great freedom to come and go without comment.

It was quiet, convenient to Westminster, and blessedly and completely free of women.

Until now.

Once on Aidan's floor, which truly was solely Aidan's but for old Lord Aldrich, whose room lay at the far end of the hall with a view of the street, and who was deaf as a post and nearly as blind, the three made their way to the first doorway in the dim hallway. The flick of a key in the lock and they were safe inside, home free.

Free to do what, Aidan wasn't so sure. "Now that we've got her inside, O Criminal Mastermind, what do you propose we do with her?"

Colin let the little girl slide casually from his hip down his extended leg until she landed giggling on small booted feet. "Do it again!" she cried, holding up her arms.

He absently ruffled her hair. "Later, smidgeon. Go play in Uncle Aidan's bedchamber. There's a candy in his bureau somewhere."

Aidan watched in consternation as the tiny female person scampered off to violate his privacy with great energy. "I haven't any sweets in my bureau."

Colin shrugged. "Oops. Anyway, she'll be occupied for half an hour and we can decide her fate out of her hearing."

Aidan wasn't any too thrilled about the sweet safari taking place amongst his collars and cravats, but time to think was essentially a good idea, even if it had come from Colin Lambert.

"Are there any clues in the bag?" he asked Colin.

There was pitifully little in the small, worn satchel, which held a pathetic number of small, worn items. A few patched underthings, much-darned stockings, raveled ribbons, and another faded little dress. Colin held up a scrap of muslin. "This is the smallest pinafore I have ever seen."

They repacked the bag, discouraged. It seemed that no one knew whose daughter little Melody was, especially not Melody.

"What is your plan then?"

Colin opened his hands. "I got her within the hallowed halls, didn't I? Now it's your turn to play genius."

Aidan frowned at the doorway of his bedchamber. There were thumpings and bumpings going on. "Should we check on her?"

Colin shook his head. "It's not when they're noisy that you ought to worry. It's when they're quiet."

No danger there. The thumps were now punctuated by a lilting monologue he couldn't quite understand. "I thought you were an only child."

Colin leaned one shoulder on the wall. "I had a slew of younger cousins. They spent years crawling all over me."

That image gave Aidan a mingled flash of revulsion and envy. He had cousins, but Lady Blankenship had kept them at a distance. He'd once longed for company. Now he felt rather grateful.

Colin snapped his fingers. "Your cummerbunds will survive. Back to business. What are you going to do with her until Jack gets back?"

Aidan held up a hand. "When did this become my problem?"

"When I couldn't keep her in my rooms on the second floor because I've crotchety old gents on all sides. Besides, you've twice the room in here."

He'd been hornswoggled, no doubt about it. Damn it. "We'll write to Jack. Fetch him home as soon as possible."

Colin nodded. "Well enough, but he won't get the letter before his ship docks at London anyway. All that will ensure is that he comes directly to Brown's upon disembarking."

God, it could be days, possibly even a week. Or longer.

Colin simply gazed at him. "What are you going to feed her?"

Aidan drew back. "It requires special food?"

Colin shook his head. "*She* requires the same food as you and I, only a bit more simple. Meat without sauce, carrots, bread and butter, et cetera." He held up a finger. "And milk."

Aidan folded his arms. "Wilberforce is supposed to believe I've suddenly taken a fancy to *milk*?"

Colin clapped him on the shoulder. "There, you've got it." He grinned. "Have a lovely evening with your new playmate, old man." He turned to leave.

Aidan panicked. "You're not leaving me here with that—that child, are you? I don't know a thing about it!"

Colin paused, his hand on the doorknob. "A child is just a person, Blankenship. Shorter and a bit busier, but still a person."

"I don't know anything about people, either!"

Colin blinked. "I can't believe you just admitted such a thing. Who utters things like that?"

Aidan was saved from further hazing at Colin's hands by a shattering crash followed by a frightened wail. Without losing an instant, both men ran for the bedchamber.

CHAPTER 3

Lady Madeleine shut her bedchamber door behind her and turned the key in the lock, though she lived alone. Then she pulled the threadbare draperies on the window closed as tightly as possible. Then she blew out her last stub of a candle and undressed in the dark anyway.

She was being foolish, of course. There was no one here. She was alone in her shabby little London house, just as she had been for the past four years and more.

She only *felt* as though she were being watched. A silly fear—oh, how she wished that were true.

Unfortunately, she'd become more and more convinced over the past few days that she was, in fact, being watched. No matter how she tried to convince herself that that man, Critchley, hadn't seen her three days ago on Bond Street, she couldn't quite manage to renew her peace of mind.

She'd only stepped out of her own familiar neighborhood for an afternoon, and that only to sell her second-to-last item of value. Up until then she'd held onto the locket her husband had given her, not out of sentiment—heavens, no!—but because the piece was too distinctive and unique. Necessity had prompted her to sell it at last and she had nearly been spotted!

In her gown and wrapper, which were probably inside

out, she sat on her bed and tucked her cold toes beneath her. With a small bone-handled brush, she began to brush out her long dark hair. When she was done, she braided it with quick practiced movements in the dark.

Matters had become quite grim. Her coal was all but gone and, despite the fine weather, her little rented house was not terribly snug. She had barely made it through the past winter. She'd not survive another one in London.

Sitting there in the dark and chill and silence, she forced herself to face the truth. There was no reason to stay in London and plenty of reasons to leave. If she had been recognized, then it was past time to flee. Even if she hadn't, there was no chance that after all this time she would see Aidan de Quincy on her doorstep again.

So, time to pack. It wouldn't take long. She'd sold almost everything, piece by piece. Gone were the jewels from her husband's coffer and gone were all but one of the gifts that Aidan had given her three years ago. Diamonds and rubies were nothing to her, but the memories . . . well, those were hers forever, like them or not.

She shivered. She'd always been slender, but now she was worn to the bone and the chill could set deeply.

I look a proper scarecrow, I'm sure.

Vanity was so far in the past it was less than a memory, yet she could not help feel a twinge of loss. She'd never been a famous beauty, but she'd been rather pretty once. Not that it had done her a bit of good. Pretty had its price, which she'd paid.

The chill ate through her worn coverlet and she shivered again. She was still paying the price for being pretty and foolish.

She'd rather be wise and scarecrow-scrawny and free.

Quickly, she picked up the candle again and knelt by the puny pile of glowing coals to relight it. Her last candle, her last coal, her last night in London. Setting the stub on her nightstand, she felt beneath the bed for the old carpetbag she'd stored there.

As she folded her few things into the bag, she planned. If she could save her single reserve, a strand of pearls, she would be able to use it to make a new start somewhere else—somewhere she might dare to take humble employment without fear of being recognized by one of London's elite.

If she could talk her way onto a ship as a chambermaid or cook, she could survive long enough to go somewhere different, somewhere distant and safe. Perhaps even somewhere foreign and tropical.

Somewhere she should have fled to years ago, if she hadn't met Aidan de Quincy in a filthy alleyway.

When Aidan and Colin rounded the doorway into the bedchamber, they both drew back in horror—and from the eye-watering cloud of scent.

Little Melody sat wailing like a siren in the middle of a circle of destruction that defied the imagination, knowing how quickly she'd created it. The pile of books that had lain close at hand to Aidan's bedside were strewn about, pages ruffling gently. The tray of toiletries which had rested upon his dressing table had been pulled down. Shattered bottles and jars oozed bath scent and hair cream. The bedcovers lay in a tumbled pile on the floor at the edge of the spreading goo, soaking it up.

Melody sat at the center, the jewel in the crown of disaster. She had smeared her face and arms in what looked to be Aidan's hair cream, she smelled as though she'd bathed in the expensive cologne that Aidan's mother had given him but which he never wore, and it seemed she'd finished the job with a thick dusting of talcum.

From the eye of the hurricane, she gurgled another red-faced wail and held out her arms.

"Pick her up." Aidan urged Colin.

"Hell, no. You pick her up."

"I'll pay you a hundred pounds to pick her up," Aidan promised desperately. Melody's wails escalated. Sticky arms reached up.

Colin took a step back. "That's not *my* hair cream. And she reeks. What were you thinking, to let her play in here alone?"

I'll kill him. Somewhere, someday when I can make it look like an accident . . .

Inhaling deeply, Aidan held his breath and advanced toward the wailing child. She really was terribly upset, poor little bit. Gingerly, he put both hands under arms and picked her up, holding her at arms length. She dangled there, reeking and dripping blobs of hair cream onto the carpet.

Aidan grimaced at the miasma of scents rising from her. At his expression, Melody giggled through her tears.

"She needs a bath," Colin declared from the safety of the doorway.

Aidan turned to him in horror. "I can't bathe a girl child! It wouldn't be proper!"

Colin rolled his eyes. "We're a bit short on ladies around Brown's, idiot. It's you or it's Wilberforce—and then he'll throw her out."

Aidan closed his eyes for a long moment, concentrating very hard on pretending that his life had not become so complicated. "Firstly, order one, no, two, buckets of hot water. Secondly, send down for a tray of simple food. Thirdly—get out of my sight before I stuff you into that old dumbwaiter and tell the world I haven't the faintest idea what happened to you."

Colin smirked. "I wouldn't fit."

Aidan slid him a slow meaningful glance. "I could make you fit, given a quarter of an hour and a freshly sharpened knife."

Colin's smirk faded. "Right. Hot water." He turned toward the bell pull and stopped. "A bloke doesn't order another bloke a bath!"

Aidan ignored him. Melody had stopped wailing. Unbelievably, she seemed quite content to dangle from his hands while she industriously smeared his cuffs with goo. She was a stalwart little thing, wasn't she?

Colin snapped his fingers. "I've got it. I'll order it all from my room and bring it up to you when they go back belowstairs." With that he was gone.

Aidan decided that the only place he could sit was the soiled carpet. He hadn't sat upon the floor since he was a boy. It felt odd not to be so tall. Settling Melody a safe distance from the broken things, he reached for an item of his strewn clothing on the floor and began to gently wipe the worst of the powder-crusted goo from her little hands before it traveled further. "You're a menace," he said gently.

She hiccupped and her face was still blotchy under the smeared mess but she seemed quite calm now. "I'm a girl," she pointed out in a reasonable tone. "*You're* a mens."

That surprised a short bark of laughter from him. He tilted his head. "You're a very smart girl."

She took the fine linen shirt from him and began to smear—er, wipe his cuffs clean. He gazed down at her. "You like to explore, don't you? You like to dig right into new things."

" 'Splore." She paused and looked up at him as if she was thinking over the new word. "Nurse Pruitt said I have too much cursedy."

"Curiosity. That's impossible. There's no such thing as too much curiosity. Nurse Pruitt sounds like a right fussbudget."

She giggled. "Fussbudget."

He took the shirt back—it was a rag now—and continued his mission to uncover the real Melody. By the time Colin appeared in the doorway, out of breath and lugging two pails of steaming water, Aidan had the child mostly de-crusted and down to her dingy little chemise. Colin pursed his lips in approval. "She looks better than you do."

A few moments that seemed like hours later, a pink and naked and *clean* Melody splashed quite contentedly in the middle of the large washbasin, safe and warm by the fire. Aidan took of his soaked jacket and threw it on the growing pile of permanently ruined clothing. "Now the carpet."

Colin blanched. "I can't, man. I'm done in!" He looked nearly ready to cry. "She's a monster," he whispered.

Aidan lifted a corner of his lips. "Well, the carpet won't fight back. We can hardly ask the staff in to clean it up, now can we?"

Colin resisted. "But . . . I've never cleaned in my life."

Aidan raised a brow. "You've mucked out your horse's stall, haven't you?"

Colin shrugged. "Once, perhaps, as a boy."

"Same principle. Scrape up the mess. Scrub down the rest." Much the same as he'd done with Melody, now that he thought about it. Perhaps this child thing wasn't so difficult after all.

An hour later, Aidan too was ready to cry uncle. Yet somehow he found the strength to struggle grimly on, determined to see the madness through. At last he sat back. "There. All done."

Colin leaned forward from his chair by the fire, where he sat smoking Aidan's tobacco and savoring Aidan's brandy while doing absolutely nothing of use. He frowned critically at Aidan's latest attempt at a braid. "You mucked it a bit there."

Aidan looked down to where Colin pointed and nearly cried at the sight of the long dark lock which was most certainly not caught properly up in Melody's lopsided braid. Since grown men did not cry, Aidan did what all men did and scowled fiercely.

Melody giggled and then mimicked his thunderous expression, with her delicate brows nearly meeting and her little chin thrust forward belligerently. Aidan doubted that it was an attractive expression on him, but on her it was adorable. He fought the urge to turn to sugary goo. Colin was apparently having difficulty as well, for Aidan caught a glimpse of smitten adoration on his face before he abruptly turned away with a cough.

"Marshmallow," Aidan accused him gruffly.

"Speak for yourself," Colin retorted. "You melt like candle wax."

They both grumbled deeply, satisfied at having fulfilled their manly duty of name-calling and denial of sentiment.

"That's a brilliant bit of mimicry," Colin said lazily. "She looked positively primitive, just like you."

Colin was only needling, yet Aidan felt alarm jolt through him, unfortunately tainted with uncertainty. Melody pulled her braid forward and examined it.

"You mucked it, Uncle Aidan," she pointed out calmly. "It's all bunged up."

Aidan blinked at the vulgarity, then looked at Colin in panic. Alas, Colin had buried his face in his brandy snifter, where he sputtered quietly. Aidan cleared his throat and gazed down at Melody. "I apologize for the damage, little one, but . . . one ought not to say words like 'muck' and 'bung'."

She blinked her large dark eyes at him. "You said it, Uncle Aidan. So did Uncle Colin."

"Er . . . well, we ought not have. Sometimes gentlemen use bad language, but they should never do so in the company of ladies. I deeply regret that, and I know Uncle Colin does as well—"

The sputtering by the fire became louder, so Aidan raised his voice. "But you must remember that ladies *never* use crude language."

Melody blinked. "I'm a lady?"

Aidan smiled. "You most certainly are." Any daughter of Jack's, legitimate or not, could be raised quite nicely on such connections. Society's rules were easier on "natural" daughters than sons, especially if they were openly claimed by their fathers.

Which Jack was going to do promptly on his return, or Aidan would beat him soundly until he did.

Pleased, Melody dreamily considered her new status. "Do ladies get pretty dresses?"

Aidan smiled. Feminine to the core. "Of course. The very prettiest."

Melody dimpled with pleasure. "Do ladies get cake?"

Aidan laughed. "Indeed."

"Do ladies get a kitten?"

Aidan found himself nodding. "Yes, that would be—"

Colin broke out in howls while Aidan did his best to backtrack on his inadvertent promise. "Now, Melody, I don't think it's a very good idea—"

Melody bestowed an angelic smile on him and threw her arms about his neck. "Thank you, Uncle Aidan!"

If Colin didn't stop sputtering into the brandy, he was going to need a dunk in a cold tub. Aidan wasn't about to be bested by a vixen he could pick up with one hand!

Yet gooey sentiment threatened again. He could only glare helplessly at Colin, who now lay draped over the chair, gasping. "You're no help at all, you know that?"

Colin recovered enough to send him an unapologetic salute. "It was just so much fun to watch you go down in flames."

"Heartless wretch."

"Spineless dupe."

Aidan stood. Melody still clung to his neck, her little feet dangling beneath the giant night shirt. Aidan hefted her on one arm and patted her awkwardly on the head. "A kitten then, as soon as—" *As soon as your papa comes home.* But there was no way to promise that when they didn't know for sure until Jack returned. "As soon as we've got you settled properly. It wouldn't do to bring a kitten into this room, would it? Kittens need to play outside."

Melody yawned, considered his logic for a moment, then acquiesced by laying her head comfortably on his shoulder. "A white . . . kitten . . ."

Just like that, she was asleep in his arms. Aidan felt his heart stutter just a bit as she became oddly heavier in her relaxation, going entirely limp upon his chest.

It was an entirely different sensation than holding her awake. Awake Melody was like a coiled spring always in danger of being loosed. She was loud and busy and bursting with energy. Sleeping Melody was soft and tiny, her baby features lax and sweet; even her freshly bathed little feet were limp and soft, with toes like small pink peas.

Strange emotions assaulted him. Helpless alarm—what should he do now?—mingled with a sense of being insanely honored by her unconditional trust in him. No one had ever depended upon him so utterly. No one had ever bestowed upon him such simple and absolute faith.

It was outrageously daunting. How could he ever live up to such a thing? He looked up at Colin. "This is a mistake," he whispered frantically. "We can't do this. We have to give her back!"

Colin scoffed. "Back to whom? Do you think she'd be better off warehoused in some crowded orphanage?"

Aidan's panicked thoughts circled. "No. Not orphanage. School!"

Colin folded his arms. "She's barely off the wet-nurse and you want to send her to school? Are you mad?"

Aidan shook his head. "No, no. Of course not." God,

there had to be an answer! "What if we do something wrong? What if we break her somehow?"

Colin glared at him. "Coward!"

"Shh!" Aidan lay Melody down on the giant bed. She looked no larger than a doll on the vast mattress. "Sleep now, poppet." He brought the crimson coverlet up to her little chin and fought the urge to drop a kiss on her brow. He ought not to get attached. He ought not to allow such a complication.

Then he gave up the fight and leaned down to brush his lips over the downy curls at her temple. When he straightened, he glared at Colin, daring him to mock the gesture.

Colin only gazed at him for a moment, then looked down at Melody, who had now gone thoroughly limp, her little fingers curled loosely at her chin.

"What was her mother thinking, to cast her off this way?" Colin murmured, his low tone not masking his anger.

Aidan wasn't nearly so surprised. "Heartless women in London are as common as snails in the garden," he said with a snort.

The lovely widow Madeleine, for example. Madeleine of the dark eyes full of secrets and lies, the insincere touch, the deceitful lips . . .

But he never thought of Madeleine anymore. He'd recovered from her poison years ago.

As he shooed Colin from the bedchamber and resigned himself to a night on his sofa, he firmly put away thoughts of Madeleine and ridiculous new suspicions of Melody's origins.

Or, at least, he tried.

CHAPTER 4

Far from London, a man prepared to leave on a journey. He ordered his horse brought round, for he no longer owned a carriage fine enough to transport him in the manner to which he'd become accustomed.

He'd lost everything. He now lived in the gatekeeper's lodge at his own gates. The manor was a scorched ruin and the farms were a wasteland. He did not have the money to rebuild so vastly. He had debts mounting enough already.

He dressed in his best riding habit—which, due to his lack of enthusiasm, was only a bit worn where no one would notice—and ordered the footman, who was really no better than a horse groom but now served as his valet, to pack his things into the leather panniers that went behind his saddle.

When his horse was brought around, he mounted with a grimace. He wasn't fond of riding, but a man who rode to Town might be considered a sporting fellow, too youthful and impatient to bear the tedious ride on wheels.

Town life awaited him, which he'd once enjoyed, but now saw only as an escape from the dreary ruin his existence and his estate had become. He needed a speedy inflow of cash most direly. Gambling might do it, but he'd been badly cheated too many times and hardly had enough left with which to start a game.

There was no choice but to sell his minor title and connections to the highest bidder and wed that shipping magnate's horse-faced daughter. A shudder of revulsion went through him at the thought. He could hardly bear to expend himself on something so unattractive when he'd once had the most beautiful wife in the county.

As he mounted his horse and rode away from the blackened ruin that had once been his very fine house, he eased his mind with thoughts of his former delicate, smoky-eyed wife.

Beautiful and obedient—at least, she'd become so with a bit of training. Those had been such satisfactory times. The more vulnerable and eager to please she had become, the easier it had become to exploit that vulnerability. After all, had he not fed her and sheltered her and provided her with the finest of everything?

And then to have her say, directly to his face, that she intended to betray him? Hot tendrils of rage threatened to escape the tightly locked cage he kept within himself. Had she really thought he'd allow her to unmask him to the world?

He was fond of that mask. It was a handsome one by birth and he'd spent a lifetime learning to use it well. There was little he craved that he could not get by persuasion . . . but persuasion wasn't quite as satisfying as it had once been, not since the Incident.

He'd been an ordinary man before. Well, an ordinary aristocrat at any rate. He'd kept mostly to the conventions of Society, at least outwardly, never realizing that he had the potential to be more, the potential to achieve total mastery of his world, the potential to hold the godlike power of life and death in his hands.

He smiled as sweet memory eased back the hot burn of betrayal. That was a moment he very much looked forward to enjoying again.

It was really too bad his pretty wife had died so young. Such a waste, losing her in the blaze like that, burned to ash—like kindling—like paper. He let out a sigh of deep regret. After all, he'd missed the whole thing.

It must have been a lovely sight to see.

The next morning, Aidan was up and dressed before Colin tapped upon his door. Better to say, he was still dressed, having not gone to sleep at all.

He'd spent some hours of the night composing letters to be mailed out to various ports of call that Jack might make before landing at London. Unlikely that any of them would get to Jack before then, but worth the effort nonetheless.

The rest of the night he'd spent circling about a single thought. It was a thought he did not want to have—a thought he refused to have!—yet it would not go away.

He greeted Colin absently and went about gathering up Melody's few things to get her dressed. Aidan found her sad, dilapidated little buttoned boot, still a bit sticky from last evening's adventures. It was hardly worth cleaning. When he got his hands on this Nurse Pruitt he was going to drag her before the magistrate.

Yet who was truly to blame here? A nurse gone unpaid? Melody's mother for hiding her away and then refusing to pay? Or her father, for never even bothering to inquire as a man should after . . . well, after.

As he had never bothered to inquire after Madeleine.

His job of dressing her finished, with not too many mistakes, he hoped, he straightened and gazed down at little Melody. The daylight made her dark hair gleam and her little fingers were busily tying far too many knots in the frayed bow on the front of her little dress.

She spoke so well and she was so bright . . .

Perhaps she was older than Colin believed her to be. She could be small for her age, if she hadn't been cared for properly. Perhaps she was a little older . . . just enough older . . .

Old enough to be mine.

He narrowed his eyes and pounded his fist on the doorjamb. "Damn and blast!"

"Damn and blast!" The girlish piping echo made both men freeze, then guiltily turn their heads. Melody gazed brightly at them, then narrowed her eyes and pounded her fist on the nearby bedpost. "Damn and blast!"

Colin snorted. "Are you sure she's not yours?"

Aidan's gut went cold because he realized that at that moment, no, he wasn't completely sure of anything.

And that meant that he was going to have make sure. And to make sure, he was going to have to see *her* one more time.

Madeleine.

Distaste roiled through him. It *was* distaste, revulsion, disgust even. It was in no way—and would never be— anticipation. Absolutely not.

That was his explanation and he would die defending it.

By dawn, Lady Madeleine had her affairs in order, her few things packed in a small valise, and the last strand of pearls from Aidan in her reticule, ready to be bartered for a berth on a ship.

She'd found a discarded newssheet from the previous day that listed the departure dates and destinations for the larger ships leaving the London Docks. There was one leaving for Jamaica that very day. Foreign and warm to be sure!

All that she waited for now was the morning crowds to swell so she could lose herself in them. She brushed away a strand of falling hair and counted slowly backward from five as she put her hand on the front door latch. She hadn't been out in days, fearing recognition by that insect, Critchley. Three . . . two . . . one.

The early spring air that touched her face was cold and smelled of city soot and cart-horse droppings. She allowed herself one short, sentimental glance about the house where she'd once spent the happiest hours of her life.

It was nothing but an empty shell now, furnished only with the items with which it had been rented. The bright days and succulent nights of the past didn't live within its non-descript papered walls. She was taking her memories with her.

All of them, good and bad. Whether she liked it or not.

Raising her chin and straightening her shoulders, she tightened her grip on her sadly under-filled valise and took a step into the outside world.

"Going somewhere, my lady?"

Scarcely one step outside, Madeleine whirled to see the short, stout, gaudily clad figure of Oran Critchley waiting, leaning in what he probably thought was a casual manner against the wall of her house. Deep-set, piggy blue eyes swept over her greedily. His wide, greasy countenance did not delude the observer. He was precisely as he seemed—self-indulgent, filthy, and grasping. Unfortunately, any hope of a smooth escape was dashed by the smug knowledge in that sneering face.

Critchley had at one time been her husband's closest companion. One could not say friend. Partners in malcontent, perhaps.

Madeleine turned immediately to flee back into her house, but she wasn't quick enough slam the door on Critchley and all the memories he brought with him.

He pushed past her into her narrow front hall and then, taking her firmly by the arm, closed the door on the world outside. Madeleine's heart sped and her stomach turned over, for Critchley had never been overly fond of soap. She swallowed hard but did not speak. She would not give this cellar crawler the advantage.

His grip still punishing her arm, he pressed her back against the door and came close, grinning at her with yellowed teeth and poisoned gums. She drew back from his stinking breath, but not before she noted the odd irregularity in his pupils. He used a number of substances that altered the mind, if she recalled correctly. Drinking was the least of his vices.

"You ran from me the other day," Critchley whispered, his breath hot on her cheek. "I saw you turn away and hurry off into the crowds. I could have dropped dead of surprise on the spot, you know. Why did you fly away after the fire, my lady? What sort of woman would make us all mourn her death and mock us from afar?"

She wouldn't do it. She wouldn't ask him what he

wanted. She wouldn't plead with him to leave and forget he ever saw her. She certainly wouldn't beg him not to tell anyone what he knew!

Except that she rather suspected that she would do all three, if only she could make the past go away again. If only she hadn't been so bloody stupid all those years ago. If only she'd hadn't done what she'd done—lived what she'd lived!

"After I lost sight of you, I wondered what your business was on that street. It didn't take long to find the locket you'd sold—you know the piece, I'm sure. Gold, was it not? With a wild rose motif, I believe. You see, I'm quite familiar with it, since it was I who helped poor dear Wilhelm choose it for you. I knew it must be true then. Lady Madeleine lives."

Madeleine felt ill. She'd held onto that blasted locket precisely because it was too distinctive. Only true desperation had prompted her to sell it at last.

She ought to have thrown it into the privy instead.

CHAPTER 5

Critchley rubbed his body against Madeleine's. "So clever to fake your death. Who knew such a sweet, naive young girl could become such a masterful conniver? Now, I can allow everyone to continue to believe in your demise, or I can tell them the truth about you. I can hardly resist it now, just anticipating how you'll explain arson and murder to the authorities . . ."

"I did nothing."

He raised a brow. "Nothing? Then why hide out for years? You give yourself away. What of the jewels you stole? What of your poor dead lady's maid? Are you quite sure you have not the slightest stain upon your conscience?"

Guilt swept her, rivaled only by the fear twisting about her throat.

"Time is running out, my dear. Rumor has it that he is on his way. You have but a week to deal solely with me. After that, matters will be out of my hands."

The past three years of isolation and regret had taught her one thing, however. By god she knew when to shut her mouth! She turned her face as far away from Critchley's foulness as she could and disdained to give him one more instant of her attention.

He twisted her arm hard. She inhaled sharply but did not cry out.

"Too good for me then? Too much the lady to even look at the man who is going to save you? I could keep your secrets . . . or I could tell the world. Your husband trusted me once. Perhaps you can trust me now?"

She almost looked at him then. Trust someone who was twisting her arm from its socket while he pushed his slovenly body against hers? What an idiot.

No, she would definitely be better off if he ripped her arm off and let her die of it. Altogether a cleaner and more desirable death.

Even as she fought back tears from the pain, she wanted to spit on him. Disgusting worm.

The worst of it was that she had no one but herself to blame. Her choice, her own will had led her to wed a monster.

Wilhelm's façade had been complete, of course. She'd had no idea—no one did. How could anyone even surmise that such a thing was possible behind the charming smile, the easy friendliness, the handsome, noble face.

He'd been so kind, so accommodating. His interest in her needs and wants seemed complete—his selflessness almost to a fairytale extreme. No effort was too much, no detail of her life too small for him to relish. She'd been embarrassed to accept at first, not daring to believe that such a man could be real.

Her mother had been charmed, her father enthusiastic. Everyone in the small circle of family and friends had been so captivated that it almost seemed that they wondered how such a rather ordinary girl had snared such a catch as he.

Had he perhaps been as kind and generous as she'd believed and her own faults had somehow changed him? Had she been such a complete disappointment that his behavior was excused?

The world might think so. She knew he was thought to be so exemplary a man, so outstanding a catch, that the girls of her county had vied for his attention. Every family warred for the chance to host a dinner for him. Every squire eyed him for his daughters, every gentleman sought him for cards, or for shooting, or simply for an evening of good male conversation and cigars.

And yet, although he was in great demand socially, he'd never seemed to have any real friends. All his connections were loose ones—ones of Society, of power, of influence, to be sure—yet no one was held tightly, no one was allowed to see the man within.

No one but her. And Critchley.

Her arm vibrated with agony, lest she forget her disgusting blackmailer. Oh, his clothes were fine and well made, but the various stains and stenches gave proof to his decadent lifestyle. He was rather more than portly, and no longer as young as he had been when she'd seen him last.

"Your ways are aging you, Critchley." Her gut was shaking with fear, but she kept her spine straight and scorn in her voice. She might buy some time, possibly even persuade him to let go for a moment—which she would use to bash him over the head and run for her life! She could likely outpace him, slug that he was.

Critchley self-consciously passed a hand over his balding scalp, disarranging the oily strands he'd strategically combed over it. Then anger flared in his small, greedy eyes and his round face flushed red. He raised his hand sharply as if to strike her.

Madeleine didn't draw her head back. She knew that to show fear to men like Critchley only fueled their violence. Of course, defiance did as well, but at least she could live with herself afterward.

"You've strayed from your pen, Critchley." She stood her tallest and gazed down her nose at him. "Are you sure you're allowed to be out?"

He grinned then. His rotted gums swelled around blackening teeth. "Shall I let myself out for you, pretty Madeleine?"

The fear in her belly threatened to rise into her throat and choke her, but she must keep him talking so she could think of how to get away.

She'd happily brain him with a candlestick, but she'd sold them as well. All she had within reach were her own fists. She shivered at the thought that he'd probably like that very much.

He spotted the shiver and wheezed a chuckle. "Little Madeleine, so scared and all alone." He moved closer, pressing himself more firmly to her, sure of his success. "I'll keep your secrets for as long as you like . . . if you keep your promise."

Her promise? What promise could he—

Oh. That promise. Oops.

She'd promised him her body. She'd lied, of course.

It wasn't a lie at the time.

True. Once upon a time she would have said and done anything if it meant she could disappear. Now, having survived as a free widow for most of the past five years, the very thought of bowing beneath a man's thumb again made her want to retch.

Of course, Critchley made her want to retch simply by existing.

Now, as he pressed closer still, she wondered faintly if vomiting on him would make him go away. One never knew what Critchley's level of tolerance sank to.

When his fleshy hand moved toward her breast and his wet mouth descended upon her neck, she rather thought she was going to find out, whether she chose to or not.

Suddenly, a confident hand at the door knocker shattered the creeping silence of the house. Critchley started, lifting his head to stare at the door. His grip slackened on her arm.

Madeleine knocked his hand aside and ran for the door.

She opened it in a rush. It could be anyone, she didn't care—anyone that could give her the remotest chance of slipping away from Critchley—please, God, anyone at all—

There, tall and dark and looming on her doorstep, stood the man she thought she'd never see again.

Aidan.

For a long, breathless moment she could only stare at him, which was no real punishment because he was, and had always been, the most handsome man she'd ever known. Nearly black hair and night-sky blue eyes were a devastating combination, but combined with a tall, broad-shouldered form and chiseled features, they were very nearly lethal.

The laugh that broke from her lips was part surprised

gasp and part panicked howl at this particular twist of fate. The expression on Aidan's face—his beautiful, striking face which her memories had not, in fact, embellished in the slightest—turned from grim determination to appalled confusion.

Welcome to my world, my love.

It wasn't that he hadn't changed. He had, though his thick dark hair still curled over his forehead and down over the back of his collar—he always forgot to have it cut short—and his blue eyes still riveted her female attention. Intelligence and feeling lived in those perceptive eyes, belying his apparent lordly indifference. He was certainly the same height he'd always been, yet now he seemed like a cold, immovable tower. He didn't bend to her as he might once have, attentive paramour that he'd been. Now he stood stiffly, gazing at her with eyes as impenetrable as night.

Grim lines had cut themselves into his face on either side of his mouth . . . the mouth which most definitely was not smiling, nor looked as though it had in a very long time.

Aidan, where have you gone? Did I do this to you?

She hoped not—but she was afraid she might have been the one to harden his handsome features into forbidding granite. He seemed . . . darker? Definitely more somber than the charming knight who had saved her in that alleyway.

And now he was about to save her again.

Whether you like it or not, my darling.

Then she felt Critchley move closer behind her to take her arm in a painful, hidden grasp once more. "What do you want?" He gazed suspiciously at Aidan, the very picture of a man interrupted by an unwelcome visitor to his home.

Aidan's gaze flickered between them. She knew what he was thinking. First, that she'd moved on from him to another man. Second, that she'd lost any modicum of taste or selectivity.

She narrowed her eyes at him. *As if I'd give this cretin the lint from my drawers.*

Aidan had always seemed to know what she was thinking. That perception of his had brought them closer than she'd ever known a man and a woman could be— although in the end it had torn them apart. Her fault, of course. Even knowing that he'd spot the deception, she'd lied anyway.

Now, it seemed that Aidan was still somewhat attuned to her, for his expression hardened as he looked Critchley over. "I have business to discuss with Mrs. Chandler . . . confidential business."

Bless you, you stubborn, gallant man. Despite his well-deserved scorn for her, he still could not resist the role of knight errant.

Critchley tightened his grasp until her arm went entirely numb. She didn't make a sound, only held Aidan's gaze. "Mr. Critchley was just leaving," she said, forcing a serene tone. "I'm sure I have a spare moment to discuss your business."

Now there was nothing Critchley could do that wouldn't invite further investigation into his presence, investigation that a man like him would not appreciate. Really, when someone chose to live a sordid life of criminal blackmail, one ought to realize the difficulties one might therefore encounter. Some men had no acuity whatsoever.

Critchley had no choice but to release her arm—although not without a last painful wrench behind her back—clap his hat upon his head, and step past her out the door. Aidan politely stood aside, somehow managing to impart both gentlemanly disinterest in someone of a lesser caliber and masculine delineation of territory. The two men circled slightly, never taking their eyes off one another.

Woof.

Of course, Madeleine knew to keep such irreverence to herself. Men lacked a proper sense of the ridiculous sometimes.

She also knew the only reason she felt such a giddy rush of lightness through her body was that Critchley was gone, for the moment anyway. It had nothing to do with the fact that Aidan stood so near she could smell the sandalwood-scented soap he used. Having rid herself of Critchley, she now needed to get rid of Aidan as quickly as possible.

It was time to leave. Her ship was due to undock by noon. She might already be too late.

Forcing herself to ignore the inconceivable fact that Aidan de Quincy was standing on her very doorstep, Madeleine tightened her grip on her valise and began to step around him. Heavens, he smelled good!

Despite the fact that he was definitely, absolutely over her, Aidan was at the edge of his self-control. The scent of her was fair to driving him mad. He could hardly think for the heat pulsing through his body. He'd thought himself well and truly cured—what a terrible joke that was.

The first sight of her was like a blow to the gut. It was

as if he'd had the breath knocked out of him, and yet as if he'd finally remembered how to breathe.

She was as beautiful as ever. She ought not to be. Her evil acts ought to show upon her face. Instead, she looked lovely, all willowy grace and deceptive vulnerability. Her eyes, so huge and dark, so bottomless—he'd nearly fallen into them all over again.

Then the memory of his humiliation, still hot and cringe inducing, swept him, and he could scarcely look at her. How unbearable that she could still have so much power over him.

Then that fellow had the temerity to pretend ownership of her! Love her or hate her, Aidan wouldn't leave any woman in the hands of such a scoundrel.

Yes, she was as lovely as ever. Except . . .

Ah, yes. There were no more teasing smiles or husky laughter. The light that was Madeleine's lust for life had dimmed. She seemed . . . careful?

Well, that was fair enough. He'd been a bit short on *joie de vivre* himself.

She picked up her bag and began to march past him. His chest spasmed at the thought of letting her walk away.

It wasn't the ache of loss. It couldn't be. It was because of Melody. He still required the answers he'd come for. He needed to know if Melody was his child.

That, and only that, was what made him reach for her at that moment.

As she passed Aidan, the tentative touch of his hand on her shoulder stopped Madeleine as Critchley's cruel grip never could have. She felt the world slow until her heartbeat resonated like the bells in a church tower.

If she closed her eyes, she would see that hand smoothing over her naked skin, feel the hard yet tender heat of it scorch her most delicate places . . .

But her eyes were open now and they would stay that way, by God!

CHAPTER 6

Madeleine took a deep breath and turned to face him, taking a single step to move out from under that undemanding touch. Aidan wasn't a grabber. He wouldn't stop her if she turned to flee him. As long as she remembered what she was about, she could afford to spare him a moment.

Then she would be on her way.

Yet her determination didn't change the fact that as she gazed into his eyes, the sounds of the busy street around them faded away like a dream. She heard her own heart and she swore she could hear his as well.

I missed you so.

His shadowed gaze—when had he become so somber?—moved over her slowly, then fixed on the valise in her hand. "You are going on a journey?"

Oh, yes. She was fleeing for her life. How silly of her to forget, even for a moment. She raised her chin. "I am leaving London."

His dark eyes met hers once more. Would she always feel such a jolt from his gaze? It was a good thing she would be far from here by the time the sun had set.

"You do not intend to come back." A statement, not a question. She didn't bother to answer.

"What is it you require, my lord?" He did not deserve

her impatience, but if she did not turn and leave him now she might very well fall upon her knees and beg him to take her back into the house and make love to her until she lost her mind. Which plea would no doubt cause him to pull away in revulsion.

Wouldn't that simply complete this splendid day?

"I have something of great importance to discuss with you. I realize that we did not part on the best of terms . . ."

Dear lord, he'd chosen now to apologize? Sickening urgency grew in her belly. Every instinct she possessed cried out for her *run*.

"It has come to my attention that there may have been consequences to our assignation . . ."

As he spoke, Madeleine's gaze flickered past him to spot Critchley loitering at the corner. Fear twisted her gut. Oh, God, how was she going to slip away now? Aidan asked her something. She moved to one side to use his big body to hide herself from Critchley's view and murmured an abstracted assent.

"Bloody hell!" Aidan burst out.

Madeleine blinked in surprise, fixing her attention upon him once more. He was furious! What had she said? "Ah . . ." Swiftly, she played his words back through her mind. Something about three years gone by and had she perhaps forgotten to mention having his child—

Oops. She held up both hands against Aidan's towering rage. "Now, my lord, I fear you have misunderstood—"

His eyes narrowed. "I understand perfectly well. You hate me so much that you would send my daughter to live in squalor!"

Aidan had a daughter? For a moment she was stunned to realize he thought she'd had his child. Of course, it wasn't an impossible misconception. It was a rather lovely thought, really.

Yet, conceived by him at that same time? A child who wasn't hers, obviously. Which could only mean that Aidan had had another lover during their time together.

The bastard. The *liar!*

You're hardly the pot to call the kettle "liar."

Irrelevant. Besides, *he* didn't know that! Which meant that while he'd believed her to be faithful and true, he'd been taking another woman to his bed! To make it worse, it sounded as though he'd abandoned that wanton creature as well!

She folded her arms and faced down his fury with her own. "You walked away, if you recall. *You* decided we were finished and *you* removed yourself from my life. I owe you no explanation whatsoever!" All true . . . for once. She must not forget the damage her heart had sustained as well. For a single moment she had been less than the perfect woman of his fantasy, and so he had deserted her.

Never taking his furious gaze from hers, Aidan snapped his fingers in the air. In seconds, his carriage pulled up alongside them. Bloody hell, the man had style.

"Get in," he growled. "It's high time you met your responsibilities."

At that moment, Madeleine remembered Critchley dawdling around the corner and climbed swiftly into the carriage without argument. As she settled into the unaccustomed luxury of velvet cushions and expensive springs, she was already trying to figure a way out.

She could work this out with Aidan on the way—and perhaps even finagle a ride to the docks. He owed her that at least—imagine thinking she could ever abandon her own child! What an idiot!

You're only angry because now you must imagine his talented hands on someone else's skin.

Too bloody right! And she was going to stay angry until she made him pay at least a little!

Not to mention that she would have claimed to give birth to a litter of kittens if it would get her out and away from prying eyes watching . . . always watching.

Aidan hesitated a long moment before following Madeleine into the carriage. It wasn't even his own. He'd hired a hack from the club. The Breedloves had the use of the Blankenship carriages for the moment. For a ridiculous moment he wished he had his own transport—that he had the upper hand upon his own turf.

He tightened his grip on the strange door handle, fighting the trembling in his hand.

Get hold of yourself, man!

Her eyes had flashed when she'd rightfully berated him for his neglect. He blamed himself every bit as much as he blamed her. Yet through it all, he'd been unable to ignore the high color in her cheeks, the way her hair always tended to fall from its pins on the left side—so endearing, that little flaw—and the thinness of her wrists within her gloves, and the way her gown had faded away from its seams. Sympathy twanged beneath his fury and confusion.

Was she penniless, then? That man had not been her lover. The scorn in Madeleine's face had told him that. Creditor? It would explain the note pinned to Melody's coat. "The mony stopped coming."

She has no current protector. That simplifies matters.

Relief, that was all that thought inspired in him—simple relief that he wasn't going to have to detach some rich old man or wealthy callow youth from her clutches before he shipped her off to live at the Blankenship estate. It was not satisfaction, nor the irrational hope that no man had touched her since him.

He would not be such a fool as that again.

Madeleine wasn't going to like his plans for her. He only hoped that reconnecting her with her child would inspire some glimmering of maternal instinct within her cold soul. If she could only see that it would be best for Melody, he was sure she'd agree to take up residence there until the child was grown.

If necessary, he would make it financially rewarding for her, but she *would* go.

A pretty bird, kept in a gilded cage, whom you visit for your own pleasure? Does that sound like the woman you know?

Ah, but he didn't truly know Madeleine, did he? She'd made that perfectly clear years ago.

He took the step into the carriage, his fury now well set in stone. As he settled into the seat opposite her, he forced himself to gaze directly at her, his expression hard.

She tore her gaze from the street and raised her chin. "So flinty, my lord. Are you willing to hear what I have to say now?"

"No," he said curtly. "Not a word until we reach Brown's."

Her brows drew together. Ignoring his command, she leaned forward. "Your gentlemen's club? I shan't be allowed in."

"I managed to get your daughter inside. I believe I can do so for you as well."

Her brows rose. "Really?" She glanced out the window on the near side, then leaned forward to look out the opposite one. Was she still worried about that greasy creditor?

Finally she sat back with an air of relief. "Brown's will do for now," she said primly. "But you will have to listen sooner or later, my lord."

How could he listen when his mind was full of the past? Fresh hunger vied with old pain, still sharp. He still craved her, damn it!

From the instant he had first touched her hand, Aidan couldn't stay away from his fey, sprightly Madeleine. Far from sad, the widow seemed determined to suck the marrow from every moment as if she truly didn't believe she would have another chance.

When they tumbled into her bed that first night, she was breathless and pliant in his hands. For a strange moment he thought virgin, but of course she wasn't. It did cross his mind that her late husband hadn't been much of a lover, but he didn't ask and she didn't volunteer.

It was as if there was no past. There was only each breathless moment, more thrilling than the last.

When they talked—and they did talk, occasionally!—it was of childish dreams, of likes and dislikes, of passion and ideas. No past, no future.

By unspoken agreement there was no one else allowed in their world. They were new and pure for each other and it made them brave. They gave each other what they had never given before.

She'd brought out the wild creature in him. He'd never

been such a lover before. In fact, before Madeleine, he'd been so damned gentlemanly in bed that he'd scarcely broken a sweat! She had a way of sweeping away his righteous boundaries, of laughing away his moral inhibitions and unleashing a man he'd never realized lived within him. She'd made him see his own darkness, his own towering passions, his own possessive animal nature that lived beneath the façade of reason and civilization. He'd reveled in it then, though he'd denounced it later.

Yet he couldn't forgive her for it. How was he to go back to being the man he'd been before, tightly wound and quietly forlorn, knowing what he knew about himself?

Instead, he'd become hard. Grim, even. Jack had complained of it, but even his friendship could not ease the burden of being a passionate, primal man with no outlet for that passion.

Now, he could only glare wordlessly at the creator of his misery. *Beautiful, fragile devil in a faded dress, what am I to do with you?*

Madeleine gazed down at her hands, pretending fascination with the strings of her reticule. Aidan was glaring at her again. She could feel the repressed animal inside him, ready to rise up and spring at her.

She wasn't afraid. No matter how enraged he might become, Aidan would sooner leap out a window than strike a woman. No, what she ought to fear was her own weakness.

Letting her eyelids droop, she allowed herself to feel his presence like heated pressure upon her skin. She could imagine setting aside her things, undoing her bonnet, and moving catlike across the carriage to sit astride his lap, riding the jolting motion of the carriage until they both cried out in completion—

With shock she realized that she'd dropped her reticule and was even now slowly tugging at her bonnet ribbons! She hurriedly masked the motion, pretending to tuck a fallen strand of hair away. Madness, that's what this man inspired in her!

She would hide at Brown's only long enough to explain this terrible misunderstanding and then she would be on her way!

Her way to where? She would miss her departure time now and there wasn't another boat to Jamaica for days. She would have to maintain the lie at least that long, for she could hardly expect the furious glowering man opposite her to nod understandingly at her lies, then allow her to stay at his expense for three days!

Blast it, why had she gotten into this carriage? Because he'd ordered her to?

No, because you wanted to be near him.

Sentimental idiot, passing up her chance for escape so she could moon over a man who hated her!

He hadn't always been so hard. Madeleine still sometimes reddened in the light of day, suddenly recalling an outrageously delicious moment with Aidan from years before.

She had not known she possessed such a wicked animal nature, nor that she would explore it so shamelessly. When she thought of the things she allowed him to do— the things she'd done to him!—her knees would go unexpectedly weak and she would have to sit.

Oh, my love, I want you to do it all again . . . and again . . .

"Are you unwell?" His jaw was hard but his tone was formal, his shadowed expression carefully neutral.

"I am fine." *I am not fine. I am fevered, short of breath and I can feel my own pulse between my thighs. Does that seem well to you?*

Memories of that first night together overwhelmed her. The first taste of his mouth, the first touch of his hand upon her breast, her thigh . . .

The first moment of having the depth of him inside her, unlike anything she'd known before.

Those firsts—those panting, sweat-dampened, aching firsts—were burned upon her memory like brands. For the rest of her life, the first night with Aidan would live in her memory as the moment she had woken as a woman.

The Madeleine she had once been would have been appalled at making love to a man she'd known for only hours, a man not her husband.

She might have blamed it on the sheer romance of that moment of rescue, or she might have chalked it up to her own loneliness and fear of being truly on her own for the first time in her life, but Madeline always told herself the truth, if no one else. She'd thrown herself into Aidan's arms that very evening because she'd fallen in love with him in that single insane moment when he said, quite earnestly, "You ought never to walk alone."

Finding Aidan had been a gift—the gift of herself when she was with him, a self she'd never truly known before. With him, she did not exercise her wit in order to charm or entertain. Nor did she repress her thoughts or impressions. She was merely, and ultimately, herself. She was able to be out loud the woman she'd always been in the privacy of her own mind.

And in the privacy of my own mind, I love you still.
Idiot. Recall that daughter that isn't yours?

Fine. She would go get a look at that daughter and take away an image to keep in her mind when she was wont to dwell on Aidan's virtues. After all, this was a man who abandoned her simply because she wouldn't allow herself to be owned. What became of his midnight whisperings of devotion then?

Marriage—what a horrible concept, undoubtedly dreamed up by men for the benefit of men! She was better off on her own.

Even when that man was Aidan?

Even more so, for she would lose her will altogether anytime he should so much as touch her hand. She would adhere to her plan. If she could not catch the ship today, there was another in three days time. In a few days, she would slip away again, this time forever.

CHAPTER 7

The hired carriage, woefully unmarked, took Madeleine and "my lord" off down the street, leaving Critchley behind. Still burning from the humiliation of being stared down by that beefy colossus, Critchley snarled as he dabbed at his sweating face with a mildew-speckled handkerchief. Who did that rotter think he was?

That single moment had been enough to transform Critchley back into the pudgy, sullen boy he'd been in school, and he hated the blighter for it. Memories swept him of the bullying and pranks he'd endured before Wilhelm had selected him as a companion. Of course, Wilhelm's bullying and pranks had been every bit as severe and humiliating, but those had mostly been in secret, and at least young Critchley had belonged at last.

Now he was lost again. Having lost Wilhelm's favor, he now slunk about London, gambling away most of his meager family allowance at the games and races he was unable to win, and spending the rest on absinthe and the hookah. He'd never been the brightest, at least that's what his father had said once, but recently his mind had seemed to wander more and more.

Seeing Lady Madeleine had brought what was left of

his mind into nearly sharp focus. Lovely, delicate, vulnerable Madeleine . . .

She had obsessed him since the moment Wilhelm had brought her home. He'd known immediately why Wilhelm had chosen her above all the others. She was more than beautiful, more than simply sexually desirable. Young, sweet Madeleine had a glow about her, as if she were alight with innocence and purity. It emanated from her and pulled at Critchley like a natural force. Ugly moth to the lovely flame, he'd made a fool of himself from the start.

Wilhelm had laughed so. He'd delighted in giving Critchley every detail of her deflowering, of her cringing and crying, and then came stories of her becoming a jaded sexual addict, eagerly begging for all the most humiliating acts. That the bloom was off the rose did not matter much to Critchley. It only fired his weak imagination with lurid detail.

Wilhelm had even offered her to Critchley once during a rare lucky run at cards. Then, when Critchley had dared to actually arrive in her ladyship's bedchamber, perspiring and fervent, Wilhelm had been waiting with two burly footmen, who had beaten him soundly and tossed him from the house. It had taken Critchley months to beseech his way back into favor, and then only by way of subtle blackmail.

And then Lady Madeleine had come to him herself. Disguised as a housemaid, she'd arrived in his guest room before dawn one morning with a proposition. If he would steal her from this house and take her safely to London, she would lie with him willingly. Of course, at first she'd offered him jewels instead, but Critchley knew desperation when he saw it. It had taken some doing to convince her that one night with him was a small price to pay for a lifetime of freedom, but in the end she'd quietly agreed.

How he'd mourned her when he'd thought her lost forever. How he'd mourned his lost chance at heaven between her thighs.

He'd never had his night with her, yet here she was, a free woman living in London after all. To his somewhat muddled thinking, that meant he was owed, by God!

And now here he stood on this shabby street corner, his hand still burning from its brief, luscious encounter with her breast, and his face burning with humiliation once again. His mind clearing in direct proportion to his anger, he scowled at the disappearing carriage and turned his fury into effort at discovering the minor detail of that giant bastard's identity.

He would have what was owed him . . . and so would Lady Madeleine.

Hidden away in Brown's, Melody lay on her belly on the carpet, her chin propped on her hands, her feet waving idly in the air. The coals glowed in the fireplace and the floor was warm, not like at Nurse Pruitt's where she'd had to wear rags wrapped about her legs in the winter. Still, Melody wriggled restlessly.

Uncle Colin wouldn't let her move because he said she'd only set disaster in motion and that wouldn't do because he'd just got her clean again.

She hadn't meant to dribble the porridge down her pinafore. The porridge here was much nicer to eat than the thick, chewy mess that Nurse Pruitt made, but it was also harder to keep on the spoon.

Sighing loudly, Melody began to roll over onto her back.

"Ah! Don't move!"

She froze obediently and waited while Uncle Colin saved the pitcher from falling off the washstand she'd just kicked with her feet. She blinked up at him. "Sorry, Uncle Colin," she said sadly.

He picked her up and held her high so he could look her in the eye. "Captain Melody, it was a near miss but we have saved the ship from sinking again."

Penitence happily banished, she dangled, twisting her feet eagerly. "Is it the *Dizzonor's Plunder*?"

"Aye, captain, 'tis the *Dishonor's Plunder* indeed. But we hove to and hoisted the mains'l. All is right at sea once more." He hefted her to his hip. "Listen, Mellie—"

She held up one finger. "Cap'n Melody."

He grinned. "Captain Melody," he corrected. "Uncle Aidan has gone to look for your m— for someone. He'll be back soon, and when he comes I want you to be clean and ready. So just play quietly, all right?"

She looked at him. "With what?"

"Er . . ." He looked around, turning them both in a circle. "With . . ." He moved to the wardrobe and began to open drawers. "With this!" He pulled out a long white piece of cloth and handed it to her.

She took it. "Thank you," she said seriously.

"You're welcome," he said and put her back on the floor where she had started. "Go on now."

Melody looked at the long cloth for a minute, then started to wind it around her arm. "Look, Uncle Colin, I'm broken!"

"That's good, pet," he said absently.

Melody frowned at him where he stood looking out the window. Then she balled up the white cloth and threw it on the floor. "Don't like it!"

He turned and looked at her then. "Why not? It's a wonderful cravat—I mean, it's anything you want it to be." He knelt on the floor with her and began to do something with the cloth. "Look, you can practice knots. Pirates tie knots, you know."

"Pirate knots?"

He coughed. "Well, not exactly . . . but I do know a few neckcloth styles. This one is called an Osbaldston. Watch me."

Melody watched but it didn't look like anything but a fat knot like Uncle Aidan had tied around his neck this morning.

Uncle Colin untied it and started another one. "This one is called a Gordian—"

Melody shrieked and grabbed the knotted cloth. "It's a doll!"

Uncle Colin frowned at her but she was too excited to care. "See, she has a head and arms and legs and she needs a face, Uncle Colin, make a face, make a face!"

He made that sound he made when he was trying not to laugh. "And here I was worried you lacked imagination." He got up and rummaged through Uncle Aidan's desk. He came back with an inkwell and a quill pen.

"Uncle Aidan is going to kill me, you know," he said as he drew eyes and a smile on the smaller upper portion of the knot. "I think this is his favorite cravat."

"Her name isn't Cravat," Melody insisted as she took the doll back and hugged it, forgetting to keep the fresh ink away from her pinafore. "Her name is Gordy Ann!"

* * *

Slipping a child into Brown's under his coat didn't prepare Aidan for the task of sneaking a grown woman into the club. Perhaps he ought to bring Melody out again . . . but then where would he take her?

No, the priority here was to sort this matter out once and for all. Besides, reuniting mother and child in the street didn't seem . . . well, proper.

"Stay here," he ordered Madeleine. Her eyes narrowed at his tone. Damn, he'd forgotten how she despised anything that smelled even faintly of authority. His jaw clenched as her stubborn chin rose a fraction. He hadn't the time for a battle now. "Please," he uttered from between gritted teeth.

Her brows went up and her lovely lips twitched. "That hurt, did it?"

She was laughing at him. She always had. His gut twisted. Once upon a time her irreverent viewpoint had freed him, had allowed him to be a man he'd never known he could be. Now it only reminded him of the way she'd laughed away his proposal, laughed away his nakedly offered heart.

He turned away before she could read his pain. How he loathed that she could see into him so plainly, as if he were no more obscure than a clean-running brook.

The way cleared. He'd never been more thankful for the skeletal staffing of the club. They had scarcely climbed one floor before Aidan heard the alarming sound of feet running down the stairs ahead and above them. One of the younger footmen must be in a terrible hurry to avoid Wilberforce's wrath.

There was no time to do anything but react. Swiftly

Aidan pulled open the nearest door and yanked Madeleine through behind him—

Directly into the main club room!

He froze. Madeleine impacted softly against his back, then he felt her freeze as well. Aidan winced, awaiting the inevitable uproar. None came. The few occupants of the vast club room continued to read, snooze, and play chess as if nothing whatsoever was amiss.

From where she stood mostly concealed behind him, Madeleine tugged at his sleeve. "Are those two gentlemen dead?" she whispered.

Aidan turned his head to where Lord Bartles and Sir James continued their allegedly decade-long chess battle before the fire. "They don't look any different than usual. I believe Wilberforce gives them a poke occasionally, just to be sure."

She made a small, dubious noise. "Yes, but has he poked lately?"

"Shh."

He felt her go on tiptoe to whisper into his ear.

"I'm only asking because once I found a toad behind the kitchen stove, dry and hard as stone but as lifelike as could be, albeit wrinkled. And they are awfully close to the fire."

He felt her go back down on her heels but within a moment she was back, pressing against him in distracting ways in order to reach his ear.

"And they are very wrinkled."

His ears began to buzz and his neck burned hot where her soft breath touched his skin. It had really been entirely too long. Reaching behind him with both hands, he found her waist—after a moment of delightfully mysterious fumbling that made her catch a quick intake of breath and quickened his own pulse further—and pushed her gently back down and away from him.

He turned his head slightly. "Check the stair," he said out of the corner of his mouth. "Just open it a crack."

He heard the faint click of the door opening behind him, then a quick tug at his coattail. Backing carefully, he followed her into the stairwell once more, then turned to face her.

She was gazing at him with pursed lips. "You fit right in here," she said. "It seems everyone is stuffed and mounted. Is it a condition of membership?"

Aidan didn't dignify her impertinence with an answer. He merely grabbed her hand and continued up the servant stair to his floor, and then down the deserted hall to his door.

Madeleine was fascinated. She might very well be the only woman ever to step foot in this club! She almost felt as though she ought to take special note as the representative of her sisters everywhere.

It was a very handsome place. A great lot of polished wood. Men did seem to love wood.

The hallway was soothingly masculine in blue and gold. Patterned carpet ran the length of the hall, ending at a window draped in blue velvet. It was lined with doors on both sides, rather like a hotel. In fact, it was exactly like a hotel.

So much for the secrets of men.

Aidan opened the door nearest the stair. Madeleine leaned forward curiously. What would Aidan's quarters tell her about Aidan?

There was a spacious sitting room with a grand window. Light streamed in over a carpet of subdued blues and danced upon the few furnishings. She saw a tufted velvet sofa of deep blue and a wingback chair of brown leather. A round rosewood table with four chairs held court near the window. It was a comfortable room, if a bit severe.

Then flash of red caught her eye, pulling her attention through a door on the far wall that opened into a bed-chamber. Her brows rose at the picture of lush brocade bed draperies woven of a rich, decadent crimson silk that was framed by the open doorway. The matching coverlet lay sensuously rumpled on the huge bed, naughtily offering a peek at snow-white sheets so fine they might have been made of silk as well.

My goodness. It's the bed of a rakehell!

Madeleine made a tiny sound of protest as Aidan thrust her into his room, but that died away the moment she saw the tiny person sitting on the lap of another fellow, one nearly as attractive as Aidan, if one liked one's fellows fair-haired and splendidly gorgeous. As handsome as he was, he paled in comparison to the black-ringleted angel perched on his knee.

Aidan's child. Baby-soft hair as dark as his, wide eyes in a slightly easier shade of blue, long dark lashes, and a stubborn little chin . . .

Aidan's child, perhaps, but never hers.

CHAPTER 8

Aidan left Madeleine's side to kneel before the little girl. "Melody, my dear, this lady is—"

Oh no. I lied. Don't say it, don't tell her—

The truth compelled her to open her mouth but the danger outside kept her silent.

"This lady is your mother."

Big baby eyes blinked up at her slowly. Madeleine held very still. Even her breath halted. Surely a child would know its mother, wouldn't it? Yet how did she know? What did she know of children, other than having been one an eternity ago?

The two men were obviously waiting for her to fall upon her knees and clasp the small, confused person to her bosom.

So sorry, gentlemen, but you see, I lied.

Yet even through her discomfort, she could feel the safety of Brown's enclosing her like a warm coat, shielding her from the cold rain of discovery.

I lied, but if you could see your way to allowing me to stay anyway . . .

It was wrong to lie, but the deed was done. The child had been presented and now waited with somber eyes to see what her "mother" would do. It would be a worse sin to let this moment pass without reassuring the wee thing.

That's what Madeleine told herself as she slowly knelt before the little girl, who stood not much higher than her knee. "Hello, Melody."

"Hello . . ." The child trailed off and glanced up at Aidan for guidance.

"Mother," he prompted.

Melody looked doubtfully back at Madeleine. She, for one, seemed less easily convinced. Smart child. "M—"

No, it was too much, even for Madeleine's begrimed soul. "Maddie," she filled in for the child. She settled down on her heels, her hands in her lap. "That will do for the start."

She felt Aidan's flinch more than she saw it. "Maddie" had once been his pet name for her, one that no one else had ever used, not even her father. Even Aidan had only used it in tender, intimate moments. Toward the end he'd taken to whispering it into her hair when he thought her asleep. *Be mine forever, Maddie.*

"Maddie," repeated Melody with a nod. She and Madeleine eyed each other for a long moment. Then Melody stepped forward to wrap her little arms about Madeleine's neck.

The small, warm body trustingly fitted itself to hers. Unexpected tears sprang to Madeleine's eyes. She closed them tightly as she carefully enclosed the child in her arms. A grunt of satisfaction came from Aidan's general direction.

Yes, Aidan. Everything is wrapped up and orderly, in its proper place.

That man truly needed to unwind.

"Well," Colin said brightly, "now that Mrs. Chandler is here, I suppose we are off nurse duty."

Madeleine looked up at him. "I don't see why. I know nothing about children."

Colin eyed her strangely. "Except for bearing them, of course."

Ah. Right. "Yes, of course." Blast it, it looked as if she was going to have to pay for her keep then. No matter. Anything was better than the cold world outside, the one that contained Critchley.

Exhaling briskly, she sat back and held Melody at arm's length. "Well, first of all, let's get that hair properly braided, shall we?"

Melody nodded soberly. "Uncle Aidan mucked it."

Madeleine bit down on her lip. "Indeed, he certainly *mangled* it."

"Mangled it," Melody repeated carefully. "He bloody mangled it."

"Told you," Colin muttered.

Aidan cleared his throat sharply. "I think it's time for Melody's nap."

Colin stared at him. "It's but an hour past breakfast."

Madeleine stood. "Never mind. Melody and I shall freshen up, shall we?" She held out her hand and felt that same warm glow when the tiny one fitted into hers.

"I already went," Melody confided in a loud stage whisper as they passed into the bedchamber. "But you can use my chamber pot. It's blue."

Madeleine tried not to hear the muffled snickers behind her. Sir Colin was going to be a handful, she could tell. She wasn't even sure who he was. Aidan had spoken of his friend Jack a few times, but she couldn't recall a single mention of Colin. Perhaps he was a later addition to Aidan's circle.

Aidan watched his new family disappear into the bed-chamber and gazed at the closed door for a long, strange moment. Family.

"I'm going to have to marry her."

Colin lifted a brow. "Have to? Wasn't there a time when you wanted nothing more?"

Aidan worked his jaw. "Old news. Things have changed. Damn it."

"You seem disappointed. Did you have someone else in mind?"

No, there was no one else. There never had been and Aidan had begun to fear that there might never be. He removed his surcoat and tossed it over the back of his chair. He pulled at his cravat. Everything he wore seemed to confine him and restrict his breathing. He threw himself into the chair and buried his hands in his hair. "Damn it."

Colin snorted. "Such theatrics. What's the difficulty? You needn't wed for money or property, anyway. She seems likely enough. Pretty, if you like the type. A bit lean, but get her with child again and she'll plump right up."

With child. For an instant the vision tempted Aidan. She must have been so beautiful. He could picture her glowing, smiling softly and secretly the way women did when they were carrying.

And he could imagine getting her that way . . .

Having Madeleine in his bed forever, belonging to him at last? Soft, sweetly giving Maddie, with her warmth and breathless passion, twining her limbs about him, twining his heart in knots, binding him to her until he couldn't breathe without her, tearing him mercilessly to bits while she uttered that false, tinkling laugh—

"Damn it!"

"You're repeating yourself. It shows a lack of imagination." Colin looked skeptically at the bedchamber door. "Besides, I thought we agreed she must be Jack's."

"Probably isn't definitely."

"But this woman . . . why wouldn't she simply tell you?"

"Because . . ." *Because I walked away. I insulted her and told her never to contact me. Because my pride forced me out the door and never allowed me to look back.* "Because we didn't end on good terms."

"Meaning you were an ass, of course."

"Of course," came a husky contralto voice from the bedchamber doorway.

Aidan reluctantly turned to look at her, knowing he would see that damned teasing glint in her eye. However, her gaze was dark and somber. She lifted her chin as she took two steps into the room. "Then again, he wasn't the only ass that day."

Aidan swallowed back a sharp rejoinder. Her admission was as good as an apology—and all that he was likely to get from his stubborn, bloody-minded Madeleine.

Not yours, boyo.

Yes. Mine. Whether she likes it or not.

Still, he hesitated to make his wedding plans clear. Whether he was wary of being rejected again or simply giving everyone time to adjust was not a question he truly wanted to ask himself. Suffice to say *he* needed some time.

Melody galloped into the room, using the bedchamber fire broom for a horse. Her little hands were black with soot and so was her only pinafore. She circled the room, enthusiastically giving out a creditable neigh.

Aidan felt his shoulders sag. Even Colin moaned slightly. "But we just got her clean."

Madeleine looked defensive. "Well, it isn't as though these chambers hold a fully supplied nursery," she snapped. "If she's happy with a knotted neckcloth and an ash broom, I think you two ought to count yourselves fortunate!"

Colin stiffened. "We've done bloody well so far!"

"Bloody!" Melody caroled the vulgarity sweetly as she spun in a wobbly circle that sent hobbyhorse ash in an arc through the air to sift gently down to the carpet. "Bloody, bloody, bloody!"

Madeleine folded her arms and raised a brow. "Oh my, yes. Such admirable fathers both."

Sir Colin snickered, but Aidan only glared. Madeleine ignored both reactions and put on a polite face. "Now, would one of you gentlemen mind showing me to my room?"

An awkward silence fell. The only sound was the thumpity-thump of Melody's little boots as she galloped her hobbyhorse back into the bedchamber. Madeleine looked from Aidan to Sir Colin.

Sir Colin snickered. "Good lord, is that the time?" Three steps later he was gone, the door closing decidedly on the tension in the room. As far as Madeleine could see, there were no clocks in sight.

That did not bode well. She faced Aidan straight on. "My lord, where precisely shall I be staying at Brown's?" She had a very bad feeling she knew the answer. He wouldn't dare, would he?

CHAPTER 9

"You are staying here," Aidan informed Madeleine stiffly, "in these rooms, with Melody . . . and with me."

He would dare, it seemed. Chilly apprehension warred with undeniable warmth inside her.

He wants you still.

Not bloody likely. She lifted her chin. "I don't see why that is necessary. You have arranged Melody's right to be here. Why can you not do the same for me?"

He flushed slightly and turned away, seating himself in the large chair by the fire—the king assuming his throne. "Melody appeared on the doorstep only yesterday. I cannot take her to my address in town, nor can I excuse myself from the House sessions just yet. Her existence here is temporary, as is yours—" Goodness, that sounded rather dire. "—and for the moment it is . . . well . . . a secret."

Madeleine took her bottom lip between her teeth as she considered that. "So you intend to hide your secret baby and your secret ex-mistress in a gentlemen's club on St. James?"

He looked over his shoulder at her with a slight twist to his lips and that particular gleam in his eyes—the one that meant she was overstepping. It always stirred a devilish bit of her that couldn't help but push further. "Or am I to be mistress once again?"

He turned his body more fully toward her and leaned back in the chair at an angle, stretching his arms and then twining his fingers behind his head as he gazed at her. He looked big and masculine, composed, but still somehow poised to spring into motion. His body fascinated her still, for who but she knew what lay beneath those perfectly tailored coats and well-fitted breeches?

His other lover.

Well, yes. Still, she didn't think he'd been all that active a player. Men such as that became notorious, even to women who could only afford to read the gossip sheets they found drifting in the streets. That wasn't to say he could not have had a discreet affair in the past few years. A man like him . . . a man with shoulders twice as broad as hers that tapered to slim hips and long, muscular legs that led up to a hard, muscular—

Right. She was trying to make a point. Fighting her own speeding pulse, she dragged the memory of the last words said from her memory. Hmm, best ignore that remark about mistresses . . .

"I must admit," she said casually, "it is the last place anyone would look." Including Critchley. She might be mad for going along with this—but in its very madness it was brilliant. "I take it I shall not have the run of the club, then?"

He had the decency to look a little embarrassed at last. "We cannot let the staff know you are here. I do intend to arrange alternative accommodations as soon as . . ."

She narrowed her eyes. "Do be specific, my lord."

He hardened his jaw as he stood to face her again. "As

soon as I am sure you can be trusted with Melody's welfare," he growled. "You have not shown a natural maternity thus far."

Despite the ludicrous nature of the accusation, considering that she had been a mother for precisely a quarter of an hour, Madeleine was offended. "Says the man who found his child yesterday morning!" She strode up to him. "Tell me, Papa Bear, how is your paternity faring so far? Giving a bath and tying a knot doll hardly qualify you to judge!"

Oh no. She was too close. He towered over her, his broad shoulders blocking the light. For a moment she was back in bed with him, covered by him, impaled upon him, wrapped around him as she shivered helplessly in the throes of yet another orgasm.

Shoulders like that could shelter a woman for the rest of her life—if she was mad enough to lie and cheat and sell her soul to get them.

No. She must not stand where she could feel him, where she could breathe him in, where she could reach out to touch him so easily.

Step away. Move.

She did so, one painful step at a time. Turning away, she forced her feet to carry her to the opposite side of the room. "How . . ." *Get your mind off those shoulders, you idiot!* She cleared her throat. "How shall Melody and I get on? If the staff is not to know we're here, who will bring our meals?"

Even as she spoke she restlessly picked up a child's jumper that was crumpled in a corner of the settee. As she absently fluffed and folded it, she kept moving. She could feel Aidan more than see him, but she knew he was circling as well, keeping his distance but never taking that intensely hot gaze from her.

"Colin has gone out to purchase edibles," he told her in a low voice. "I believe we can use them to stretch the dinner orders."

Aidan watched her put the knitted thing down, feeling it like a blow to his gut when her gown clung her firm shapely buttocks as she bent. He could envision her as if her gown did not exist. He could see those perfect heart-shaped ivory cheeks with the matching dimples above. He could see the crease that hid such secret places . . . unless she was bending, as she was now. Then he would see the pink petals of her creamy slit framed in dark silken curls.

"So it's naught but buttered buns?"

He choked. "What?"

She cast him a glance over her shoulder and moved away once more. "I'm simply asking if we're to eat nothing but things Sir Colin can sneak in his pockets. Could you ask him to fetch me a nice long sausage?"

Aidan closed his eyes. "Colin shall *not* be delivering you sausages."

She turned to him, her eyes wide. "Why not? It should last me a good long while."

"Never mind the sausage!" Good God, he was going to snap, right here, right now. Taking his lust by the throat, he choked it, beheaded it, buried it, and built a crypt. Inhaling deeply, he squared his shoulders. "I shall see to the matter. I'm sure I can increase my orders to the kitchen without drawing suspicion."

She shrugged. "Very well then." Moving behind his chair, she lifted his discarded coat and shook it out. Folding it absently, she pressed it to her bosom with one hand while the other stroked down the velvet, smoothing out signs of his careless handling.

Aidan would have cast his fortune into the waves to be that coat. To feel those hands stroking over him, to press himself between those ripe, rounded breasts, to taste that milky skin—

"Milk!" She nodded emphatically. "With cream, I think."

She was trying to kill him. That was it. She was intent on murder—Death by Excessive Lust—in vengeance for his abandonment.

He twisted and flexed his neck, but the tension of his near-bursting blood pressure refused to lessen the pounding in his head, among other places. "Milk, you say?" His voice was nothing but a rasp.

"Oh, yes. Children must have milk. And cheese. And fruit—you'll have to find oranges, or more apples," she said, pointing to the nearly empty fruit bowl on the table. "There is only one left. I do love biting into a crisp, sweet apple. Somehow it seems to make everything alright." She squeezed his coat to her bosom, her gaze far away as the pressure pushed her breasts high. "Too bad it's far too early for melons."

Melons. Oh my God. She was demonic. "How . . . unfortunate for us all."

She narrowed her eyes at him. "You're mocking me." Tossing his coat back down to fend for itself, she turned her back on it. "What of the housekeeping duties? Am I to be your chambermaid as well?"

Abruptly his lust rose from the dead, bursting from its crypt to take *him* by the throat. *The Lusty Lord and the Cheeky Chambermaid.* Not that he was elitist. He would be just as happy to play the part of Lusty Footman or Lusty Stableboy, as long as it was Madeleine in the low-cut chambermaid costume with a feather duster and a distinct lack of knickers . . .

They circled in silence for a long moment, their gazes locked. *No. We cannot. And yet . . . I think perhaps we will.*

The room became small as they moved about it, restlessly touching things, fighting the draw. She could feel his warmth. He could smell her skin.

Spiraling closer . . . until they stood face to face, less than a yard apart.

He remained silent, gazing down at her. Madeleine abruptly became aware of two things. One, that they were alone together for the first time in more than three years. Two, that her longing for this man had not lessened in the slightest in those intervening years.

She could not break their locked gazes, perhaps because she didn't want to. He worked his jaw and she noticed his breath coming harder. Her own heart galloped like Melody's horse as she felt her skin flush.

Step away. Move.

This time her feet would not obey. *I cannot.* She was physically tied to him by a rope formed of heat and lust and heartbroken craving. A burst of fire exploded between her thighs and she squeezed her knees tightly together in response.

Am I going to go up in flames right here, simply from standing arm's length from him? It seemed a distinct possibility.

Slowly, as if he fought it every inch of the way, Aidan's

hand came up, cupped as if he already felt her cheek in his palm.

Yes. Caress me. One touch of your hand and I shall ignite the very air in this room. Reach for me, for I cannot reach for you. Take me—

Melody galloped back into the room. "I'm dirty!"

Aidan dropped his hand, springing back from Madeleine even as she jerked away from him. He used his other hand to rub the dampness from his heated brow. His empty hand closed into a fist, denying his moment of weakness.

He looked at Melody, blinking back the fog of lust. "I concur," he growled. "You are indeed dirty. It seems to be your natural state, Lady Melody."

Melody's brow crumpled at his gruff words. "I'm s-sorry, Uncle A-a-aidan." Those big blue eyes blinked once, twice, then welled with one giant tear apiece.

"Oh, for pity's sake, my lord, look what you've done!" Madeleine knelt beside Melody and took her into her arms. "Don't mind Uncle Aidan, mousie. Papa Bear is new at the job. You and I shall set it right." She straightened and led Melody from the room, casting one last scathing look over her shoulder as she left. "Now, where's that washbasin?"

Remorse did much to dampen his lust. It certainly wasn't Melody's fault that he wasn't strong enough to resist the siren's call. Aidan opened his fist and gazed down at his palm. So close . . .

So close to losing your mind again. So close to letting her break you again!

He closed his eyes.

So close to heaven.

Or to hell.

He would give anything to be sure of her, one way or the other. The mystery that was Madeleine had haunted him for years. Perhaps, instead of being a profound bother, this was his opportunity to solve it at last.

CHAPTER 10

The afternoon passed with excruciating slowness. Aidan found himself unable to leave his rooms, despite his restlessness.

His rooms at Brown's had always seemed spacious enough. There was a large bedchamber with room for all his things. As with the better rooms, there was a sitting area, which he preferred to call a "study" once he'd filled it with his books, where a man could sit and think and gaze out the window over his morning coffee and a hearty breakfast.

A single man could while away his time nicely in the two chambers with a view of the garden.

So why did he feel as though he couldn't breathe for the closeness? The walls seemed to seal them in, hiding them, lending the hours an illicit tension. Madeleine was very quiet, moving and saying little except to Melody, yet he found himself fascinated by the slightest arch of her brow, the merest wave of her hand. What was she thinking? Was she thinking about him? Was she regretting that day, years ago?

Did you miss me the way I missed you?

It was intolerable. Part of him longed to ride away,

out of London, far from the sight and scent and thought of her.

Of course, nothing had changed. Aidan still could not leave London because of important matters due soon in the House of Lords. The Breedloves still occupied his town house, and he still wasn't convinced of Madeleine's maternal commitment. She seemed fond of Melody, but that was all.

With no respite in sight, he was forced to be aware of her like a prickling upon his skin. When she walked past, he caught a peek down her bodice. When she stood by the window, gazing into the winter-worn garden, he found himself mesmerized by the light on her hair. It was all he could manage not to reach for her, to fall willingly back into the old blindness, the old credulity.

Would it be so bad to go to hell in that particular handbasket?

Madeleine felt exposed and vulnerable knowing that wherever she moved in the rooms, his gaze was upon her. She usually abhorred being watched, but such attention coming from Aidan felt rather . . . warm. He didn't grab, he didn't coax, he didn't try to steal anything from her. He actually seemed just as helpless in the face of their predicament as she herself did.

Yet the fact remained that it was impossible for them to exist in the same two rooms in some neutral, companionable fashion. She closed her eyes against the dreary view outside and again she saw a moment from the past—her hands buried in his thick dark hair, his head between her thighs—

This was impossible. There were simply too many naked, slippery memories!

What's more, little Melody was beginning to feel the tension. One minute she was scolding her cravat doll, the next she burst into frustrated tears because she slithered off the settee, banging her bottom on the floor.

Madeleine sighed and went to scoop her up. "You're just fine, mousie. Nothing but a little bump." Melody buried her damp, slightly snotty face in Madeleine's neck and wailed. Madeleine looked to Aidan, whose expression of concern mingled with confusion.

"Is she injured? Should we take her to a physician?"

Madeleine refrained from rolling her eyes. "You'll not fix it that easily." She rocked her body in some unfamiliar yet instinctive way as she stood there. "I think it's a bit unnatural to keep her cooped up in here. Perhaps she needs diversion."

He brightened. "I could read to her." Then his face fell. "But I don't think she wants to hear Homer or Plato."

She smiled at him. "No, I think not. But it would be a good idea for you—us—to aquire a more childish library."

Us. The word fell into silence and they both looked away.

I ought not to pretend I will be here then. I ought not to let him think we'll be a family. I ought to tell him the truth. And then what? Sleep in a doorway for three days until the next ship, keeping one eye open for Critchley and the other open for bandits and rapists?

As for Aidan, his thoughts ran along similar, if opposite lines. *I should inform her of the marriage plans. I should arrange for them both to travel to Blankenship Hall.* Yet he couldn't do it, couldn't risk seeing that wary, revolted expression upon her face again. He needed matters to stay just as they were, just a bit longer. He needed to know if she was woman or witch before he allowed himself to fall into her hands again. He needed to know her innermost heart.

He was bound to her now, compelled to keep her always. It wasn't about her being hardhearted, it was about him not being wanted, about stripping himself naked and needy and then being rejected. He knew somewhere deep inside himself that she wasn't evil. She wasn't a whore. She was simply a woman who didn't love him—to the degree that she wouldn't even keep his child! Ouch!

There was simply too much to lose in this game.

"Shall we play a game?"

He started. "Please stop doing that."

She blinked at him over Melody's tousled head. "Doing what?"

He shook his head. "No matter. Go on. A game, you say?" He gazed doubtfully at Melody. "I doubt she can read the cards yet."

She smiled widely at him, a laughing open grin. "Think a bit further back, my lord. What did you play when you were very small?"

God, so lovely. How could anyone so sweetly beautiful be anything but good? "Er . . ." He hadn't played when he was small. He'd been nannied and tutored every waking moment. Only once had he managed to escape the restrictive supervision. He'd run off to the stream on the far side of the park, fallen in and gotten soaked, caught a salamander, and then spent most of the afternoon hiding from servants searching for him. It had been one of the best days of his childhood.

No stream nor salamanders at hand . . . "Hiding?"

She brightened. "Of course! Hide-and-seek!" She smiled at him daringly. "I'm very good, my lord. I fear you'll not keep up."

He gave an answering twitch of his lips. "I have an advantage. These are my rooms."

Melody had lifted her head. Her face was tearstained and she sucked woefully on one finger, but her eyes were eager. "Hide now?"

Madeleine shifted her to hold her face to face. "Would you like to hide first or find first, mousie dear?"

"You hide. I find you."

"All right." She grinned at Aidan and loudly whispered to Melody, "Find Uncle Aidan first."

"Cheater." Aidan folded his arms and looked arch. "I hold myself to a higher standard."

Melody giggled. "Funny man."

Aidan raised a brow. "I am not. I am a very serious man." He put either hand up to his ears and wiggled his fingers at her.

Melody chortled louder.

Madeleine huffed. "No fair trying to sway the judge." She put Melody on her feet and touched the tip of her little snub nose with one finger. "Hide your eyes. I'll count for you. When I say 'ten,' you can uncover your eyes and try to find us."

Melody wrinkled her nose. "I *know* how to play." She covered her eyes. "One . . ."

Madeleine laughed and ran for the bedchamber.

"Five . . . two . . ."

At first she dove beneath the bed, then reconsidered. If

she were Melody, it would be the first place she'd look. There was a cloth-covered table in the study, the one that held the fruit bowl.

Still a bit too easy. She didn't want to make it hard for the child, but if Aidan was found first, then she could indulge in some lovely rude gloating, just to ruffle his feathers!

"Four . . . nine . . ."

Almost out of time! She scooted out from under the bed and ran for the closet. Giddy laughter threatened to well forth but she suppressed it. How she needed to play after all those years of worry!

"Six . . . eleven . . ."

Lifting the latch as quietly as she could, she slipped into the closet. Just before she closed it, she put her mouth to the crack and called, "Ten!"

"I *know*," replied Melody testily. "Ready not, here I come!"

Madeleine stepped slowly back, her hand extended behind her. She expected to feel Aidan's clothing . . . she simply didn't expect to feel it full of Aidan!

CHAPTER 11

For a long moment, they both stood frozen, breath stopped, hearts pounding. Madeleine didn't move, but she didn't remove her hand from him either. Helpless with curiosity and a burning urge to have, just for a moment, what she'd once had, she simply stood there, so close to him she could feel his breath upon her neck, her hand the only connection between them.

Until strong arms came about her. A wide hand covered her mouth.

"Shh." Hot breath in her ear. Madeleine's eyes closed in a shiver of pleasure. She left her hand where it was, unable to move or even breathe for fear of breaking the connection to him.

Was she touching . . . ? Yes, he hardened under her palm. His arms slowly tightened about her, pulling her back against him. She leaned into him, her hand trapped between her own rear and his thickening erection, and let her head fall back to rest on his chest.

For another very long moment, neither of them moved. She was afraid. Was he? Afraid to touch again, afraid to feel again? If she lost herself in him again, she'd never leave. That way lay disaster.

Yet somehow she'd forgotten to inform her hand of

that fact. She realized that she was rubbing him in a small circular motion, relishing the feeling of his thick, rigid flesh rising beneath his trousers.

She could have pulled his hand away from her mouth but she left it, allowing his embrace, remaining still except for that one rebellious hand. He pressed her head gently to his chest, tenderly restraining her while his other hand began to rove as well. She went instantly damp.

Touch me. God, please touch me.

At first his big warm palm rode lightly over her torso, sliding up her side, stroking slowly across the upper exposed surface of her breasts. Then up her neck to wrap wide and warm there, his thumb testing the speed of the pulse in her throat. Then his hand slid down, fingertips easing beneath her neckline with familiar accuracy. Her senses, heightened by the darkness and the years without his touch, sent shocks of pleasure through her from the simple roughness of the riding calluses on his fingers and palm. When his hot hand encased her breast, she whimpered and tried to turn her face away from his imprisoning palm. He would not allow it.

A fresh gush of hot wetness between her thighs belied her tiny protest as she submitted. He was going to touch her now and there was nothing she could do about it.

Yes.

She could worry about being independent and self-sufficient later. At this moment she ached to be mastered by him. Inhaling, she raised her chest to fill his hand. As she did so, she slid her other hand behind her to arrange a better, more encompassing grip on his tumescent organ.

He retaliated by sliding his fingertips around to her

nipple, teasing and plucking and rolling it gently. She squeezed his cock in her awkward grip. He inhaled sharply, but did not speak as she thought he might. Instead, he removed his hand from her bodice entirely.

Disappointed, she twisted against his muffling hand again. He pinned her gently back to his chest, not allowing even an instant of freedom. She heard a small, sliding sound before her and realized that he had reached forward to do something to the closet door, securing the latch somehow.

Then his free hand began to slide down the outside of her gown, over the slight swell of her belly, down until his fingers pressed the fabric into the vee of her sex. The inside layers dampened immediately.

He would feel how hot she was, how wet—he would know that she was ready, now, throbbing and eager and entirely available, no matter the consequences. It was humiliating and freeing at the same time. There was no hiding her desire. He held her last shred of secrecy right in his palm now.

His touch rotated slowly, pressing gently, rubbing her own underthings against her swollen clitoris. She jumped and struggled slightly but he only pulled her more securely against him. Her hands trapped behind her, her head pinned back to his chest, she was helpless in his gentle, implacable grip. Her knees weakened as she surrendered completely at last. Her thighs eased and he drove his hand farther between them. Using only that one hand, he bunched the fabric of her skirts high, one handful at a time, until she felt the hem rise completely and his hand could make free with her tender flesh.

Her pantalets were tied with a simple string. He made

short work of that, letting the poor damp things fall to wind about her ankles. That only added to the sweet sensation of being bound by him.

Then his fingers—God, how she'd missed those talented fingers!—slid warm and sure into the slippery folds of her. She gasped into his palm, grinding her bottom back into him helplessly as he slowly invaded her.

In and out, sliding one long finger deeply into her while his thumb worked slippery magic on her aching, swollen button. She rode his demanding hand like a demented thing, squirming and gasping and shaking from head to foot. Whimpers came from deep in her throat, only to be masked by his restraining hand. He kept her pinned to him like a butterfly in a collection while he sent her wild with his sweet, wicked violation.

I am mad. I am completely insane and yet I simply do not care.

The feel of her skin beneath Aidan's fingertips was more than enough to keep reason at bay. The heat of her body against his and the way her roving hand massaged his cock only further justified his insanity. What could he do but take this moment and this woman as far as he possibly could?

Through the sound of his own pulse pounding in his ears, he heard her moan—felt the warmth of her sigh of submission in the palm of his hand.

In his hands . . . God, how he'd dreamed that he'd feel this way again.

She felt it, too, though she claimed not to love him. She was melting to his touch like wax to flame. His wayward hand captured the nectar from her slick, hot petals—proof that she wanted him, proof that she lied at least in part.

Love, he knew not. Lust and hunger and heat—that he knew she needed from him.

She would marry him and he would own this lust and heat and hunger forever. Perhaps someday it would be more. He wasn't a gambling man, but he was willing to wager his future on it.

Finally, he spoke, a deep rasp in her ear. "Come," he ordered. "Come to me *now*."

She did so instantly, as if his hot breath on her skin were all she'd lacked to fulfill her. She came gasping and shuddering and gushing hotly into his palm.

"Good," he said soothingly, bringing her down slowly with gentle, easy strokes, then slipping his fingers from her completely and letting her gown fall once more. "Shh. Breathe now."

He released his hold over her mouth, sliding his hand down to her waist to support her until her head cleared. Even as she reveled in the satisfaction that only he could give her, even as she appreciated his considerate embrace while she recovered, part of her loathed her own weakness. He found her hand and pressed his handkerchief into it. She took it wordlessly. He turned his back, despite the darkness, while she tended herself.

Finally he spoke, his voice low. "I feel as though I should apologize—"

She interrupted with a short breathless bark of laughter. "One more word and you'll not make it out of this closet alive," she whispered furiously. She straightened her clothing, smoothing her rumpled skirts with shaking hands. She would not make herself vulnerable to him again. "This did not happen," she whispered. "Is that perfectly clear?"

The only problem with her breathless denial was that

it made Aidan want to reach for her again. His absurdly endearing Maddie . . . what was he to do with her?

And what was he to do with himself? What madness seized him to strip her of her dignity just to hear her sweet moans?

In the moment that she'd joined the game, she'd laughed—the same sweet husky sound he'd been smitten with four years ago. In that instant, he wanted her back just the way she was before.

At least now he knew that he had not imagined her response to him back then. He passed a hand over his eyes. It smelled of her deepest, darkest secret—whatever her heart might say, her body could not resist his touch. He knew that, had always known that, and had used it against her just now.

How could I do that?

How could I not?

Having Madeleine trembling in his arms again—how had he survived so long without that? He'd wanted so much more. He'd wanted to drag her from the closet and tumble her into bed, craving the sight of her as well as the feel, needing the taste of her as well as the sound of her sighs. If it weren't for Melody outside—

"Melody!"

"Don't fret, Aidan. She hasn't made a sound."

Oh no. *It's not when they're noisy that you ought to worry. It's when they're quiet.*

"Quickly!" He reached for the garter he'd looped about the door catch to secure it. "Are you decent?"

"Allegedly."

They exited the closet to find the sitting room empty

and the bedchamber as well. Then Madeleine saw that the main door was ajar. "Aidan!"

Aidan's heart sank. Melody on the rampage in Brown's Club for Distinguished Gentlemen? "Oh, dear God."

Madeleine frowned. "This place isn't safe for children. We have to find her before she hurts herself!"

I'd be satisfied to find her before she burns the place down. He pulled on his coat. "Stay here. I'll search for her. Perhaps I can catch up to her before—"

She'd folded her arms and stood glaring at him. "Are you insane? Do you think I'd leave finding her to a man? You lot can't find your own socks in your own drawer!"

Aidan opened his mouth to deny it, but really, she had a point. "Fine. You search this floor. Old Aldrich is deaf as a post and blind as a bat. You could probably climb into his lap before he'd notice you."

"Nonetheless, I shall endeavor to restrain myself," she said dryly, but she was right behind him as he ran from the room.

CHAPTER 12

Leaving Madeleine to search his floor, Aidan raced down the stairs, then pulled up abruptly when he saw one of the more mobile fossils glaring at him as he walked by. Tugging his weskit straight, he tried to assume a more sedate demeanor.

"Young ruffians," the old man muttered as he carried on to his rooms. "Ne'er-do-wells, all three of you!"

Aidan did not stop to debate his place in the *haute ton*. As soon as the crusty old patron had rounded the corner, Aidan threw on reckless speed. Casting wildly down the hall, he stuck his head into every empty room and a few that were not. He checked every niche and crawled shamelessly beneath every table. He even checked Jack's room, which was as cold and impersonal as Jack had left it.

You are the worst father in all of England. Your child needed you and where were you?

In the closet with the worst mother in all of England, actually. Unfair to blame Madeleine, perhaps, but his rising panic bid fair to making him irrational.

"Melody!" His hoarse stage whisper echoed in empty room after empty room. In the last room on that floor he would have begged on his knees to hear a reply.

No Melody. Oh, God. If she wasn't here, she must be—
Down in the club.

Flying from that room, he skidded to a stop just outside. "Oh . . . Hello, Wilberforce."

The head of staff stood in the middle of the hall, the portrait of bland helpfulness. Aidan must have imagined the waves of suspicion he felt flowing from the man. *Guilty conscience.*

"Good afternoon, my lord." Wilberforce nodded a very correct bow. "Is there something you require, my lord?" He glanced at the doorway to the unoccupied room Aidan had just left.

A thousand reasonable excuses ran through Aidan's mind and then flew right back out again. To hell with it. The uproar would no doubt start rising momentarily anyway. Melody was probably regaling the entire membership with tales of her chamber pot accomplishments even now. "No, thank you, Wilberforce." He inhaled deeply and ran right past the man, taking the stairs two at a time to the main club floor.

Once there, he realized that there was no one in the main room but Lord Bartles and Sir James, those white-haired fixtures who perpetually dozed before the fire, their chess pieces apparently untouched for decades.

Right. He might as well fear detection by the ivory knights and ebony pawns! Tossing caution to the wind, Aidan freely searched the room. He tossed aside draperies, tipped chairs and crawled under furniture.

When he found himself, dusty, perspiring, and panicked, wedging his big body under the heavy oak liquor cabinet, he was forced to admit that he, a lord of the realm, a man of mature age and education and experience—a man of reason and logic, by God!—had in the past thirty-six hours entirely lost control over his life.

To a baby.

Madeleine waited for Aidan to clear the way, then followed him into the hall. Pausing, she looked about her. There were a number of doors in this wing, but only the farthest one at the front of the house had a tray outside it, waiting to be picked up by the staff. Aldrich's room, then.

The others opened easily to her touch. Melody might very well be in one. They were furnished much more sparingly than Aidan's room, thankfully, so it was short work to lift the dust covers and determine there was no curly-haired imp hiding beneath.

Madeleine didn't bother calling out, for if she were playing hide-and-seek, she certainly wouldn't fall for such an obvious ploy. Melody was very bright, as of course Aidan's daughter would be.

Another woman's child. Another woman's bed.

Not her affair, to be sure. She longed to ask Aidan about it, for he might very well give her the truth, but she couldn't very well do so without revealing her own lie. She'd woven herself a tangled web this time, indeed.

Once Madeleine cleared every room, she stood in the hallway, perplexed. She'd been so sure Melody wouldn't roam far, for it wouldn't be playing the game properly. Melody had been so adamant that she knew the game, she wouldn't like to get it wrong. Another quality she shared with her father.

She spotted another door, at the end near Aidan's room. It was concealed in the paneling like the entrance to the servant stairway. She doubted that Melody would have noticed it, but she was learning that there was little she could put past that clever little monkey.

The catch worked the same way as the servant stair, revealing another stair leading upward. Aidan's room was on the top floor. Therefore, this must lead to the attic.

It looked dark and dusty, and she wasn't fond of that creeping, hair-rising-on-the-back-of-her-neck feeling that attics and cellars always gave her, but she ought to check nonetheless.

Carefully leaving the door wide, she put one hand on the railing and went up the steps far enough for her eyes to clear the next floor. Yes, it was an attic—a very neglected attic, in fact. A few trunks and chests and a single bent coat tree loomed in the dimness, but the space was mostly bare. With all those empty rooms in the club, she supposed there was no shortage of storage. Why carry something all the way up here when one could dispose of it much closer?

Well, it was clear from the unblemished layer of dust on the floor that no little boots had scurried across it recently. Melody was not here.

Relieved, Madeleine descended the stairs quickly and pressed the concealed door shut behind her. Gazing down the long hall to the draped window at the end, she saw no little feet poking out beneath the velvet.

But there were a few draped tables along the length, holding vases that no one bothered to fill any longer. With a sigh, Madeleine got on her knees before the first one and poked her head beneath the cloth. If someone were to come upon her now, they would see nothing but her rear end!

* * *

Aidan poked his head beneath the last tablecloth, aware that he presented a ridiculous picture of nothing but a perfectly tailored but rather dusty arse.

"Well, now. One doesn't see this every day."

Colin. Of course. Aidan closed his eyes in resignation. Crawling backward, for Melody was nowhere to be seen, he emerged from his search to see Colin standing next to him in the entrance hall.

Colin carried a cloth bag heavy and bumpy with the supplies he'd been sent for and wore an expression of dry amusement, his eyebrows high and his eyes glinting as he munched on a bun he'd purchased.

I'm never going to hear the end of this.

"You realized that you're never going to hear the end of this, don't you?"

Aidan straightened and took his time dusting off his knees, elbows, and rear. His panic warred with his pride. Admit to Colin that he couldn't be left alone with a child for an afternoon? Or come up with some brilliant excuse for his bizarre behavior and retain a modicum of self-respect?

There was another possibility. He could run screaming from this place and this situation, board a ship to the Far East and become a bearded hermit who lived on rice and insects.

Tempting . . .

In the upper hallway, Madeleine stood frozen, her back to the wall, the large blue and white Chinese vase she'd just been peering into clutched to her bosom in panic. A bent and wobbly creature who could only be old Lord Aldrich slowly shuffled down the hall toward her.

She held her breath and prayed, however uncharitably, that the gnomish Aldrich was every bit as blind as Aidan had claimed. As he drew closer, he turned to peer closely at her, his rheumy eyes magnified by the thick lenses of his spectacles. Unmoving, her heart pounding in her ears, Madeleine waited for the outcry. A woman! A woman in the club!

Surely he wasn't going to be willing to overlook her presence. Her throat dry, she tried to swallow, tried to form the words to beg his tolerance. He looked her up and down, his lips twisted in displeasure.

Oh, blast. Here it came.

"Hmph!" He sneered at her, speaking a bit too loudly, in the manner of those with loss of hearing. "Tatty bit of modern rubbish!"

I beg your pardon?

Aldrich winked.

Impossible. It must have been a twitch, a tic surely. Never a wink!

He grimaced and turned away, muttering. "Philistines. No one appreciates classical artistry any longer." He shuffled on, his cracked voice rising as he ranted to himself. "The Greeks—now that was sculpture! The Romans, not bad, not bad . . . but the Byzantine era, lovely stuff, truly lovely stuff . . ."

Her breath leaving her in a long, painful wheeze, Madeleine let her frozen knees go. She slid down the wall, clutching her wonderful sculptural vase and giggling helplessly to herself. Sitting tailor fashion on the carpet, she leaned her head back against the wall and laughed until the tears she wasn't prepared to admit to leaked from her eyes.

After a long, relieving moment, she wiped her cheeks, let out a breath, and regarded the vase fondly. "Tatty modern rubbish, my hat!"

At that moment, she heard a giggle and looked up. There was someone tiny and clever hiding behind the drapery after all. She stood, returned the vase to its place on the hall table, and then peered behind the slightly balding blue velvet.

There was a window seat there—which was the first place she would have looked had she realized there was a deep embrasure!—and sitting quite comfortably upon it was Melody.

"There you are! You were supposed to be seeking, you imp! Have you been watching me all this time?"

Melody nodded, giggling. "You're funny."

Relief aside, now Madeleine remembered their need for secrecy. "Let's get you back before someone sees you." She swept Melody into her arms, sneaking a glance through the window at the street below. Was it evening already?

People, men mostly, strolled by singly and in groups. This was St. James Street after all. None of them seemed inclined to look higher than themselves, and likely wouldn't have been interested in the odd girl child hiding in a club window anyway. Relieved anew, Madeleine turned away.

Just as she did so, a movement in the corner of her eye caught her attention. She ducked to one side before peering out the window again. What she had thought was mere shadow within a doorway across the street had taken shape. Was that a man, gazing up at them? She blinked and peered closer but now could only see the slanting shadow of a doorway in the deepening dusk.

Her imagination was running wild again, just like a few moments ago when she'd thought it worthwhile to search inside a Chinese vase! At any rate, the shadow she had seen was tall and thin, not short and round like Critchley.

Now she must find a way to let Aidan know the search was over. Smiling, she thought she knew just the thing.

Colin was enjoying himself a little too much. "You can't explain yourself at all, can you?"

Aidan fumed. Even so, he was ready to confess if it meant help finding Melody. He opened his mouth to tell all, but a sound distracted him.

Thump-thump-thump.

A shiny green apple leisurely bounced down the stairs and rolled to bump gently against Aidan's boot. Both men watched it spin slowly for a long moment.

Colin tilted his head. "And yet another sight one doesn't see every day."

Somehow it seems to make everything alright.

Melody was safely found. Clever Madeleine!

"Ah!" Aidan bent, snatched up the apple. "I wondered where that got to!" He rubbed it on his weskit and took a big bite. He raised a brow at Colin and swallowed. "Shall we retire?"

Colin eyed him narrowly. "Are you sure you want to eat that?"

"What do you mean?"

Colin gazed nonchalantly at the ceiling. "Oh, I don't

know. It just occurred to me that you might want to resist temptation for a bit longer. Have you eased your doubts about Mrs. Chandler?"

Right. As Aidan followed Colin up the stairs, he chucked the apple into the nearest Chinese vase. The very last thing he needed was more temptation!

CHAPTER 13

Back in Aidan's rooms, while Colin displayed his trophies, Melody began tucking into the bread and cheese with the appetite that only being truly naughty could supply. Aidan waited impatiently for Colin to leave again so that he could speak to Madeleine about what had "never happened."

Colin, however, was stubbornly refusing to take the hint.

"So tell me, Mrs. Chandler, about this woman you hired to nurse for Melody—did it not occur to you to wonder what would become of your child when you stopped sending her pay?"

Since this was a very good question and one that he himself had not remembered to ask, Aidan remained quiet.

After a quick glance at Melody to see that she was engrossed in her supper, Madeleine gazed evenly back at Colin for a long moment.

"When there is no more money, there is, undeniably, no more money," she said, keeping her voice low.

Aidan had to admit she had a point. Madeleine had not been living high while her daughter stood neglected. They were both of them in need.

"But you were leaving," Aidan felt compelled to say. "You said you were leaving London."

Madeleine seemed to realize that she was not going to be able to avoid the questions and raised her chin nervously. "I hope—had hoped to find a better situation elsewhere."

"Alone." Colin's flat tone showed what he thought of that.

Madeleine stared him down. "Do you think it would have been easier to do with a child to care for?"

Colin's gaze narrowed. "You're evasive."

"Of course I am." Madeleine's gaze matched his. "You're prying."

Astonishing, to Aidan's eyes, Colin was the first to look away. Madeleine might be many things, but weak wasn't one of them.

"I don't recall Aidan mentioning you when I knew him before, Sir Colin," Madeleine said suddenly. "When did you and Aidan become friends?"

Never, Aidan almost blurted, but that would have been rude. True, but rude.

Colin didn't seem to mind being rude. "We aren't," he said tersely. "We simply have a friend in common."

Madeleine smiled. "Jack." She glanced at Aidan. "You spoke of him so often, I feel as though I know him."

"You wouldn't know him now," Aidan said quietly from his place near Melody. "He has changed a great deal." He stood abruptly and turned away to gaze out the window at the dark garden.

Madeleine made a low sound of dismay. "What did I say?"

Colin murmured a denial. "Jack has not been the same—"

Aidan interrupted without turning around. "Not since I abandoned him, left him to go to war alone."

Colin raised his voice slightly. "You did not abandon him. You have an obligation to your estates and your dependents. It would have been irresponsible for you to leave them. Jack should not have followed that fool cousin of his when the idiot abandoned *his* responsibilities to go play soldier!"

Aidan closed his eyes against his own reflection in the window glass. "We had talked of becoming soldiers together someday, officers in our own regiment, but I knew I could never go to war. I knew it and Colin knew it as well, but Blakely was army mad and Jack was always at Blakely's back, come hell or high water."

Hell had come quickly enough. Two young aristocrats with forged commissions. What chance had they? "Blakely never made it home from the bloodbath, and Jack came back a shadow of himself." A gray, brooding, Jack-shaped reflection that never laughed again.

"Which is not your fault," Colin repeated.

"So staunch," murmured Aidan, "for someone who is not a friend." He turned to see that Madeleine had left the room with Melody. Fixing Colin with his gaze, it occurred to him for the first time that Colin might blame himself for not being able to talk sense into Jack. "It wasn't your fault, either, you know."

Colin's face was hard. "Wasn't it?"

"It was Blakely's fault for being a self-indulgent cretin."

"I could have convinced him when you failed. I was too busy gloating over your failure and missed my last opportunity to speak to him."

Aidan blinked. "You've been carrying that for three years? Colin, he wouldn't have heard you. Blakely was going and there was no way to stop Jack from protecting Blakely."

Colin scowled. "We ought to have shot Blakely in the foot."

Aidan barked a short laugh. "Now you think of it."

Colin gave an answering grim smile. "If he wasn't dead, I'd kill him myself for forcing Jack over there and then dying in his arms, thus leaving the world to congratulate Jack for his 'good fortune' in inheriting Blakely's entailment and estates. How is a fellow supposed to come back from that?"

Aidan had no answer. They both gazed into the fire but there were no answers there either.

In the bedchamber, after they'd both changed for bed, Madeleine tucked Melody into the center of the big mattress and snuggled Gordy Ann into the crook of her little arm. "Would you like Uncle Colin to buy you a real doll tomorrow?"

Melody tucked Gordy Ann beneath the coverlet, smoothing the crimson silk gently in imitation of what Madeleine had just done. "I don't want a real doll." Then she seemed to reconsider such a swift refusal. "I want a kitten!"

Madeleine smiled. Best not to make promises she wouldn't be here to keep. "I adore kittens. What is your favorite kind?"

"White," Melody said decisively. "Black. Orange."

"Do you know what I like?" Madeleine whispered. She leaned closer. "My favorite kind of kitten are the odd-looking ones. You know, the ones with big ears and crossed eyes and rather too much tail?"

Melody giggled. "I want one of those."

Madeleine smiled. "That's right, mousie. Don't ever give up." She leaned down to give the tiny girl a kiss. It seemed the most natural thing in the world, but when she straightened, Melody was frowning at her.

"Maddie, are you really my mama?"

Madeleine pressed a palm over the twist of shame in her belly. Would the lies never end? "I . . ." She swallowed and smiled. "Today I was yours. May I be yours tomorrow as well?"

Melody thought about it for a moment. "Uncle Aidan is my papa."

Madeleine smoothed back a curl from the pale little face. "I believe so, yes." She wondered why Aidan hadn't told Melody to call him "Papa"? Perhaps he was still afraid to let anyone in, even his own child. Again, probably her fault for breaking his heart.

Another long moment of silence from the tiny girl. What was going through that clever little mousie mind? Slowly Melody smiled and then closed her eyes, snuggling Gordy Ann closer still. "G'nite, Maddie."

"Goodnight, mousie."

When Maddie put the burning candle safely high and left the room, Melody waited a really long time before opening her eyes. Then she brought Gordy Ann up to lie on the pillow so she could see the drawn features in the dimness. "When you grow up, you'll live in a big house way up high and have a papa and a mama . . . and another papa . . ."

Suddenly worried, Melody frowned. "I don't know if you can have two papas. I think maybe there's a law."

Aidan sat in the dark sitting room. Colin had taken the candle away when he'd left moments ago. Aidan preferred the dark. So much more effective for brooding.

A light laugh traveled from the bedchamber to the study through the closed door and taunted him with memories. Oh, that's right. *She* was here, filling his ears with that soft, delicious chuckle, filling his eyes with the bare skin of her softly rounded arms and the sway of her hips just grazing the fabric of her loosely draped gowns, filling his nose with the scent of flowers and warm woman that rose from the back of her neck . . .

His imagination—nay, tantalizing *memory*—took over, and she filled his hands with the warm heavy bounty of her breasts, filled his mouth with the salty-sweet taste of her, encased his cock with the hot, wet heat of her—

"Are you all right?"

He jerked upright in his chair and opened his eyes to see her standing in the doorway of the bedchamber with the lighted candle shining behind her. Though she was perfectly decently clad in gown and wrapper, they were of the finest lawn and very nearly transparent against the light. Every curve, every soft, lovely luxury that had once been his to savor was outlined in a halo of sheer drapery and golden light. The faint memory of gifting her with that very set of intimate garments only inflamed the throbbing in his groin.

She tilted her head and frowned into the darkened

room where he sat rigid, trapped by the pounding in his chest and paralyzed by the agony in his groin.

"Aid— my lord, is all well with you? I thought I heard you groan."

Groan? He wanted to roar! He wanted to bound to his feet and sweep her into his arms! He wanted to press her to the wall and grind into her soft body while he invaded that irrepressible mouth with his tongue! He wanted to do everything he'd ever done to her and more—he wanted to perform every despicable act he'd ever heard of and some he was willing to make up as he went along!

She took one step toward him in concern. *Please, stop!* He pushed himself to his feet and moved away from her, to the window, where he tried to cool his lust by letting his forehead drop against the chill glass. God, if she came even an inch closer, all hell would surely break loose!

Hell or heaven? Sweet, hot, transcendent heaven in her arms . . .

No! She's the devil in dark velvet, remember?

Her voice came low through the darkness. "I know what your problem is."

Oh, I sincerely doubt that.

"It's this room. I'm going mad in here as well." She worked her shoulders restlessly. "If I could only go outdoors for an hour . . ."

He gazed at her faint reflection for a moment. She was right. It was only the room, closing them in—and perhaps a bit of male libido too long denied. Natural enough. "I think I can do something about that." He turned to the door, then looked over his shoulder. "Well, are you coming?"

She glanced back at the door to the bedchamber. "What of Melody?"

He smiled, a slight twitch of the lips. "We won't go far."

Madeleine couldn't resist that smile. She followed him into the silent hallway after tightening the belt of her wrapper and slipping into her shoes.

CHAPTER 14

Aidan's objective, whatever it was, took them through the door next to his rooms, the one that she'd entered while looking for Melody. When she hesitated at the base of the dusty stairs to frown up at the darkness above, he held out his hand. "Don't you trust me?"

She slipped her hand into his large warm one. Instantly the grim portal seemed much less intimidating. "I'm not afraid of the dark," she pointed out in her own defense.

"I know you aren't. You prefer it. It makes you feel free."

She glanced at him in surprise. "I never told you that."

She heard him chuckle. "I spent many nights with you. Some things become obvious."

His warm recollection startled her. They had been so careful not to speak of the past. So many things they didn't speak of. So many secrets and forbidden topics.

It was a wonder that they managed to hold a conversation at all.

He took her through the large attic room, guiding her carefully around the bent and broken coat stand to the large window beyond.

She'd never stood so high. The house she'd grown up

in had no more than two storeys, as did the rented one she'd just left. Her husband's house had been a grand three. She now stood five whole storeys above London!

The garden below was a small dark rectangle but the glow of the city could not be hidden, not even by the years of soot on the window. It blurred the lights in the squares and houses and buildings for a quarter of a mile into a radiant smear.

"Goodness!" she breathed.

"It gets better." Aidan reached forward and undid the window latch. It opened with a protesting screech that cause Madeleine to clap her hands over her ears.

He took her out of the window, like some strange tale, into another world. There was a moment of true fear, though he held her quite safe, where she had to step from the window across a narrow ledge to the roof edge just beyond.

Only one step and a brief scramble up a few feet of the mansard-style roof and then he released her to stand quite easily on the flat section of roof. A waist-high decorative railing ran around the entire edge for show rather than safety. It was like a balcony overlooking a magic city, a world she'd never known.

"There," he said, standing behind her and pointing over her shoulder. "South of us. With all the windows ablaze. That is St. James Palace. Remember? That darker area just past it is St. James Park."

She remembered strolling down Pall Mall with him the night they met, but though she'd walked right past the palace, all she remembered was Aidan.

He was so close to her that she could feel the heat of

him through the thin layers of her gown and wrapper. Though the spring night air was cool, she felt heat rise in her cheeks.

The moonlight broke through the thin hazy clouds and coated the view in enchantment. It was ridiculously romantic, a fact that they both recognized but did not dare say out loud.

He was close to her, not touching but hovering protectively. She knew she'd come to no harm.

"Jack showed me this when I moved to Brown's with him. There was a time a few years ago when you could find me up here every night."

Memories . . .

Perhaps . . . perhaps they could speak of it after all. "When I refused your proposal."

She looked over her shoulder at him as he gazed out at the lights. "It was the only place where I felt I could breathe," he said.

"You must know I never intended to hurt you, Aidan." She turned her gaze out to the glow of the city. "I'm not that woman any longer."

"Nor am I."

She snorted. He shook his head with a slight smile. "I mean to say, I'm not that man any longer."

She turned her back on the rooftops stretching away into the night and stood with her hands behind her on the railing. Her eyes, dark and shadowed in the moonlight, examined his face. He swallowed and turned his gaze from hers.

"I like the man you are now," she said quietly. "I like seeing you with Sir Colin. I like watching you with

Melody. You were lover and companion to me, but I never saw you as a friend and a father before. Perhaps I never knew you at all."

"You knew me."

She nodded. "Yes, part of you. Just as you knew part of me. Our time together was almost like a warm correspondence—"

Very warm.

"—in which you receive someone's words and even their intimate thoughts, but you never see their deeds. Limited. Confined to what we wish the other to know. One can lie more easily in that situation, I think."

Indeed.

She turned around again and leaned out over the railing, bracing herself on her hands. "It's a part of London I've never really seen. I wonder now if we can ever truly know someone until we see them in their world."

"You never wished to see my world."

"I wished. I simply didn't allow myself to ask."

"Why not?"

Silence. Of course. Mysterious Madeleine, woman of secrets. If he could open those beautiful, cautious lips with anything short of force, he wouldn't hesitate.

She let out a long breath. At the end of it, he thought he heard, "I'm sorry, Aidan."

She was, he could feel it. Yet not sorry enough to tell him anything of herself. Not sorry enough to let him in. Never sorry enough to risk whatever she thought she'd lose by opening up to him.

What could possibly be so precious to her? She had nothing that he could see. What was there to lose?

The answer was close . . . he could almost feel the

words about to drop into his mind. What an odd sensation. It was as if he already knew the answer, and only needed a reminder.

She broke the moment. "I think it's time we went back inside," she said quietly.

He bent to help her over the difficult part. When she was safely back through the window, she pulled her hand from his quickly, as if she feared he would not release her easily.

When they reached his rooms, he turned from her. "Go back in the bedroom and shut the door," he growled.

He heard a soft exhalation, as if she'd given up on what she'd wanted to say, then a soft rustle of fine fabric, and then, blessedly, the click of the bedchamber door closing.

She could not be trusted. He must not forget that she had never trusted him either. He'd charmed his way into her house and into her bed, but he'd never managed to find his way into her heart. She never told him she loved him, never told him anything, least of all why she refused to marry him.

And if he couldn't maintain his distance, he was going to lose his heart again without gaining a single shred of knowledge of her first.

And that would be the end of him, he feared.

A man rode into London, exhausted from his journey, bitterly envious of everyone he passed in their carriage—though he took care to look as if he was having a marvelous time of it all. His body ached, especially his right arm and hand. He was scarred, burned, from his claw-like hand to just above his elbow. He hid it from view as much as possible, but the scars were always there, like a betrayal—a way for people to see too much of what he'd rather keep secret, too much of the man he was inside.

To gild this perfect hell of a day, he had barely enough silver in his pocket to pay for one night's lodgings.

Still, he was not completely without resources. There was one fellow in town who owed him a favor—or at least was amenable to a little bullying. He needed to present an acceptable front to the bloody shipping magnate or the pompous upstart might not hand over his spoiled mule of a daughter.

It didn't take long to track Critchley down at his grimy little boardinghouse in the Seven Dials. Such creatures always sank to the bottom. Finding the door to Critchley's room locked, he made short work of it with a swift kick that split the doorframe.

The room's occupant was out, which suited him fine. Unfortunately, a quick search revealed nothing of value—until he noticed a loose stone at the edge of the crumbling fireplace. It lifted out easily, revealing something wrapped in a stained handkerchief. Removing the small bundle, he drew back at the smell of sour sweat emanating from the cloth.

"Really, Critchley," he muttered, "Would it kill you to bathe more than once a year?"

Standing, he carried the bundle closer to the grimy window. When the soiled linen was unrolled, something dropped into his hand, glowing richly gold. "Aha! That should pay for a meal or—"

His gut went cold, part fear and part fury. It was a locket, a fine piece worked in gold with an elegant floral motif etched on the front. The beautiful chain slithered through his fingers as he stood there, his breath trapped in his chest.

Madeleine. My Madeleine.

His fist closed over the locket until his knuckles went quite white. "Critchley, old son," he breathed. "You are keeping secrets from me. You ought to know by now that isn't wise."

A moment later, the locket was wrapped back in the cloth, the bundle was back in the stone gap, and the man was halfway down the stair to the street below.

"May I have this dance, milady?"

Madeleine turned to twinkle a flirtatious smile at the handsome earl bowing to her. "Why, I shall have to ask my husband, my lord."

The earl smiled, an engaging gleam in his own eyes as he straightened. "I am certain he won't mind, dear lady. After all, I know him well."

He swept her into his arms with such graceful urgency that the ladies she'd been speaking to sighed in unison. They entered the waltz pattern with ease. He led her about the room with strength and care, but then again, that was the way he did everything—even the way he made love.

She blushed at the thought and ducked her head, but he noticed immediately. Chuckling, he bent to whisper in her ear. "Remembering last night, are you?"

She flamed red-hot, and not just in her cheeks. "Last night was an aberration," she told him tersely. "I shall never allow such a thing again."

"You adored it."

"I was willing to experiment. I shall be sure not to do so in the future."

He tightened his embrace and threw in an extra turn, just to pull her more firmly against him. She could feel him, proud and ready against her belly. The flames grew.

"You are such a liar, my lady," he taunted in her ear. "I'll wager that by the time we get home this evening, you'll be begging me to do that to you again. And more."

She pushed him to a proper distance and continued the dance, her face averted. The shimmering twirling gowns and brilliantly glinting chandeliers blurred to a jeweled smear before her unfocused eyes. "Very well then," she said, her breath coming fast. "But only once more."

He laughed and spun her again in masculine conquest. She was fluid submission in his arms, too achingly aroused to do anything but follow his lead.

Later, in the vast and sumptuous bed—most worthy of an earl—he pulled her naked form beneath the covers to twine hotly with him, skin to skin. "Only once?" His murmur was a hot, deep thrill as he nibbled gently on her earlobe. "Would you care to renegotiate that number?"

She strove to maintain her high and mighty tone. "It is not my duty to do the counting. I am above such things." She failed completely at such arrogance, for each word was a breathless pant.

His fingers were invading her hottest, wettest places even as his mouth moved down to conquer each nipple in turn. The roughness of his cheeks and the heat of his mouth turned her skin into a single live nerve as he kissed his way down, down . . .

Hot tongue inside her, hard to her softness, wet to her

wet. He pushed her thighs apart with his hands and she submitted, no will of her own, no thought but the hunger for his talented tongue to work its magic upon her. She opened to him shamelessly, for what use was shame when such blissful fulfillment was so close for the taking?

Up, down, around . . . flicking over and under, in and out . . .

He pinned her gently when she started to writhe, but there was nothing he could do to stop her rising cries. She buried her hands in his thick hair, urging him onward, greedy . . . oh, so greedy for that moment . . .

Then the tide rose within her, sweeping her thoughts away in rolling waves of pleasure. She gasped his name, calling to him. With the timing of long practice, he rose to lie above her, braced upon his hands.

She reached for him, clung to him. "Now!" she begged him.

He aimed himself deftly and then, just as her orgasm had crested and barely begun to fade, he filled her in a single, long slow thrust.

It worked. It always worked. She was off again, rising like a Chinese rocket flare, this time shuddering in his strong, warm arms again and again as he thrust into her, filling her to almost painful limits, taking her cries into his own mouth as she rode the wave up, higher than before, up and over into the crashing surf of her ecstasy—

CHAPTER 15

Madeleine woke, heated and breathless, her body throbbing from the wicked, wicked dream.

Such dreams had ruled her sleeping hours once upon a night. As the months and years ticked by and she remained alone, they thankfully came less often. And they were so much more than mere dreams.

The ball, that was sheer fantasy. She and Aidan had never gone about in public after that first evening together. She had never danced in his arms or been envied by women of Society. She'd been a hidden mistress, a secret, by necessity.

The rest . . . well, that had not so much been dream as memory. Delicious, wicked memory, to be taken out and reviewed often in the solitude of her own cold bed.

She opened her eyes abruptly. She was not in her own bed!

Ah, yes. She was tucked safely away in Brown's Club for Distinguished Gentlemen, far from Critchley's reach.

And in Blankenship's bed.

She rolled over and buried her face in the pillow, breathing deeply. The faint woodsy scent of him made her close her eyes in mingled pleasure and pain. How could one man smell so good when all the others merely smelled like . . . well, *men?*

She stayed that way, shutting out the world until her body ceased its high, edgy humming and the heat seeped from her blood. She'd made it through one day so far. She could make it until the next ship left for Jamaica.

From the next room came a masculine voice and a high, piping childish voice muffled by the intervening door. Melody was up and about.

Madeleine sat up and looked about the room. Melody's nightgown was tossed negligently on the other side of the bed, the washbowl had been used, and the smudged toweling, stained with a last bit of soot from the ash broom, hung haphazardly from the hook on the washstand.

Someone had washed and dressed Melody in the room while she'd been asleep? Pulling the sheet higher over her bosom in alarm, Madeleine decided not to think on that one too closely.

Hurriedly, she rose and dressed in her oldest gown, pulling her hair back into a simple braid to fall down her back. After all, she wasn't going anywhere, she thought with a rueful smile.

As the hours chimed by that morning, Aidan found himself reluctant to leave the cozy rooms. After they had shared out his breakfast tray, the three of them fell into a relaxed mood that felt suspiciously like . . . well, *family.*

Melody lay upon her belly on the floor with a pencil and some of Aidan's discarded estate papers, drawing "kitties" that looked rather more like potatoes with whiskers and tails. He praised each one warmly as she offered them.

Madeleine presented a particularly charming picture of domesticity as she sat by the window sewing—at least until he realized she was slicing up one of his shirts with abandon!

"Er—"

"Melody needs a few more underthings." She shot him a slit-eyed smile. "Unless you feel up to shopping for them?"

He swallowed. "Ah, no. That's quite all right." There were some worlds into which even the bravest of men did not advance. The world of little girls' underpinnings existed somewhat even beyond that.

She turned back to her work, smiling to herself. He heard something that sounded like "Thought not, you great pansy," but decided it must have been the wind.

He leaned back in his chair by the fire with his news-sheet and reached for another piece of toast from the plate nearby. There was nothing left but crumbs.

He blinked sadly at them, his stomach growling.

"You'll get no pity from me," Madeleine said without looking up. "I only had one bite of the eggs." She bit off a thread and then smiled at him. "Go and drum up some biscuits or something, will you please?"

He brightened. "I'll steal Colin's breakfast, shall I?"

"Too late," said a voice from the doorway. Colin sauntered in, chewing on a triangle of toast. "This is the last of it."

Aidan nearly whimpered. "I'll give you a hundred pounds for that toast."

Colin grinned and tossed the last nibble into his

mouth with satisfaction. "I should say not. I'm a growing boy."

"Growing closer to an early grave," Aidan muttered resentfully. There was no hope for it. He was going to have to bestir himself and seek out the steely-eyed Wilberforce, keeper of the keys to the kitchens.

As soon as Aidan stood, Colin took Aidan's chair and snapped open Aidan's newssheet.

Aidan opened his mouth to protest. *Oy, move your arse! This is my domestic bliss!* But it wasn't yet, was it? He couldn't claim his family until he worked up his courage—er, made the logic-based decision to propose to Madeleine again.

I am a great pansy.

At that moment, she glanced up and smiled at him, a brief and happy smile that made him think of the thousands of fireside mornings before him if she actually said yes this time.

What of all your hurt and betrayal? What of all those things you think she is?

He could have been wrong. He'd been wrong once or twice in his life. He was sure he could remember some occasion if he truly thought upon it.

What of all the secrets she still keeps?

Ah, yes. There were still those, simmering in the air about her, like heat waves rippling from the desert sands.

And what if, like the desert sands, this sweet, laughing, warm Madeleine was nothing more than a mirage?

What purpose would that serve her? What reason could she possibly have to carry on so? None that he could conceive of.

Another mystery or a reason to trust her further?

She glanced up at him again, this time with a playful scowl. "Go, mighty hunter. Kill a teacake and drag it back for me before I take a bite out of Sir Colin."

Colin bowed flirtatiously from a seated position. "You may nibble on whatever you like, my lady."

Aidan narrowed his eyes. Colin had better keep his buttered buns and sausage to himself, by God! "Hmph." Turning, he pulled on his coat and tugged his sleeves straight. "I'll be right back."

Wilberforce was in the dining room, supervising the laying of the linens for the coming evening. Two young footmen fluffed the tablecloth high, letting it fall over the table while the head of staff watched with a critical eye.

When Aidan entered, Wilberforce turned to him immediately, though he'd made no noise. "May I be of service, my lord?"

The two footmen froze instantly, the cloth still hovering somewhat heavenward. Aidan looked askance at the tableau. Were they truly so terrified of Wilberforce that they would not let the linen touch the rosewood tabletop until the butler turned to watch them once more?

One of the footmen shot him a wild-eyed pleading glance, clearly beseeching him to hurry it up. Right. "Yes, Wilberforce . . . I, ah, find myself a bit, ah, more peckish of late . . ."

"Of course, my lord. I shall take care of it by the noon meal."

"Hmm. Yes . . . well . . . what I really mean to say is . . ." He was a terrible liar. He'd had no practice at it, dammit! He was a peer, a wealthy man, all he needed to do was order something and it appeared before him! He cleared his throat. "I'll need another breakfast immediately."

Although he'd scarcely had a taste of the first meal, he found himself sucking in his belly when one of the footmen glanced in that general direction. Wilberforce was far more self-disciplined. He didn't so much as flicker his eyes from Aidan's face. "Of course, my lord. Is there anything particular you would prefer this time?"

"Toast." His stomach growled. "A great deal of toast. And a teacake. And . . . ah . . . a bit of . . . milk." Grown men did not drink milk. God, everyone was going to know he had a child sequestered in his chambers!

Wilberforce didn't blink. His eyelids didn't even shiver. "Of course, my lord. I shall have it brought up immediately." He folded his hands before him. "If I may ask, my lord . . . ?"

Here it came. They were truly pinched now. "Yes?"

Wilberforce did not break his eternal blandness. "Is there something amiss with the bell pull in your chambers, my lord, that you needed to seek me out yourself?"

You mean besides the fact that I had to tie it up to keep it from curious, sticky little fingers and the fact that I don't want anyone coming to my rooms to answer it?

"Ah, no . . . I simply . . . ah . . . felt the need for a bit of a walk." Ridiculous statement, but he forced himself to stare Wilberforce down as if he were making perfect sense.

Perhaps the butler was used to bizarre requests from the crotchety fossils at Brown's, for Wilberforce only bowed easily. "Of course, my lord. May I assist you in any other way?"

The tablecloth still hovered, but it was beginning to quiver in the air. The rigid footmen begged him with their eyes. Aidan waved a hand as he backed from the dining room. "No, thank you, Wilberforce. Please, carry on."

"Thank you, my lord." Wilberforce turned back to the footmen, and the tablecloth sailed with stately grace onto the table as if the scene had never been interrupted.

With the oddest feeling that he'd not gotten away with a thing, Aidan made his way back to his chambers.

When the Earl of Blankenship left the room, Wilberforce gazed into space for a long moment. The two footmen fidgeted worriedly for a long moment.

Finally young Bailiwick found the courage—or possibly he simply couldn't bear the suspense any longer—to ask. "Sir? Is there something wrong with the tablecloth, Mr. Wilberforce?"

Wilberforce dropped his thoughtful expression and fixed young Bailiwick with a freezing stare. "Monkeys."

Bailiwick swallowed in alarm. His gaze flickered about the room but there were no monkeys to be seen. "Sir?"

But Wilberforce had already dismissed him from his attention and was gazing after the earl. "Monkeys, indeed," he murmured.

CHAPTER 16

When Aidan made his way back to his rooms, he found Melody was now perched on Colin's knee, listening to some story—which apparently left Madeleine wide-eyed with dismay, for she sat with her sewing clutched forgotten in her lap as she listened.

He sat next to her on the sofa. "What is it?" he whispered.

She turned to him, her brow furrowed. "I believe we've just had our second beheading, our third keelhauling and if I'm not mistaken, we're about to have another garroting—yes, I was right. There he goes again!"

Aidan brightened. "Ah, pirates!" He settled down to listen.

Madeleine blinked at him. "But Aidan, do you think that's appropriate for a baby's ears?"

He shrugged. "I haven't the faintest idea. She seems to be enjoying it."

Melody was, indeed, completely engrossed in the bloodthirsty tale. In fact, as he listened, it seemed to be little more than violence and gore. Aidan enjoyed it immensely.

When Colin wound down with a final violent battle— that left Madeleine with one hand covering her mouth in horror and had a body count so high Aidan was beginning to wonder where the extra pirates had come from—Aidan applauded with great enthusiasm.

"You ought to write that down," he urged Colin. "You'd sell a thousand copies!"

Colin let Melody slide back down to her paper and pencil, where she immediately began to draw potatoes with sword hilts sticking from them. Colin scoffed openly at Aidan's suggestion. "Nonsense. It would hardly aid my reputation as a scholar. No one would ever take my papers seriously again."

Madeleine leaned forward. "You're a scholar, Sir Colin? What do you study?"

Colin leaned back, happy to have another audience. Aidan prepared to drift off into a doze now, as he usually did when trapped into listening to one of Colin's dreary lectures.

"I'm working on a formula to calculate the population growth of the next century, based on life expectancy, birth rate, declining social values, median temperatures, and the evolution of the gin mill."

Madeleine frowned. "I understand life expectancy and birth rate, but what do all those other things have to do with one another?"

"Nothing," muttered Aidan. "Colin is full of horse apples."

Madeleine slapped gently at him. "Shh. I'm listening." Aidan grinned, enjoying her newfound ease with him. Even with Colin droning on and on about the temperature of gin and society or some such claptrap, sitting there with her felt good. It felt . . . right.

It feels married.

Yes, well, about that . . .

You haven't done a thing about that and you know it. Have you appealed to the bishop for a special license?

No.

Have you even begun to arrange better housing for you all or to secure transport for them to Blankenship?

No.

And what about that long overdue proposal?

Shut up. I want to sit here with her and simply be.

He stretched his arm over the back of the sofa, not quite touching her. She smiled absently at him, then turned back to listen to Colin. He gazed down at Melody, who was now stabbing repeatedly through the paper, using her pencil as a sword, to create an even more gory image.

A blissful family scene. A knock sounded on the door. He smiled as he rose to his feet to answer it.

A blissful family scene, complete with teacakes.

Outside the club, St. James Street was nearly deserted, with only the postboy and a number of servants to be seen. The traffic of morning deliveries had long passed, and since no self-respecting member of Society stirred before noon during the Season, there was nothing interesting going on whatsoever.

Critchley watched Brown's from beneath the shadowy doorway across the street. He was mightily bored. Stuffy old warehouse full of stuffy old near-corpses, waiting for death like kindling waiting for the fire.

The thought made him grunt with sour humor. The place needed a good house fire, that's what. A good bit of rushing about would put the spice up all those tired old arses.

He yawned and blinked away the grit of little sleep and much self-indulgence. He'd been here for hours already. He checked his pocketwatch. Well, nearly one, anyway.

She hadn't come out since she'd gone in. She wasn't going to start now, he wagered. He'd found her once. Actually, twice. He could find her again if she left.

Although . . . it had been a bit difficult to pull the memory of Blankenship's identity from his befuddled mind. What sort of earl went about in a rented hack?

At first he'd checked the man's town house but it was currently infested by an obnoxious accumulation of spawn. Critchley was almost absolutely sure that Blankenship had no offspring. The place was most likely overrun with relations for the coming Season.

So where did Society bachelors go when their country bumpkin relations came to mooch from the larder? Why, their clubs, of course.

Yes, he'd been very clever indeed up till now. He ought to be rewarded, that's what. He yawned again. He'd start with a bit of a kip.

Pushing off from the wall, he ambled away from Brown's Club for Distinguished Cadavers with relief. Rolling his bulk before him rhythmically, he strode off down St. James Street, his gaudy waistcoat glinting like tin trash in the afternoon light.

Lord Aldrich von Kitt screwed the spyglass more tightly to his eye and leaned closer to his window. The fat man who had been watching the club was leaving. Aldrich rather liked the fellow, or at least liked watching him. His girth and lurid waistcoat made him so very easy to keep in focus. If he left, there would be nothing interesting to see on St. James Street for hours yet.

Time passed so damned slowly while Aldrich waited to die. He'd been old for so long he'd lost count of the years. He'd lost his elder brother; he'd lost any chance of inheriting anything from that brother; he'd lost his wife; and he'd lost the only woman he'd ever loved—who rather unfortunately was not his wife.

That was how it went sometimes in Society. He'd gotten a portion from the estate, but that wasn't good enough for Esme's father. He had sneered at Aldrich's offer and thrown him out. Aldrich had married someone he liked well enough, but they'd had no children. When his wife passed away, he'd sold the house they'd lived in and moved to Brown's, planning to die soon himself.

That had been nearly twenty years ago.

If it weren't for the spyglass, those years would have passed at even more of a snail's pace. Luckily, he could see better with the glass than he could with his own spectacles. His fourth-storey room had such a marvelous view.

Now, Aldrich watched the fat man amble away with regret. The fellow hadn't done much of interest, but his mere presence there, watching the club with that sneer on his face, boded well for some future excitement. That man was seriously annoyed with someone in the club. Aldrich rather thought he might know who. Those two young pups, Blankenship and Sir Colin—

Wait. Another man stirred on St. James. Aldrich quickly switched to his good eye—well, to the one that was slightly less bad—to peer down at a tall, thin man stepping out of the shadow of a doorway just after the fat man had passed it. The thin man cast a single intense glance up at Brown's, then followed the oblivious fat man away, staying carefully a casual distance behind him.

Aldrich watched them both until they'd turned the corner at the Palace and left his sight. Then he straightened his aching back and let the hand holding the spyglass fall to his side. His thick spectacles slipped down from his forehead to rest in their usual place upon the bridge of his nose while he stood there lost in thought.

Someone was watching the watcher.

Fascinating.

"Maddieeee!"

The shrill sound cut through the drowsy morning peace in Aidan's sitting room.

Madeleine sprang up from her sewing to answer the wail from the bedchamber. Aidan was right behind her. Colin came along more slowly.

"That's not what they sound like when they get hurt," Colin offered as he caught up to where they were huddled over Melody.

Madeleine shot him a repressive glare. "My lord, will you please shut it? This is important." She turned back to comfort Melody, who held what used to be Gordy Ann but was now nothing more than an unwound and grubby cravat clutched in her hands.

Melody looked up at Colin with overflowing eyes. "I mucked her, Uncle Colin! I mucked her real bad."

Madeleine rolled her eyes. "The language you two ruffians taught her," she scolded them in a whisper. Then she turned back to Melody. "Uncle Colin will fix Gordy Ann, mousie. You'll see."

Colin ambled up to the rescue. "The master knotsman is at your service, milady." He swept a deep bow, making Melody giggle through her tears. She handed Gordy Ann's remains over to Colin with mournful ceremony.

"Now let us see . . ." Colin murmured as he spread the cravat out on the floor. It was stained and sooty in places, and there was an odd smeared area where Gordy Ann's face used to be.

Aidan protested. "I say, that *is* mine!"

Madeleine waved him silent and waited with Melody in her lap as Colin began to tie. No one said a word for several long moments. Finally Colin looked up.

"Stop watching. I can't do it if I'm thinking about it."

They pretended nonchalant indifference, except for Melody, who had her pinafore crumpled in her tiny fists as she fixed her tearstained gaze on Colin's hands.

"There!" Colin said with satisfaction. "A perfect Gordian knot!" He put the knotted thing in Melody's eager hands with a flourish. Rising to his feet, he dusted himself off with great ceremony. "Nothing to it, of c—"

"Not Gordy Ann!"

The three adults turned to stare down at Melody, who was glaring at Colin with suspicion. She waved the wad of linen at them. "No face!" She tossed the offending thing away, her scowl black and her bottom lip trembling.

"Oh, my," Madeleine muttered to Aidan. "If I ever had any doubt she was yours . . ."

"Thank you very much," Aidan retorted. He knelt once more at Melody's side. "Pet, if you don't like Gordy Ann anymore, I shall buy you a real doll—"

"Don't want a real doll!" Melody's voice rose to a frustrated howl. *"Want Gordy Ann!"*

Colin picked up the cravat and straightened in alarm. "Aidan, the entire club will hear her!"

"I doubt it," Aidan said absently. "They worried about a repeat of the Great Fire. It's solid stone, through and through." Nonetheless, he picked up his wailing, kicking, shrieking daughter with gentle hands. "Shh, pet. Don't worry. We'll fix Gordy Ann, I—" He paused because both Madeleine and Colin were waving their hands in alarm. He frowned at them and kissed Melody's forehead. "I promise."

Colin passed a hand over his face. "Oh, God, you've done it now."

Madeleine folded her arms and glared at him. "Brilliant."

Aidan gazed back at them in consternation. "What did I do? She stopped crying, didn't she?"

"Do you know what a promise means to a tiny child?" Madeleine shook her head. "I certainly hope that we do not fail in recreating Gordy Ann, or you will have shattered her trust in you."

"Oh." Aidan looked down at the child in his arms. "Oh, da— dash it all."

"Precisely." She let out a breath and took the knotted cravat from Colin. "I shall untie, Sir Colin, and you shall tie. Between the two of us, we ought to be able to find Gordy Ann again."

It took a great many tries. Melody would not be distracted. She remained focused on the proceedings, all the while clutching Aidan as tightly as she used to clutch the doll. He tolerated it patiently, as intent on keeping his word to her as she was on getting her playmate back.

Colin tied, and tied, and tied again. Each time, he would present it to Melody, who would shake her head forlornly and bury her face in Aidan's neck. Madeleine dutifully untied again and again, encouraging Colin with brief advice. "Perhaps if you begin from the opposite side this time . . ."

Wearily, Colin tied yet again. He held out the knotted thing toward Melody without much hope.

Her shriek made them all jump. "You found her! Uncle Colin, you found Gordy Ann!"

Colin looked down at the wad in his hands. "I did?" It looked like every other attempt, except for the single vital detail—the smeary face was again at the head of the knot.

Colin handed over Gordy Ann and wiped his brow. "I'd rather play the tables with loaded dice," he moaned. "What are the odds I could do it again?"

Madeleine paled. "Oh, heavens. Don't even think on it!" She knelt next to Aidan and Melody. "Darling, can I have Gordy Ann for a moment?"

Melody clutched her doll more tightly. "Why?"

Madeleine smiled and reached out a hand to smooth a dark curl back from her little pink, damp brow. "Mousie, I only want to make sure that Gordy Ann won't ever come apart again. We'll sew her just a bit, shall we?"

With that promising entertainment, Melody was off Aidan's lap in an instant, happily skipping off to the other room where Madeleine had left her sewing.

CHAPTER 17

Aidan watched Madeleine go, as entranced by her clever-ness as he was by her swaying hips, which were delight-fully showcased by his current viewpoint seated on the floor.

Her mind was marvelous in its quickness. He'd never realized she was so swift to solve things. Her cleverness, her sensible perspective . . . she made things simpler somehow.

He stood and brushed absently at his backside, un-aware of the curious smile etched on his lips.

Colin watched his smitten friend with a wary eye. Aidan had best take care or he'd be as wound about Madeleine's little finger again as he already was about Melody's.

Who would have thought the highly reserved Earl of Blankenship would ever make such a fine family man? Jack was going to lose his mind with laughter when he saw.

Except that Jack didn't laugh anymore.

Maybe seeing Aidan so giddy—well, giddy for Aidan, who'd always been such a stick—would help Jack get over that blasted Clarke girl.

Then again, it might inspire an opposite reaction. Co-lin himself had been having disturbing thoughts lately—

thoughts about going backward, about finding *her*, the one woman who had ever meant anything to him, about making one last stab at persuading her to love him . . .

Which was nonsense. That matter was well over and done with, and Colin had long since lost interest. Indeed, he'd lost interest in her so completely that he'd lost interest in women in general.

Yet the thought would not die.

It had worked for Aidan. Might it not also work for him? Lost in thought, Colin turned and left the rooms unnoticed by Aidan or Madeleine.

"Bloody hell," piped a tiny voice.

Both Madeleine and Aidan whirled to see Melody standing in the center of the sitting room with her hair ribbon in one hand, the end of her unraveling braid in the other and her brows drawn together in mystification. "It comed out again, Uncle Aidan."

"Oh my goodness," Aidan said mildly. "What a pickle."

Madeleine hid a smile behind the tips of her fingers as she watched the big man kneel on the floor and braid a tiny girl's hair with quick, easy motions. Even on his knee, he had to lean quite far down. Most adults would have picked the child up to make it easier, but Aidan seemed to think Melody had a perfect right to stand while he knelt.

Melody, for her part, kept perfectly still until he held his hand over her shoulder. "The ribbon, if you please, Lady Melody."

A quick knot and a quite respectable bow later, Melody was off again. Aidan watched her scramble onto the sofa, petticoats atwist, little boots all over the upholstery. He smiled and stood, absently brushing off his knee.

"So gallant," Madeleine told him when he returned to her side. *So heartbreakingly endearing,* her heart corrected her.

Aidan blinked. "What was gallant?"

"Oh, nothing." He was becoming a wonderful father right before her eyes. It was both surprising and painful to see it.

Her dream came back to her embellished tenfold. To dance with her husband at a lovely ball, to come home to their growing child, to delight in her increasing beauty and cleverness together as the years went on . . .

A pretty dream. Only don't forget that, unlike other women, you must wake up before the end.

Very true. Women with dirty little secrets were never rewarded with sparkling new lives.

She looked at Aidan. Nor were they granted a man who was all that was good and fine and ethical. He was everything she'd ever longed for and could never have. He would be horrified at the things she'd had to do. He would never want a fraud like her.

Aidan met Madeleine's dark gaze and went very still. There was so much in her eyes . . . so many interpretations of the emotion in those dark brown depths. As always, he felt the pull of her mysteries, the need he had to delve into this woman, to know all of her.

All she wouldn't share with him.

Recalling his resolve to unearth the true Madeleine, he decided it was time for a few questions.

Striving for a casual tone, he leaned back on one hand. "Did you not wish for children with your husband?"

She did not look at him. "One cannot always have what one wishes for."

More evasion. Dismissing casual for something a tad more forceful, he leaned forward. "When you were leaving your house yesterday, where had you planned to go?"

"I was simply moving on. London had not worked out well for me."

"That man—"

She looked at him then, straight into his eyes. "He does not concern you, Aidan. Nothing that happened after you left me concerns you."

She had a point.

"I didn't know my father," he blurted. *God, what am I doing?* His mouth went on, spilling himself out. "He was much older than my mother, who was his third wife. He died when I was younger than Melody. When I was a child, I don't remember seeing my mother for more than a few moments every evening.

"If I clung to her she would peel me off and force me back to my nurse. If I wished to stay in her presence, I had to learn to keep my needs to myself."

Her eyes widened slightly at his sudden expansiveness, but she said nothing, only nodding slightly in encouragement.

"If I broke a toy, it was swiftly replaced, whether I still liked it or not. I never knew . . ." He shook his head. "Earlier, when you knew what to say to her, when you knew just what to do—" He spread his hands a bit desperately. "I don't suppose that's written down somewhere, studied by people who somehow forgot to mention it to me?"

She shook her head with a small smile. "If it is, I was left out as well." She looked down and smoothed her skirts. "Did you love your mother, when you were young?"

He shrugged. "From afar, perhaps. I remember wanting

to, desperately. I don't know that I've ever become all that well acquainted with her. Even now we tend to speak about politics or Society news rather than anything personal."

He turned his gaze to Melody once more. "I don't want to raise a child so. I don't want her to be as I was . . ."

"As you were?"

Her sympathetic gaze awaited him when he turned back to her. When he hesitated, she only sat patiently, idly winding a thread around one finger.

If you wish her to let you in, perhaps you ought to go first.

"I grew up in a house of women. Some boys might have ended up the spoiled darling of the doting mob, but that wasn't the case at Blankenship. I learned early that good boys didn't run, or yell, or track dirt."

Lady Blankenship was the queen, and all there were her faithful court. The queen rarely deigned to notice him, therefore the staff did their best to follow.

He was a very lonely boy.

Until the day he was packed up in a businesslike manner and driven briskly away to school. He hardly had time to become alarmed, so he had disembarked the carriage that day with his usual reserved, watchful manner— into chaos.

"At school, there were boys everywhere, running, yelling, even somewhat dirty. On first impression it was heaven. Until it turned out that I had no idea how to be a real boy. I was too clean, so I was labeled a prig. I was too serious, so I was denounced as a bore. Worst of all, I was too careful, so I was roundly considered to be a coward.

"Luckily, I was well grown enough to discourage any

physical bullying, but I found myself helpless against the jeers." His response had been to withdraw further, which only reinforced their impression of him.

Jack had saved him. Laughing, open-hearted Jack who tackled Aidan on the lawn and tickled him into gasping. At last, Jack let him up grinning. "Knew you weren't made of wood."

Jack was the cousin and heir to Lord Blakely, son of the Marquis of Strickland. Highborn Jack had no real expectation of gaining the title, for his uncle was a hale man of forty and Blakely was a sturdy boy at the same school—and Jack's primary partner in crime.

"Some said the worst of their scrapes were Blakely's ideas, but Jack never voiced a word of blame. His loyalty, once won, was absolute."

Sometimes, however, it was bestowed upon some very incomprehensible objects—namely the brilliant but astringent young Sir Colin Lambert.

From the first, Aidan and Colin circled each other like wary hounds. Jack doused them both with unconditional camaraderie and relentless jests, forcing them to get along for the sake of the only true friend either had ever known.

Jack's friendship also raised them in the estimation of the other lads and Aidan's early misery at school was soon forgotten. "It took a while, but at last I began to join the human race."

Madeleine smiled gently at him. "You seemed quite human when I met you in that alley."

He snorted. "Well, that was not one of my shining moments. If I'd been any clumsier, I would have landed on his knife and made a murderer of the poor fellow."

She laughed, a soft, full, contented sound. It made something inside him thaw further. He reached out—was that his hand?—and took hers.

"I know we are still beginning . . . again . . . but I wish you would tell me—"

She slid her hand from his grasp and turned to Melody. "No, dearest, you mustn't stick my pins in the carpet. You wouldn't want to find them later with your toes, would you?"

Aidan waited for her to retrieve the pins and come back to him, but she didn't return to her seat. Instead, she began to busily tidy the room, folding the new pinafore she'd made for Melody and packing her sewing things back into the small wooden box she'd brought with her in her valise.

Ah. There would be no secrets from Madeleine today.

He felt empty, as if he'd poured himself out for her only to watch his soul seep unnoticed into the sand. An old wound began to ache anew within him. God, why did only Madeleine have the ability to hurt him so?

He stood abruptly. "Let me have those," he said, taking Melody's things from Madeleine. "I'll put them away." He walked into the bedchamber and shut the door.

Madeleine watched him go with hot eyes. How she loathed lying to him like this! He'd just cracked open his heart like an egg, and she couldn't return the favor. His hurt throbbed inside her like it was her own wound.

What a rare man. Even when he was hurt and angry, he remained considerate and thoughtful! How she wished she could keep him forever.

Tucking her sewing box into her pocket, she leaned

her forehead against the cool glass of the window. If she could ever tell the truth, what would she say?

I married a monster. I burned down his house and killed someone to hide my escape. I ran away.

That would go over splendidly.

CHAPTER 18

When Critchley reached his own rented rooms—not the sort of thing he was accustomed to, but having a pub downstairs made drinking convenient—he yawned again as he opened his door. He'd sleep through the day. When night fell, he would go downstairs for a plate of beef and ale and a grab down the gathered neckline of that plump publican's daughter. A lovely plan, just l—

"Critchley! *Bon ami,* I am so very glad to see you."

Critchley pulled up short at that smooth, friendly tone. Nothing good ever came of that charming manner. His jaw dropped and his second chin jiggled as he gaped helplessly. "Wil—" He shot a furtive glance toward the fireplace, but the hiding place beneath the stone looked undisturbed. "I—didn't expect you quite so soon." Damn it, he was never going to get his hands on Madeleine now!

"Oh, shut your gob, you witless lump." Lord Wilhelm Whittaker, master of Whittaker Hall and husband to the unlucky Lady Madeleine, sat in the room's only chair with one leg crossed elegantly over the other.

Something glinting and gold dropped from Wilhelm's fist, dangling there on a finely wrought chain. Critchley's gut went cold. Damn, he'd found that bloody wild-rose locket. No one betrayed Wilhelm, not more than once.

Wilhelm smiled kindly, his head at a congenial tilt. "Is there something you forgot to tell me, my dear friend?"

Still alone in the sitting room, high in the quietest reaches of Brown's, Madeleine closed her eyes and tried to bring up Wilhelm's face in her memory. The ugly face of fury was easy enough to recall. It was the handsome one she'd first known that she had begun to forget.

She'd been young and romantic and perhaps just a bit conceited, for she'd never stopped to wonder what a man of Wilhelm's rank and wealth would want with the daughter of an impoverished baronet. He'd admired her and fed her vanity, and she'd thought he was mad for her. "I must have you for my very own."

Her father had always indulged her irreverent temperament, applauding her cleverness even as her mother fretted over her pert tongue.

"You'll not fare well in marriage, girl," Mama had said bitterly. "No man wants to be made a fool of."

Her father had brushed off his wife's dire warning, more interested in being entertained by Madeleine's wit than worried about her chances of pleasing a husband.

Why was it so sour to admit that one's mother was right all along? Not a week after the wedding of her dreams, her husband had opened her lip with the back of his hand.

She couldn't recall what she'd said to anger him—some fresh rejoinder to a complaint, perhaps. It wasn't the blow that had shocked her the most. After all, her mother had lost her temper more than once during Madeleine's "difficult" years.

No, it was Wilhelm's complete self-possession at that

moment. He'd not lost his temper at all. He'd simply swatted her away as he would an annoying insect. Then he'd gone on to finish his complaint about his tenant as if she'd never spoken out of turn.

She'd soon learned never to do so again.

For a time she'd allowed him to convince her that his petulant rages were brought about by the extraordinary passion he held for her—she was the eye of his storm; she was the rod to his lighting.

For a time, she even took a little naïve pride in the power of that storm, for it made her special, made her powerful.

When she'd eventually realized that his passion was control and his violence was cruelty and his need for her extended only to his need to completely dominate and possess her, it was crushing to accept the extreme triteness of her position.

She was no more special than the most common village wife walking about with a bruised cheek and a wary eye. Her marriage was a farce, her heart no more wanted than last dinner's leavings. She was no one's siren, no one's goddess. She was only a very ordinary, rather gullible woman who had made the mistake of a lifetime.

She tried to play the game then, to observe and to serve, to coolly anticipate his needs so that she need not bear the brunt of his temper, to manage the house and the staff carefully so that none would suffer for her when his anger turned outward.

Her life became a checklist of accommodations and services. Had she inquired about his day? If she forgot that, he would respond with petulance or worse. Had she worn the gown he favored? Had she forgotten and worn the hat she quite liked but that he found dowdy? She gleaned her wardrobe for only the things he found attractive, wore her hair only in the ways he preferred, wrote into the menu only the foods he found delicious—and told herself that these were the things any good wife would do. One made compromises in marriage; one made allowances for men—they weren't as patient as women.

One buried oneself, gown by gown, hat by hat, until one hardly recognized oneself in the mirror.

She'd had no friends. He'd made sure of that. Whenever she'd felt the opportunity to become close with another woman, he'd found fault and discouraged further association. He kept his sphere of influence mobile, so that they never saw family more than a few times a year. He didn't care for "prying fools," so she wasn't allowed to receive callers of her own. Her few journeys from the estate dwindled down to an annual visit to her family, then even that vanished when her parents passed away.

Without friends, without any real influence in her own house—for who would defy the master when he was known to be heavy-handed?—without even the support of her parents who had died believing Wilhelm could do no wrong, her world shrank until there was nothing but him.

And when the unthinkable happened, there was no one to turn to for help. She was in trapped in an ornate and inescapable prison, and no one even realized she was missing from the world.

How could she explain such sickness to Aidan? How could she tell him what had happened to her without telling him what she'd done about it in the end?

Yet she almost did tell him. She almost gave him everything he wanted when he proposed—but she was afraid he'd never see her again. He wasn't that sort of man. He was scrupulous and ethical. He would leave her and might very well feel obligated to tell people in authority what she'd done.

In the end, however, more than her own survival, she loved him too much to involve him in her sordid, nasty problem. She loved his clean, beautiful honor and she knew he'd never forgive her besmirching it.

Now, however, her resolve wavered. Freeing Aidan hadn't actually done him good, as she had hoped. Although she realized now that he wasn't capable of infidelity, it certainly appeared that he'd immediately turned to some woman who hadn't even told him about her child!

Perhaps she'd made the wrong choice back then. Perhaps it wasn't too late to take it back . . .

Not until she had seen how marriage could be did she want it. Not until she'd woken up in these rooms with the man she loved and his child did she get a glimpse of what a normal life might be.

Turning, she saw that Melody was drowsing on the sofa, her finger in her mouth and her eyes droopy and glazed as she clutched Gordy Ann tightly. Madeleine moved to pick her up and settled back down on the sofa with the child on her lap.

I could be Melody's mother. I could love her and care for her and never would she realize she was not my own.

If only she could have this life forever, here with Aidan, like a real woman.

Yet, perpetuating her lie would cost Melody the chance to know her true mother.

That woman doesn't want her, remember?

"I do," she whispered into the silken head nestled on her shoulder. "I want you. Both of you."

When supper arrived that evening, it was a feast. Aidan was actually a bit dismayed to think that Wilberforce believed he could eat it all. With Melody and Madeleine safely concealed in the bedchamber, he stood back to let the line of trays flow in.

With any luck, none of the footmen noticed Gordy Ann—but then, what would they see but a grubby, knotted cravat abandoned on the sofa? God, he was getting as bad as Melody!

Fortunately, Colin showed up for supper just as the footmen were leaving.

"I think I'm going to need your assistance with all this."

"My fault. I told old Wilberforce that I was eating with you tonight and that I had a powerful appetite on." Colin gazed with satisfaction at the trays of plenty. "Crikey, we could have been eating like this all along? Wait until Jack gets back. We'll fatten him up in no time."

Jack. Right. Aidan thought about the letters he'd sent to Jack's various ports of call. Would he receive any of them? Was he even now rushing back to see the child he thought was his daughter?

So sorry, old son. My mistake. You're still alone in the world, but I have a new family.

Aidan looked at Gordy Ann, that smeary, ghostly wad of linen that now looked entirely like a doll to him. *Things have changed around here, my friend. We've all had to change with them.*

Madeleine and Melody joined them. "Oh heaven!"

sighed Madeleine. She looked at Aidan with delight. "I haven't had beef in months!"

Despite the pain in his heart, he could not help but laugh at the greedy glee in her face. He bowed playfully. "Have at, then, my lady."

She looked so eager and happy that he could not hold a grudge. Perhaps he'd pushed too hard, too soon earlier. After all, he had years to learn the hidden depths of the mysterious Mrs. Chandler.

It was a cheerful party for dinner. The trays over-flowed the small round table, so Madeleine set up a buffet on the sofa after covering the cushions with a sheet. This allowed even Melody to choose her own portions.

Aidan eyed the towering pile of cooked carrots on that plate, then leaned to one side to see the tiny child behind it. "If you eat all those, you'll turn into a rabbit."

She giggled. Several carrots slithered from the top to land on the carpet. Madeleine rescued the plate and set Melody up with a spoon and a giant napkin about her neck.

"Eat up, little bunny."

Colin was watching them, shaking his head in amusement. "Pour you all into a bowl and stir. Instant family cake."

Colin soon had Melody and Madeleine laughing with tales of boyhood adventures they had shared. Aidan merely smiled at the rather obvious majority of "Aidan falls face down in mud" stories. He was enjoying seeing Madeleine laugh too much to care about his own damaged pride.

She looked so lovely in this relaxed setting. When he'd

known her before, she'd spoken and listened freely but
there had always been a purpose to their meetings. He'd
had only one use for her, he realized, therefore he'd only
seen one side of this complicated woman. Madeleine re-
ceiving a lover was a different creature than Madeleine
with a family.

Now she sat with Melody pulled into her lap, wiping
carrots from the child's face—including her eyebrows!—
and laughing with Colin. She was dressed in something
faded and a bit too loosely fitted, but it only made her
cheeks seem brighter and her hair smokier by contrast. He
liked her hair down like this, a loose braid that let small
strands escape to float near her cheeks. She wore no corset,
he realized when she bent to set Melody free. He could see
her full breasts moving freely when her bodice gaped a
bit. If he took her into his arms right now, he would be rewarded with soft, warm female, no whalebone in sight.

His arms felt suddenly empty.

She caught his gaze when she straightened. His
thoughts must have been obvious, for her brown eyes went
dark and wide and her cheeks flushed. It was a charming
blush that went right down to the tops of her breasts. Perhaps even farther. It bore investigating, that blush . . .

She tried to distract him. "More carrots, my lord? I
think Melody might have left us a few." In her agitation,
another strand of hair fell from her braid, this one long
enough to curl at the base of her throat.

He reached out to brush it back with his fingertips,
relishing the brush against the soft skin of her neck. "Of
all the Madeleines I've seen," he murmured, "I think this
Madeleine is my favorite."

She looked away but he caught her chin with gentle fingers. "Don't take her away just when I've become attached," he whispered. "I'd be so alone again."

Her lips parted and her gaze rose to his. "Why would you say that?"

He smiled slightly and ran his thumb gently over her bottom lip. "I don't know. Perhaps it is only my imagination, but I fear a future without you in it."

She swallowed. "I thought you disliked me now."

"I thought I did, too. How mistaken we can be." He bent closer, his gaze lost in hers.

From behind them Colin cleared his throat. "Mistress Melody and I are going to run off to join the marauding pirates of *Dishonor's Plunder*."

"That's nice," Madeleine said absently.

"We're planning to burn down Westminster Abbey before we leave town."

"Mm-hm." Aidan smiled at Madeleine. "Have fun."

Colin grunted. "Come along, Mellie. We needn't stay where we're not wanted. Let's make a dash for my rooms."

They left a few moments later. "I've got her things," Colin informed them. "Don't wait up." He got precisely the answer he expected, which was none at all.

CHAPTER 19

In the sudden silence, it seemed to Aidan that his pulse became louder, until all he could hear was his heart's pleading. *Love me. Love me.*

He stood, pulling her to her feet, with her hands in his. "I don't think they're coming back," he murmured.

Her gaze moved from his eyes to his mouth. "No, I don't think they are."

He cupped her lovely face in his hands and kissed her lips softly. Yet when he lifted his head, her dark eyes gazed at him warily, and he despaired.

"Give me your secrets, Maddie," he whispered. "I must have all of you."

Her lids dropped, and she ducked her face from his touch. To his surprise, she did not pull away but instead moved closer to tuck her head under his chin.

"I cannot tell you . . . not yet." She must have felt him stiffen, for she clung closer to him. "Aidan, please, do not press me. There is nothing with which you can aid me, and there is nothing I can do to change what was. If I tell you that I mean no harm, that my only aspiration is my own merest survival—will that be enough?"

Would it? What was it that he feared haunted her?

When they first became lovers, she was shy, wary. She

told him her husband was older, that he rarely touched her, that she knew very little of lovemaking—yet that didn't explain her tears after the first time she shook with orgasm at his hands, or the way that in the beginning she would never allow him to stay the night in her bed, as if she couldn't fall asleep with someone else in her bedchamber.

His suspicions that her husband had not been kind were met with offhand dismissal and an airy laugh. "What a thing to say," she would say blithely, then change the subject.

He wanted so badly to protect her from whatever was troubling her. He wanted her to let him in, so sure was he that he could slay her monsters, that he was the one who could save her. She wasn't alone, no matter how hard she might fight to be.

Pulling her more tightly into his arms, he lay his cheek onto her soft hair and smiled to himself. No one who smelled so good could possibly be guilty of anything too terribly evil.

"You will tell me, you know," he pointed out. "Someday soon, you will tell me everything."

Madeleine closed her eyes and buried her face into his chest. Soon she would be gone without a word. No note, no impassioned plea for forgiveness would come close to expressing her regret. She would simply be there one moment and gone the next, and Aidan and Melody would go on.

So why not take this moment of happiness with her? Would it be so wrong to drink from this well of tenderness and joy, just for a moment, just long enough to sustain her for the rest of her days?

Slowly she tipped her head back to look at his beautiful, chiseled face. "You will always be my only love, Aidan de Quincy. That is one secret I will tell you right now."

He blinked slowly as he gazed down at her, obviously dumbfounded. "You love me?"

She laughed damply. "Of course I love you, you great idiot. I have always loved you, ever since I nearly killed you with that brick!"

He cradled her face in his large hands, smoothing her mussed hair back from her face. "Say it again," he demanded, his voice raw with emotion.

She slid her hands up his broad chest, over his shoulders and clasped them behind his neck, sinking her body into his with the ease of memory. "I love you. I love you. I love you. You probably ought to kiss me now, for I'll only carry on until you do."

He kissed her so gently it made tears spring to her eyes. With her head still cradled in his hands, he kissed her upper lip and her bottom one, her nose and her chin, both cheeks, both eyes, and at last pressed his lips to her forehead. "There," he murmured into her skin. "You've been most officially kissed."

She smiled in lazy joy and opened her eyes to gaze up at him. "But you haven't."

Sliding her fingers into his thick, dark hair, she pulled his mouth down to hers and ravaged it, pouring her entire self into the kiss, giving him everything she'd had to hold back for the past two days, for the past four years, for the entire life she'd been forced to live before meeting him.

What are you doing? Are you mad?

Yes. I'm mad enough to let myself love him just a little longer. I'm mad enough to not care how and why I have to go, mad enough to be here now, in his arms, and not look forward or back.

So shut it and get out of my way!

Aidan wasn't one to let opportunity knock and then leave unannounced. Even as her hot, demanding kiss rocked him back on his heels, he had a nice soft place on the carpet all picked out.

The coals in the fireplace glowed invitingly. Aidan swept Madeleine up in his arms and carried her there.

On the way, he bent so she could pick up a pillow from the sofa and then again so she could blow out the candles. She laughed at his playful consideration but sobered again when he gently lowered her to the carpet in front of the fire.

She'd been a fool to think she could ever armor her heart against him. No matter the consequences, no matter the pain, she loved this beautiful, honorable man more than her own safety, more than her own life.

He hadn't said the same, had not confessed his own love, but she could feel it in his touch. His hands were sure and warm, yet moved slowly, as if afraid she might disappear if startled, like a forest deer.

Resting against his chest, she closed her eyes as he slowly undid the buttons on the back of her dress. This was to be no quick tumble, she knew. This would be something they had never experienced in all their months together before.

She slid her hand up his chest and tugged gently at his intricately tied cravat. He murmured a protest, so she desisted, content that he wanted nothing more from her at this moment than to allow him to care for her, to cherish her.

When her cap sleeves slipped from her shoulders and the bodice of her gown fell away, he kissed her. First her lips, so softly it was almost chaste. Then her cheeks, her ear, her neck . . .

The heat of his mouth combined with the warmth of the fire on her skin. Languid pleasure stole through her, slowly building on the passion of moments before. She knew this man, knew that exquisite pleasure awaited her . . . yet it was all new, all glamoured in delicate emotions she'd not felt before. The infatuation of their past was nothing compared to this everlasting welling of love she felt now.

When he stroked her sleeve down her arm, exposing breasts barely contained in her thin chemise, she arched her throat and let her head fall back in complete surrender. All rational thought fled at the feel of his warm lips and hands as her gown slipped away.

All that was left was the way his hands spread out over hers, pressing them to the floor on either side of her head. All she knew was the way he never forced, never took more than he was given, how he waited for her every time.

He was patient, willing to stretch each moment into forever—coaxing, teasing, never demanding.

It was a heady ride, this balance of willing submission and sensual control. She could be free at last, herself at last, hiding nothing, reserving nothing from him.

Held but not bound, she gave cry to the heat welling inside her. He covered her mouth with his, taking her wordless cries, answering them with his own hungry moans.

Aidan felt the crack in his control widen, then tear

asunder. He was lost, self swept aside in the rush of her skin, her scented hair, her hot sighs on his face and neck.

He tugged at the neckline of her chemise. There was no time for untying bows, no thought for anything but the flavor of her nipple on his tongue.

She wriggled free of one strap and dragged her chemise down for him. He dove upon her like a hawk. A dark moan ripped from his throat at the taste of her, the feel of her tender nipple hardening is his mouth. Her hands tightened in his hair, pulling, painful, but it only fanned the flames of burning want.

Taking her waist in his hands, he lifted her, arching her up to meet his mouth. She cried out in surprise and agreement. Her hands slid to his shoulders to brace herself. She tried to wrap her legs about him but gave a wordless gasp of frustration when her skirts interfered.

He slid his hands down beneath her petticoats, running hot hands up her stocking-covered calves to her bare thighs and the thin batiste barrier of her pantaloons. Bunching the muslin layers high about her waist, he moved over her, pressing his rock hard cock, still trapped within his trousers, into her damp and vulnerable center.

Don't think, don't look back, never dare look forward. Simply be here, now, with this man because something inside you knows that here is precisely where you are supposed to be.

Even if you cannot stay.

The darkness closed upon them, keeping their secret with only the faint glow from the coals to guide seeking hands and lips and tongues. Suddenly he could not bear to be parted from her, even by the distance of mere fabric between them.

Rising from her, he tore at his cravat and waistcoat, flinging them into the darkest corners of the room. She laughed, that sweet, warm, thrilling sound, and tugged at his shirt, pulling the long tail from his trousers while he struggled with his fashionably tight boots. Her hands burned his skin when they slid beneath the linen from behind him, caressing his taut stomach and outlining the hardened plates of his chest.

"Must I cut those damned boots off you?" Her hot breath in his ear only worsened matters, for his hands began to shake with lust. If he didn't release himself from his trousers soon, he would do himself an injury!

With a strangled roar he yanked his boots free and stood to unbutton his trousers. When he turned he realized that she sat on her heels on the carpet completely naked, the faint glow from the fire outlining every curve of hip and shoulder, gilding the sides of her breasts and belly, shadowing the heaven that lay between her thighs.

Buttons flew, pinging against the wall and floor like heralds announcing that his swollen cock was free at last.

Then he was pulling her down to the carpet once more.

He was lost.

Lost in her.

Lost in the silkiness of her skin, in the scented fall of her hair, warmed by the fire. She had peeled away her gown and chemise to reveal a woman new to him—a treasure he'd never had the eyes and mind and heart to see before. So much more to this fey creature of light and dark, of secrets and sunshine. To taste of her skin here was different than here, or there. She was a feast lay before him and he was a starving traveler who had only ever heard of such bounty.

He'd been so cavalier with her before, years ago. He'd held this wondrous being in his arms and slaked his lust and thought himself fulfilled. What a fool he'd been, what a blind and selfish boor. Had he but known what he was truly walking away from he would have never put so much as a foot from the door.

She was his now. The confession of her love was a balm on that old ache, that mere wound of pride. She had gazed into his eyes and told him she loved him—and he believed her. Secretive she might be, whole parts of her hidden away, but he'd never known her to lie outright. What she did give him he would take, and he would believe in it.

As if to prove it, she gave herself to him as she had never done before. This sweet melding of skin on skin, of limbs entangled, of mingled tastes and touches and sighs—this was all new, fresh and sweet and heartachingly eager.

This was *definitely* his favorite Madeleine.

CHAPTER 20

Aidan slid down Madeleine's body, tasting her all over, from her lips to the dip of her navel to the sweet folds of her vagina and on down, rolling his tongue past the sensitive spot behind her knee, kissing the delicate bone of her ankle. She stretched out before him, one wrist carelessly tossed over her eyes, the other hand lax upon her ribs, just below the full, rounded mound of her breast. It was an artless pose, a moment of freedom and trust, and one he'd rarely seen. Madeleine of the secrets, Madeleine who hid behind the castle walls of her beauty, still and wary behind those mysterious dark eyes—that woman was nowhere to be seen.

Moving forward on his knees, he pressed hers apart, coming between them. She sighed and reached for him, her eyes opening with a smile.

He put her hands away, laying them gently back upon her stomach. "Let me."

Was that a blush, even now? She closed her eyes, bowing to his will, but could not keep from turning her face away from the fire, masking herself with darkness.

It didn't matter. He'd seen behind the mask now. He would not forget that soft and willing pose.

She tasted of the sea, salty and sweet and his alone.

This, he knew, was not done to her before him. This was his gift to her, the sweet abandon that only his tongue could bring her. As he dipped and circled, tasting and nibbling and gathering her nectar on his tongue, she began to quiver before him. As her thighs tightened in pleasure, he pressed them wide again, gently dominating the moment of her orgasm.

Come to me. Come.

Madeleine forgot her shyness, forgot herself and her lies and her past. There was only his hot tongue and warm fingers and the shimmering, aching pleasure that arched her back and made her breath short. She writhed before him, hearing her own gasping cries from a great distance. She was past embarrassment at the sounds of her own arousal—in fact, it only served to heighten it, to double it, knowing that he wanted her high animal cries, that he wanted to hear her call his name when she fell apart for him.

At the last moment, just when she thought her pleasure could go no higher, he thrust a single long finger deep into her as he sucked gently on her clitoris. Startled, she reached for him, digging her hands into his thick, soft hair as she tossed her head back and gasped out his name.

Then it found her—that sweeping tide of exquisite pleasure that never ceased to amaze her. Tossed high like a bit of driftwood on the wild seas, she fell down, down, swirling, gasping, rolled helplessly by the waves as her body shuddered around the last, potent plunge of his finger deep within her.

Then he was upon her, as if his control neared to breaking. He groaned as he covered her limp, perspiring body with his hot, urgent one. "Oh, Maddie . . . open for me," he gasped.

Still breathless, she slid one hand down between them to guide him in. He felt so large and hot in her hand. How could she have forgotten the rigid breadth of him?

Laughing a little at her own clumsiness, she wrapped her fingers about him, squeezing him experimentally. He shuddered. *"Maddie . . ."*

He didn't beg, not quite, but power rushed through her, nonetheless. She, who so recently had been helpless in his hands, now held the reins. Brave now in her revealed love, in her new knowledge of this man, in the spirit of this one last night in his arms, she angled her mouth up to his ear—and bit his earlobe sharply. He made a choked sound of protest.

She put her lips to his ear. "My Lord Blankenship," she whispered hotly. "You will *not* be gentle, you will *not* be careful, you will *not* be controlled."

He tried to draw back. She tangled her fingers into his hair, never releasing her grip on his thick erection with her other hand. "Is that understood, my lord?"

She moved her hand so that the blunt head of him slid between the slippery lips of her. She held him there, making him ride her slit, up and down, yet entering no further. The wicked pleasure of it, of stimulating herself with his aching flesh, almost made her lose her train of thought . . .

But she wanted him, the devil inside the man, the lonely, hidden, secretly wild, secretly passionate, secretly abandoned man she'd only glimpsed before. And she wanted him *now*.

"Yes!" he gasped at last. "God, Maddie, have mercy!"

She released him then, keeping her other hand in his hair and sliding her knees up to his hips. Still he hesitated.

"Aidan—"

He plunged. She cried out as his thick cock nearly split her in two. She'd thought herself ready but it had been so long—

The sharp instant of pain disappeared, leaving her at the mercy of the demon she had created. He was a whirlwind of lust, a hot, abandoned storm of it. She was helpless before the power of him unfettered. He wrapped her tightly in his arms and took her hard, thrusting deep and fast, withdrawing slowly, making her ache, then thrusting again. He wrapped one fist in her hair and pulled her head back to reveal her neck to his hot seeking mouth.

She rode the storm, winding her arms about his back, clinging with her legs as he impaled her again and again, gasping, sweating, moaning her name into her neck.

She could not resist the tide when it came again, this time as violently as a hurricane sea. His thick cock invaded her, spreading her, pounding deep until she ached from it. The pleasure/pain of his unrestrained ravishment, the wildness of him, his unmasked passion for her, the thrill of knowing it was her he wanted, he needed so powerfully—

She orgasmed again, her body tightening helplessly about him as she rode his cock, storm tossed and half thrilled, half alarmed, and entirely, completely in love with this new, raw, wicked Aidan.

He took her mouth with his when she came, breathing in her cries as she throbbed around him, shuddering in his arms. He groaned, a deep, hoarse sound as he plunged one last time deep within her, spilling into her as he held her tightly.

They lay there, locked together, shaking and slick with sweat and juices from each other, gasping in unison.

Madeleine knew for a fact that, despite all probability, she had not died from the intensity of her orgasm, for her heart pounded so loudly in her chest that she could hardly hear her own harsh breathing.

Aidan's head was dropped into her neck, where he gasped as breathlessly as she. She lifted one limp hand and slipped her fingers into his damp hair. "Are you sure . . . these walls . . . are made of . . . stone?"

A harsh bark of laughter tore from his throat. They could scarcely find air in their lungs to laugh, but they did somehow anyway, until what strength they had left was lost to weak, panting chuckles.

At last, he lifted his head to gaze down at her. The coals were too dim to see his expression, but she knew him. He was worried. She lifted her hand to his lips, forestalling the words of concern. "I'm fine. I wanted you that way. Yes, I'm going to be a little sore. No, I don't care one whit. I loved every moment of it. If I had the strength of a kitten, I'd make you do it again. So if you say you regret one single, tiny thing, I'm going to bite you again. Is that understood?"

He kissed the fingertips that lay upon his lips. "Yesh, dear," he mumbled against them. "No regretsh."

"Good." She shifted experimentally beneath him. "Now, I think I've carpet burns from my shoulders to my— to your knees. This sort of thing is all well and good for the young folk," she said primly, "but I think I'd like to find the bed now."

He rose from her after a soft, lingering touch of his lips to hers. She heard him move about the room for a moment. Testing her strength, she sat up and assessed her slightly bruised condition. With him out of sight in the shadows, she felt safe to grimace silently at the throbbing ache between her thighs. She was sorely out of practice at love-making and she would pay the price for days—and pay it gladly.

He knelt beside her in the dark. She could tell he had a dampened cloth by the way it dripped upon her thigh.

"Shall I?" he offered.

She reached for it. "Thank you. I've got it."

She probably ought to have let him care for her, but she didn't want him to know how very sore she was. As it was, she could barely suppress a hiss of pain when she dabbed at herself.

He brought one of his dressing gowns to her. "I couldn't find yours," he told her.

She wrapped herself in the costly velvet that smelled so wonderfully of him and vowed to herself to take it with her when she left. Icy pain stabbed her heart at the thought.

If she left . . .

Aidan, how can I stand to leave you now? How can I tear myself away?

How can I stay?

As he helped her into bed so gently it made tears well up in her eyes, she knew it would be hours before she could fall asleep.

Yet when he wrapped his arms about her and pulled her into the warm, naked arc of his body, she let out one long sigh and tumbled into an exhausted, deep, instant sleep.

* * *

The man outside watched as Brown's Club for Distinguished Gentlemen closed down for the night. Other clubs, some of which were little more than gambling hells, were still well lighted, still had traffic in and out of the door, still attracted small groups of young men who were done with their evenings' entertainment and wanted to find a bed while they could still see.

Not Brown's. The place was like a cemetery, only one whose members had yet to be informed.

The night was chilly and damp, a fog rising from the river to blur the edges of London and cast a veil over the filth. The man who watched didn't care for the damp, but discomfort did not stir him from his post. While the city came to a halt, he watched. While the fog crept slowly in, he watched.

What was she doing in there? How had she gotten past the door? Clever minx. She'd convinced that earl that she was worth saving and found herself a hole to hide in.

It wouldn't matter. He could be very patient when he wished to be. After all, what more enticing thing had he to do than wait?

And watch.

Uncle Colin's rooms had a view of the street, which Melody thought was nice because the garden was boring. People walked by and they were far below. It was funny when she could see them get shorter as they got closer, until they were only a hat or bonnet, and then they got longer again as they passed by.

She was very careful to do as Uncle Colin said and stay back from the glass, hiding all but her eyes with the drapery. If she didn't, he wouldn't let her sit at the window.

Uncle Colin was different from Uncle Aidan. Uncle Colin told wonderful stories of pirates and he was much nicer than Nurse Pruitt, but he didn't cuddle her like Uncle Aidan did. He sat her on his lap and spoke to her, though, just like a big person.

Perhaps it was because she'd just heard another tale of *Dishonor's Plunder* and its fearless and undying crew . . . but she thought she saw a pirate from the window.

He wasn't wearing an eye patch or a sword, but he had mean eyes, like holes of shadow, and he looked like he would use a sword if he had one.

Melody shrank down small and made sure the drapery was right where it was supposed to be. The man stood across the street, pretending to be looking at people walking by, but she could see that he was really looking at the club. She watched as he moved from his place by the lamppost to lean into a doorway a little farther down. He almost went away in the shadow, but because she'd already been watching she could still see him.

Now he didn't pretend anymore. He just watched . . . and watched . . .

Melody felt a little bit sick. She climbed down from her chair by the window and climbed into Uncle Colin's lap. He put down his pen and pulled her up to sit properly, as if he were a chair. It made the desk almost a good height for her.

"Here," he said, giving her a pencil. "You can write with me." He slid a paper closer to her and soon she was scribbling away, the bad pirate almost forgotten in the warmth of Uncle Colin's absentminded affection.

Later that night when she woke from a bad dream, Uncle Colin felt sorry that he'd told her such a scary story before bed. She didn't tell him that her dream was about the man who watched.

CHAPTER 21

Madeleine held a child in her arms, a beautiful curly-haired infant with large dark brown eyes and chubby hands busily waving. Rocking her body slightly, humming a little nonsense tune, she strolled across a beautiful bedchamber to gaze dreamily from the window out at the elegant grounds of a vast estate. "Do you see, little one? All this is yours."

Warm arms came about her from behind. Sighing with contentment, she leaned back against a solid manly chest.

"What shall we do today, my love?" she asked languorously. "Shall we take the baby on his first picnic?"

"What baby?" sneered a deep derisive voice behind her.

She whirled to see that the man behind her wasn't Aidan at all—it was Wilhelm! She backed away, clutching her child protectively.

But the child wasn't a child any longer. It was nothing more than the moldy bundle of rags she'd once used to conceal the jewels and silver she'd stolen from the house.

Wilhelm snatched the valuables away from her, flinging them out the window to fall clinking and shimmering to the lawn far below.

"You would steal from me?" Possessive hatred flashed in his eyes. "I shall teach you better."

Fear robbed her of speech and the loss of her dream child ripped her will to fight from her. When she ran to the window to escape through it, iron bars appeared across it, imprisoning her within.

Mocking laughter echoed through the room as it began to burn. She spun in panic, but Wilhelm was not to be seen. She could only hear his voice echoing through the flames and screams and death around her.

"I'll be watching you, my treasure, my own. I'll be watching . . ."

Madeleine woke with a start. Shudders wracked her body. Her heart pounded in her dry throat, so dry she could swear she choked on smoke. She couldn't breathe for a panicked instant.

Then Aidan's arms came sleepily about her and she knew the dream wasn't real. She forced herself to breathe deeply and let Aidan's full-body warmth seep into her nightmare-chilled flesh.

Still, she could not shake that dark familiar emptiness. She remembered now. That feeling was called hopelessness.

It had not been until she had escaped altogether that her true imprisonment became clear. He'd forced her to leave behind her name, her identity, and even her very voice. To breathe a single word of what she'd seen would have meant exposing herself. Therein lay danger of the most serious kind.

So she hid her face and hushed her voice and never revealed herself to anyone.

Except for Aidan.

Foolish as such a risk had been, she could not regret it. To have known pleasure and passion such as that when she'd thought her life drained of it? It was a gift, a revelation, a pearl beyond price.

Yet even then she'd known that something was missing. And now, lying in his arms again at last, she felt that emptiness again. The edges were a little blurred and the ache somewhat softer, but the hole was still there.

The hole where she herself ought to be. Wilhelm had stolen that from her . . . was still stealing it from her.

Shutting her eyes against that thought, she rolled into the heat of his big body and pressed her forehead to his chest.

Of course it's not real. Wilhelm? What nonsense. Wilhelm can't get to you any longer.

Rolling into the encircling protection of Aidan's big body, she released the fretful dream and slipped back into a sheltered sleep.

As dawn brightened the bedchamber, Aidan woke to find his arms full of warm, naked woman. Better yet, warm, naked Madeleine.

Perhaps *this* was his favorite Madeleine.

He closed his eyes briefly in thanks and then pulled her gently closer. She rolled bonelessly into him and stretched sleepily, pressing all those fascinating soft places into his hard ones.

Nuzzling her neck, he decided to investigate the possibility of an early morning lovemaking. Gently nibbling, he found her ear. She slapped grumpily at him, then chuckled. "Some things never change," she said throatily.

Encouraged, he pressed his hardening cock into the soft swell of her belly. "My lady, may I have my way with you?"

She grumbled. "I want toast."

He moved his nibbling lips from her ear to the tops of her breasts. "If I feed you breakfast, may I have my way with you?" He took a warm, soft nipple into his mouth and sucked it.

She hissed in startlement but shivered as well. Her nipple hardened on his tongue.

"Don't think this is going to get you out of fetching breakfast," she warned, but she was already becoming liquid heat in his hands. "And I'll want a nap later," she demanded breathlessly.

He murmured assent to her conditions—God, he would have agreed to anything!—and moved his hands down to cup her bottom and lift her more tightly to press against his aching erection.

"Get that thing away from me," she ordered without any great emphasis. "You could put your eye out with that."

He laughed as he took her other nipple into his mouth to coax it to equal diamond hardness. She pushed him onto his back and rolled with him, ending up sprawled on top of him with her thighs straddling his hips.

"Oops," she said mildly. "Now I've done it."

Her long dark hair cascaded about their faces as she slid down to kiss him. He closed his eyes in pleasure as the movement wrapped the head of his cock in wet, hot, compliant female flesh. "I was just thinking about this place," he moaned.

"What place?" She wriggled playfully, sending his pulse from fast to faster in less than a second. He felt his cock swell further. She felt it, too. "Oh, that place," she sighed.

He was careful, allowing her to set the pace. She was gingerly at first, sliding down upon him so slowly that his eyes nearly crossed from the effort of restraining himself. When she was fully impaled upon him, she bent to kiss him as she leisurely moved up and down, never altering her unhurried rhythm.

The kiss and the torturous pleasure went on and on, stretching time, luring him into losing himself to it, to the taste of her, to the feel of her mouth on his, to her hot wetness wrapped about him, to the firm weight of her breasts in his hands, to her nipples hardening, digging into his palms. Her hair fell about them, silken, sweet smelling and dark, curtaining them in with the pleasure and the slow, mind-stealing pace . . .

Until he abruptly orgasmed. He cried out in surprise and tightened his hands about her hips, pinning her down onto him hard as he thrust deeply up into her, pouring himself into her, lost in the ripping surprise of his pleasure.

She squirmed in his hands, her fingers digging into his chest as she shivered in her own orgasm, caught as she was upon him like a fish on a hook, forced to feel every pumping inch of him deep within her very sensitive flesh.

Afterward, she fell upon him gasping.

"Sleep," she begged. He breathed an assent and wrapped his arms gently about her, holding her there upon him. The dim room faded away as he rode his exhaustion into sleep.

Then she said, very softly, just before they were both lost to dreams . . .

"Toast?"

CHAPTER 22

A few hours later, in the morning light wandering into the room, Aidan lay on his stomach, braced upon his elbows as he gazed into Madeleine's sleepy, satiated eyes. "You rejected my first proposal." And his second. And his humiliating, pleading third.

She pulled one hand from beneath the covers and held up a finger. "I rejected marriage in general, actually, not you in particular."

He digested that for a moment. "Was your marriage so very bad?"

She shook her head, smiling slightly. "It really doesn't bear describing."

He looked into her eyes, and she gazed evenly back at him. She wasn't lying, but as always, she wasn't clarifying either.

Could he open himself up to her again, knowing that her secrets still lay between them? Could he trust her with Melody, knowing she'd abandoned the child once before?

With the rising tide of his emotions overwhelming his misgivings, could he do anything else?

"I want you as my wife," he said softly. "I will have

Melody recognized as my daughter. I want a family—this family."

She continued to gaze at him, her eyes traveling over his face as if she was trying to read him.

He knew the feeling. "I still want you, Maddie. We still have this." He dropped his head to kiss the spot between her breasts. "You say you love me. If that's true, then you must agree to be mine."

Madeleine gazed into those night blue eyes she loved so dearly and realized that if she did not marry him, he would keep Melody and send her away.

Isn't that the plan?

Ah yes, the plan. It was difficult to remember the plan and the danger she'd felt with Critchley hovering about. That problem seemed distant and faint, like the sound of rough seas when one stood safely inland.

Was this real and that life of fear only a nightmare? Or was she dreaming even now? Here, in his arms, with his need and his question still hovering in the air, his cobalt gaze careful but traced with hope—was this merely a fantasy brought on by solitude and destitute starvation?

She swallowed. "May I . . . may I think on it a while?"

He gazed at her intently. "You do not refuse me outright?"

She shook her head a little. "I truly wish to think a bit. I have . . . I have changed a little over the years, I hope, that I would not so cruelly act out of hand again. I do love you . . ." She waited, but he did not respond in kind. Stroking one hand over his cheek in silent forgiveness, she smiled softly. "I love you and I believe that Melody deserves a true family. It is only that I must . . . think." Trying to lessen his intensity, she wriggled. "And I cannot think while you lie between my thighs like this."

For a long moment he did not smile. His eyes took in every detail of her expression before he relaxed. With a small quick nod, he assented. "I have waited so long, I suppose I can wait another day."

She started to wriggle away from him but he caught her to him once more. "Maddie, I do not intend to accept a refusal. I think you ought to realize that."

He looked so serious she didn't dare smile. If he only knew . . .

Oh, Aidan, your anger doesn't frighten me. What frightens me is your honor. That was what would be the death of her.

"Yes, my lord," she responded seriously.

Satisfied, he allowed her to roll away from him. When she ran naked across the bedchamber to the washbasin, he laughed at the way she minced away from the floor's chill.

She glared at him. "Turn around."

He rolled his eyes. "Always with the 'turn around.' It isn't as though I don't know what you're about over there."

She pursed her lips. "Nonetheless, turn around. I don't care to put on a show."

Laughing, he covered his face with a pillow. "Satisfied?"

He didn't hear anything for a long moment. Just when he was tempted to peek despite his gentlemanly sense of honor, he felt her climb onto the mattress near him. He raised the pillow to see her sitting facing him clad in her chemise and his smoking jacket, her feet tucked up away from the floor. She looked adorable.

"You promised breakfast," she pointed out.

She looked so adorably rumpled that he was tempted to drag her back into bed—God, would he never get enough of her?—but he'd given his word. "Breakfast it is." Rising, he strode naked across the room for his turn at the basin.

Madeleine chewed her lower lip as she eyed this enticing view. That muscled back and that granite-hard bottom—now those she could definitely commit the rest of her life to! Her gaze slid sensuously over his wide shoulders and the way his biceps bulged when he briskly scrubbed water over his face. He ran wet hands through his hair in a careless attempt to tame it and the droplets fell to twine down over the hills and dales of his form. Heat began to gather between her thighs.

Lucky droplets.

"That's hardly fair." He was looking at her in the washstand mirror. "I didn't get to watch."

Heavens, if watching aroused him as much as it did her, she might just let him peek in the future! "That point might be negotiable," she admitted.

His brows rose. "Really?" He flexed his buttocks.

Her gaze was riveted. "Gurgle—mph!"

He laughed out loud, an open, free laugh she'd not heard in years. The sound of it was even enough to make her tear her eyes from his magnificent rear. He was grinning, his eyes flashing a shining blue.

Something careful and wary inside her melted. Aidan was happy.

Maybe . . . maybe they could be happy, together.

The wonder of that thought occupied her while he dressed and left to buttonhole a footman for their breakfast. It came in record time—causing her to suspect that this Wilberforce person had clairvoyant powers—and she hadn't time for more than dressing quickly, tying her hair back with a bright blue ribbon, and hiding the evidence of last night's tangled path of disrobing.

The food was delicious and the company divine. They did little more than exchange smiles over their eggs and toast, but the relaxed glow of his expression did more to warm her than did the tea.

She would accept. Aidan buttered his toast as he leaned back in his chair. She could not sit across from him in such sweet contentment if she were about to shoot him down.

It was time to speak to the bishop. He was wealthy enough to ensure a special license. It was only a matter of presenting the proper bribe—er, contribution.

There was also the matter of a house. Something small, perhaps. He rather enjoyed the cramped coziness of these rooms at Brown's. He wouldn't want such amiable warmth diluted down through dozens of rooms.

After a perfunctory knock, Colin entered with Melody dangling off one hand like a monkey. "I've a delivery for you."

Aidan looked at the dark circles under Colin's eyes. "You look like he— haggard." He looked down at Melody, who was swooping like a kite on the end of a line. "She looks very well."

"Oh, she's in great form. I, on the other hand, suffered from n-i-g-h-t-m-a-r-e-s." He looked down at the curly-haired bundle of energy and turned her loose to spin wildly about the room. "Hers."

Madeleine came closer, worry on her face. "Bad dreams? Was she all right?"

Colin smiled wearily. "I think so. My own fault. Too many bloody flourishes, I fear."

Aidan smirked. It was gratifying to see Colin of the many cousins be less than perfect with Melody. "You deserve it. Imagine telling such tales to a child."

Colin narrowed his eyes. "You weren't complaining yesterday when you wanted to know what happened to Captain Black Jack Harrowgate."

Aidan blinked innocently. "*I* am not going on three years old."

Colin growled and went to go pick at the breakfast tray. "Someone ate my toast," he explained with a grumble.

Melody was jumping on the sofa. Madeleine watched her with her head tilted to one side. "I was never allowed to do that. I never understood why."

At that moment, Melody miscalculated and flipped over the arm of the sofa to land on the floor with a startling thud.

"Oh my goodness!" Madeleine ran to comfort her and to divert the wailing before it began in earnest.

Colin nodded, chewing. He pointed with his toast. "That's why."

Once Aidan realized Melody was fine, just suffering from surprise and bruised pride, he turned to Colin. "I want a house."

"I don't have one." Colin held up both hands in surrender, armed with a piece of toast in each. "Search my pockets if you like."

"I must speak to my business agent in town today.

He'll know of a likely place. This club is no place for Melody. She hasn't anywhere to play."

Colin chewed thoughtfully. "You've reconsidered shipping them off to Blankenship?"

Aidan looked away. "Too far to visit during Parliament. Besides, Melody hasn't seen anything of London yet."

"She was born in London."

Aidan ignored him. "At any rate, we're moving as soon as possible. Perhaps even tomorrow."

Colin looked sad. "Perhaps I will too. It certainly won't be the same around here."

Aidan met his friend's—yes, he was truly a friend now—eyes. "You know you'll be welcome anytime. Melody wouldn't want to pass a day without seeing her Uncle Colin."

Colin was the first to look away. "Right. Sit there while you two moon at each other? Shoot me first."

Aidan growled fondly. "Bounder."

"Sap."

All balance restored by the manly insults, Aidan took quick leave of them. He picked Melody up and kissed her soundly and noisily, making her giggle. His kiss for Madeleine was faster and much more discreet, but it left her cheeks pink nonetheless.

"I must attend to some business at the moment but . . ." He gazed intently into her eyes. "I do have a matter on which I'd like to speak with you later."

He released her, but before he turned away, his gaze flickered over her shoulder to the desk just behind her. There was time for that bit of business later, when he had her answer.

On the way through the grand entrance hall, Wilberforce stopped him. "You've a message from Lady Blankenship, my lord." He handed Aidan a crisply folded sheet, sealed with blue wax and pressed with an ornate "B."

Aidan almost took a chill just opening it.

Aidan, I have arrived at Blankenship House in London. Attend me at once. Signed, Lady Blankenship.

A summons from Queen Elizabeth could not have been more commanding. He'd heard that the queen occasionally used the word "please."

He took his hat and gloves back from Wilberforce and donned them. Even the hovering maternal chill couldn't dampen his mood. He had happy matters to attend to. It would be best to deal with his mother first.

Yes, happy matters indeed.

Smiling as he left, he set his hat at a jaunty angle as he waved at Wilberforce in the entrance hall. Once on the street in front of Brown's, he inhaled deeply of the rather nasty London air, relishing every breath. His mood so occupied him that he almost missed sight of a man ducking around the corner of a building.

That Critchley fellow again.

There wasn't much doubt. Short, rotund men clad in poisonously colored waistcoats didn't appear everywhere. Yet, as he increased his pace to come even with the corner, he couldn't spot the fellow anywhere.

Well, if Critchley was looking for Madeleine, he wasn't going to find her. Entry to Brown's was definitely out of that creature's social reach.

Furthermore, within days she would be Lady Blankenship, untouchable by anyone such as he.

Oh, bother. He probably ought to inform his mother that he was getting married. If he were like Madeleine, he would send a letter by the slowest, most ancient coach he could find, just for mischief's sake.

Smiling to himself, he decided to do just that. Critchley and his vile fashion sense evaporated from Aidan's mind completely as he contemplated his mother's face when she realized she'd missed out on turning his wedding into a full-blown Society circus!

CHAPTER 23

As mothers went, Lady Blankenship wasn't so terrible. She didn't shout and she didn't strike. Then again, neither did she smile nor did she laugh. She simply chilled one into submission.

As Aidan made his way up the steps of his own house, he felt a curious reluctance to enter, almost as if he weren't quite sure of his welcome.

The Breedloves had brought their own staff along, so the door was answered by an unfamiliar face who gazed at him without recognition. "Yes, sir, may I help you?"

"Blankenship to see Lady Blankenship."

Aidan tried not to smile when the fellow nearly jumped out of his boots. "My lord! Please, come in—"

It went on for a while but Aidan didn't bother to listen. He didn't require fawning from anyone. The fellow left him for a moment to announce his presence.

How odd to be left standing in his own hall. Still, while the Breedloves stayed here, he wanted them to feel as though it was their house. Striding in to play Lord and Master wouldn't help anyone.

While he waited, he could hear high children's voices in the distance and then the patter of running feet upstairs. He noticed a small wheeled horse on a pull string half hidden beneath the hall table. Was it his imagination or did his house seem a brighter and warmer place for such changes?

Family cake, Colin had called it. Indeed.

A flash of pink caught his eye and he lifted his head to see a tiny girl, not much older than Melody, standing part way up the stair, gazing at him with one finger in her mouth. He smiled. "Hello, kitten. I'm Cousin Aidan."

She didn't speak or remove the finger, but she did come a few steps closer. Aidan watched her gaze go worriedly to the toy horse and then back to him. Ah, the little miss knew she wasn't to be playing in the entrance hall. She'd probably had to make a run for it when he'd sounded the knocker.

Aidan shook his head and put his finger to his lips. Bending, he reached the horse from its hiding place and ran quickly up the stair. He put it carefully in her hands. "Mind you don't leave it on the stair, pet," he whispered. "Someone might trip and fall."

Then he dashed back down to the hall where he assumed a very lordly mein as the Breedloves' butler scuttled back to fetch him to Lady Blankenship. "This way, my lord—er—"

Aidan only nodded and followed the man through his own house. As he passed, he saw a tousled little head peek through the banister and wide eyes watch him. He cast up a wink as he passed and was rewarded with a giggle.

Since when did you become good with children?

Perhaps since I became a father.

Well, it couldn't be that easy or there wouldn't be parents like—

"Aidan, darling, where have you been? I sent for you

hours ago." Enthroned in the best parlor like a queen in her hall, Lady Blankenship was perfectly and severely dressed for this time of day. Pale purple satin swathed her, a color she favored since it brought out the silver in her perfectly coifed hair. Never would she loll about the parlor in an old gown and a simple braid. She glanced up at him briefly. God, he hoped his own blue eyes were never so cold.

"Something must be done about the Breedloves' staff. They're simply impossible. Do you know that it took me at least ten minutes to get my breakfast this morning? Really." She held out her hand to him.

He bowed over it. "Lovely to see you too, my lady." He hadn't called her Mother since he was ten and finally realized she had no interest in the job. "I'm sure the Breedloves like their staff just the way it is."

She sniffed. "No doubt. Well, I shall suffer through the primitive conditions just long enough to launch Daphne—er, Delilah—and then it's back to Blankenship for me. I can't abide the Season."

She adored the Season, actually. She'd never missed one, not even immediately after his father died. Oh, she wore appropriate black—stylishly, of course—and she appeared appropriately wan and grieving—at every single event she could fit in—so no one could criticize her in the least.

"I simply don't know why they had to bring all of the children. Did you know that your cousin is expecting *again*? People are beginning to talk."

"People began to talk after the fourth one, my lady." It occurred to him that Madeleine's gowns were very tired indeed. Not that he minded, for she looked better in muslin than most women looked in satin, but he would enjoy making her eyes shine with a gift. Lady Blankenship had her gowns made exclusively by Lementeur, who was the very best. *I wonder what a fellow like that could create for Madeleine?* He could hardly wait to find out.

Belatedly, he picked up the tail of his conversation again. "I scarcely think number seven will make a stir."

She narrowed her eyes at him. "Do not be facetious, Aidan. *They* are not the ones who should be breeding." She flipped her fan at him. "You are the one in the family who should be making heirs. When are you going to let me make a match for you?"

Mother, I've decided that you're quite right. It is high time I wed. Will tomorrow do for you?

A snicker rose up from somewhere deep inside him— a place he hadn't heard from in years. He covered it with a cough, then smiled genially at Lady Blankenship. "Oh, I shouldn't think I'll want to wait much longer."

Obviously prepared for a disagreement, she stopped in mid admonishment and stared at him. "Are you serious, Aidan? Will you truly begin to search for a bride this year?"

Searched, found, proposed already—well, more or less. Oh my, this was going to be fun. "I think I'll be looking among the many widows in London," he said nonchalantly. "I don't wish to waste time on some silly girl."

Lady Blankenship examined this proposal and, finding no obvious traps or flaws, nodded in satisfaction. Yet she pointed one long finger at him. "As long as she is well connected—and young enough to bear you sons."

Aidan spread his hands. "But of course." He leaned back in his chair and smiled. "It won't be long before this house will be filled with children every single day. Children who will clamber into your lap with their sticky teacakes in hand and call you Grandmama!"

As he watched her cold blue eyes widen in startlement and her lips tighten in what could only be described as sheer terror, he couldn't help the laugh that rolled out. Standing briskly, he snapped her a soldierly bow and then strode from the room. "*A bientôt*, Grandmama . . ."

Back at Brown's, keeping a healthy, active child happy and occupied in a small suite wasn't an easy task. Especially when the entire matter was supposed to be a secret!

They tried. Colin told story after story, each gorier than the last. At this point, even Madeleine couldn't fight her growing interest in the exciting tales.

When even his imagination began to fade, Madeleine invented a chasing game that involved a fox and a horse. Madeleine was the fox and Colin, of course, was the horse. Melody rode hunt after hunt, until Colin collapsed gasping on the floor next to the once-again vanquished fox, Madeleine. He made pleading eyes at Madeleine. "Help?"

Madeleine stood and briskly dusted her hands. "I think it's time for bread and butter and milk."

Melody had at least worked up an enthusiasm for her snack, but Aidan's sideways proposal this morning had stolen Madeleine's appetite. She stood by the window, gazing restlessly out at the back garden.

One could truly work magic in that neglected place, she thought absently. Oh, it was painfully tidy and there were a few ordinary flowers struggling for survival, but one could tell that no one loved it.

Love. Aidan. Her thoughts always seemed to spin predictably back to him. She leaned her forehead against the cool glass, remembering the way he'd kissed her goodbye, right in front of Colin and Melody, as if he had every right to.

It was a silly girlish thing to do, to sigh over a man's kiss even after he'd left—but she felt silly and girlish and very nearly happy.

Then the memory of his strange, last look crossed her mind. She turned idly, trying to see what had caught at his attention that way. If she were as tall as Aidan and had been standing precisely *there,* she would have seen . . . the desk?

She ambled over to it, only half listening to Melody's pleading behind her for another Cap'n Melody story. Sir Colin was going to regret that storytelling skill of his someday, she would wager.

The desk was clear, holding only an inkstand just above the blotter. There was a top drawer that contained only a sheaf of blank paper and beneath it, a small key.

The key opened the other drawer. Feeling delightfully sneaky in a silly way, Madeleine unlocked the drawer, keeping her skirts between the keyhole and Sir Colin's view. The lock worked easily and she was in the drawer in a matter of seconds.

The drawer contained only one thing. A small gold box sat with its lid wide open.

In the box nestled the ring Aidan had tried to give her during that disastrous proposal years ago.

The ring blinked ruby hot and glowing in the drawer. Without even touching it, Madeleine could remember the weight of it, feel the searing heat of it in her palm.

Time slipped away and she was back there in that room, with Aidan on his knees before her and the air leaving her lungs.

I must have you for my very own.

She shut the drawer quickly but she could still feel the heavy weight of the ring—the heavy weight of her secrets. Her heart was pounding as if she was being chased. The walls felt as though they were closing in on her. Pressing a hand over her midriff to steady her breathing, she turned to see if Sir Colin had noticed her reaction.

Colin was asleep sitting up on the sofa, his head tilted back at an angle that would be sure to cause an ache later. Melody was standing on the cushion next to him, about to pour her milk into his open mouth.

Right. "Come here, mousie," she whispered. "Let Uncle Colin have his nap."

Melody wavered. "Why?"

Madeleine chose to answer the question she had the answer to. "If we let Uncle Colin have his nap, we can take a little walk outside. Would you like that?"

Melody considered the breathtaking possibilities of mayhem with the milk, weighing them against Madeleine's promise. "Outside or outside?"

In the hall or in the real world? Goodness, she was actually beginning to speak toddler!

"I remember seeing a large park just down the street." After all, this secrecy was about to end, either way she decided. Surely one little excursion wouldn't be the end of the world.

And if she didn't get out of this room, she was going to start pouring milk on things as well!

The thought of green grass and flowers and possible

real dirt swayed Melody. She carefully squatted to put her glass down on the cushion. Madeleine stepped forward to rescue it from spilling while Melody lay belly down on the sofa and let herself slide off to land on her feet.

After dressing them both in boots and coats, for the spring weather was unpredictably wet, they slipped quietly out the door and into the hall.

Old Aldrich was nowhere in sight. First, she peered out the window at the end of the hall to check the street. Then she peeked into the servants' stair, but there was no sign or sound of activity. She showed Melody how to tiptoe in an exaggerated fashion, which practice kept the child occupied long enough to make it down to the ground floor.

The stairwell opened into the hallway that ran past the kitchens. It was after breakfast but luncheon was hours away. There were only two scullery boys present and they were busy at the sinks, their backs to the hall.

It took but a moment to scurry down the hall and slip through the door to the outside.

CHAPTER 24

The trade entry was lower than street level, which gave Madeleine a chance to make sure the coast was clear at the front door above and to her left.

The sight of a proud fellow in livery who could only be Wilberforce had them ducking low, but he soon finished his business with the postboy and went back into the club.

Madeleine picked Melody up and ran for it, which lack of dignity Melody enjoyed immensely. Despite Madeleine's continued caution, they were both giggling by the time they made it to the end of the block and turned the corner toward the park.

The park seemed vast. After the two rooms, it felt as expansive and wild as the moors of the north. Madeleine turned Melody loose to run free in the pearly sunlight of the day.

Aidan's agent in town did happen to know of just the house for his employer to rent—his own. As a bachelor, he was very happy to let it immediately for a sizable rent.

Aidan walked about the cheerful and comfortable house with great approval. It was small, tastefully furnished, and in a very respectable square. There was even a patch of garden in the back that was already in bloom.

It was the perfect setting for a family. He could picture intimate suppers in the dining room, relaxed evenings sitting in the parlor with Madeleine as Melody played on the carpet, even noisy breakfasts in the sunny breakfast room with its large window facing the garden. He'd be able to pluck blooms for Madeleine's table without so much as getting dew on his shoes.

Yet by far Aidan's favorite room was the master bedchamber. Here it seems the bachelor succumbed to a slightly sensual bent. The big bed was draped in crimson velvet and gold cord.

Madeleine would look astonishing spread out on that bed, her arms open to welcome him, her skin aglow with firelight . . .

He knew then. This was to be no marriage of convenience, no simple means of legitimizing Melody's birth.

He needed her, only her.

Only Madeleine.

She understood him as no one ever had, not his family, certainly not his mother, not even Jack.

No other woman could tempt him. Hers was the only touch he wanted. Hers were the only lips he wanted. Hers was the only heart he needed. Ever.

No matter what she feared, he knew they could overcome it. Nothing was insurmountable.

It was a stunning realization. He was not a man who attached easily. He had not the gift of common friendships. His loyalty was fierce and complete once given. There was so much more than mere lust between them now. They were partners in caring for Melody. They were stronger together than they were apart. They were a family now.

His family.

He took the house. The deal was very swiftly done and the agent promised to vacate by the next morning. It seemed he had a sister he could stay with for the duration of Parliament and the Season. Aidan barely listened as the man warbled on about his plans. A warm and unfamiliar sensation was fizzing its way through his veins.

He suspected it might be happiness. However, there was one more thing he needed to secure. A special license.

Oh, yes, and an acceptance of his proposal. Thank heaven he already had the ring.

St. James Park was a large park, twice as wide as it was deep. Directly ahead of Madeleine and Melody, crossing their path and flowing down the length of the vast lawn, was a canal edged by a line of trees on both sides, rather like a country lane.

Immediately upon entering the park, Melody was off, headed down to the canal to torment the ducks. Chubby legs pumping, curls bouncing, it seemed there was nothing in the world but open green space in which to run.

Madeleine smiled and fought back the impulse to hike up her gown and follow. When had she last run for the joy of it?

Running for one's life didn't count. Nor did running from Aidan, running from the intimacy of truly being with him, without secrets, without guard. Running from . . . herself?

She put one hand to the trunk of a tree to brace herself against that sudden flash of clarity.

Aidan *didn't* love her. How could he? She was a lie, a fabrication from start to finish. There wasn't a single true thing about the woman she was when she was with him . . . except for the way he took her breath away when he stood too near and for the way her throat went tight watching his tenderness with Melody.

Must she truly carry the sins of the past forever? That seemed a rather extreme punishment.

Melody was already near the far end of the canal, squatting to poke at something on the ground. A real mother might call out for her to stand up and stop dragging her hem on the grass. Instead, Madeleine began to slowly stroll closer, idly wondering what held the child's attention so closely.

The sun came through the clouds and she paused, closing her eyes and lifting her chin into the light. It was a perfect day and she'd been indoors for so long.

In hiding for so long . . .

She was so weary of wearing black. Who was it she was mourning?

It certainly wasn't her husband.

Perhaps it was herself. Lady Madeleine seemed a lifetime ago.

On the other hand, if the old Madeleine was gone forever, then perhaps a new Madeleine could now emerge. She could build herself from the beginning. Letting the warmth of the sun sink into her and relax her to her bones, she played with that idea.

The things that made her up, the facts of her life, the girl she had been—what if she recreated those? A birthplace was just a place, after all. The names of her parents could be reinvented, her history and her path to this moment could be invented just as easily as she'd invented the name "Chandler" while standing across the street from a London candlemaker's shop.

She could give all this to Aidan the next time his eyes questioned her, the next time she watched his jaw clench as he turned away in frustration from her silence.

Perhaps if she repeated them enough, clung to them enough, those facts and figures would become real and she truly would become a different Madeleine.

What she wouldn't give to make that so—to make all the past go away and start new!

A lie of that proportion would require that she cut loose every scrap of her true self. What would she be then? Then again, what was she now but a wall of silence, a dam holding back a flood of secrets?

Perhaps it was over. Perhaps it was time to put it behind her, to become Madeleine Chandler in truth. Simply another widow, simply an ordinary woman who was free to marry, to mother a child, to live a life of truth instead of a web of lies.

Smiling at the thought, she lowered her face and blinked a few times to wash away the shimmering future which just might be within her reach. Looking ahead, she saw Melody standing on the grass with her hands cupped and uplifted, showing her discovery to a bright-coated man. Goodness, she'd best hurry over there or Melody would chatter the poor fellow's ears off.

The man stood with his back to Madeleine but as she drew closer, something cold and jagged began to twist in her belly. He was short and wide, but so many men were. He wore a sickly green coat . . . but that meant nothing, truly it didn't.

Then she caught the wobbling curve of his cheekbone and jaw. No. It was impossible for the thoughts swirling in her mind to be true. Entirely impossible—

Except, of course, that it wasn't impossible, was it?

Critchley had found her after all.

Worse yet, it seemed he'd found Melody as well.

CHAPTER 25

His rooms at Brown's were empty. They were so desolate that for a moment of sheer madness Aidan actually wondered if he'd concocted Madeleine and Melody out of nothing but imagination.

Then he spotted Gordy Ann abandoned on the floor by the window.

Stolen.

By whom? And why? No, it made no sense. No one even knew they were here but for Colin.

Colin. Aidan's fear deflated. Of course. They had gone to Colin's rooms, probably to give restless Melody a change of scene. He wasn't sure he liked having the woman he planned to wed visiting men in their rooms, but surely with Melody as a chaperone . . .

He turned swiftly, ready to barge into Colin's rooms and take his family back with an offended remark or three. There in the hall behind him stood Colin, pale and out of breath. He looked nothing short of terrified. Aidan's fear came back in a rush.

"I fell asleep," Colin gasped. "On your sofa—I was up all night—when I woke they were gone!" He dragged an arm across his brow. "I've searched the club inside and out. I even searched the street. They're not here!"

Aidan's mouth was dry. "Melody. Oh, God." He blinked. "What of Madeleine? She would have fought whomever did this."

What if she were harmed? Sick terror, black and icy, began to seep into him.

Colin cursed roundly. "How can you be so sure of her? Haven't you glued yourself to these rooms for the past three days because you didn't trust her? The moment we took our eyes from her, she grabbed Melody and disappeared!"

"Impossible."

"Entirely possible!"

He focused his gaze on Colin. "How can you think that? You seemed to like her well enough."

" 'Like' doesn't mean 'trust'!" Colin ran a hand through his hair. "I take full responsibility for this. You left them in my charge and I let you down."

"There is no blame." Aidan shook his head. "Colin, she hasn't run away with Melody. She isn't trying to get away from me. She . . ." Even now it seemed miraculous. Through his worry his heart still beat a new rhythm. "She loves me. She told me so."

Colin rolled his eyes. "Don't be a simpleton, Blankenship. For years you've been telling me that she was faithless and heartless. Now you're telling me that she's stanch and loyal?"

Aidan shrugged helplessly. "I know what you think but you're wrong. She might be in trouble and I'm dead worried about them both, but it won't be because she's trying to leave me."

Colin blew out a long breath. "I can't decide if I pity you or if I'm envious. I'm fairly certain you're being blind—but I suppose you have as much right to be an idiot as any man. Nonetheless, we have to expand our search."

Aidan nodded. "Yes. We should definitely check the park. I'm certain she took Melody to the park."

In the deceptive serenity of St. James Park, Madeleine pressed herself against a tree, then carefully leaned around it to spy on Critchley and Melody where they stood at the edge of the canal.

What should she do? Her most urgent desire was to march over there and rip sweet innocence away from the perilous maw of depravity . . . but what if Critchley had not yet seen her with Melody? Wouldn't that only betray Melody's involvement in this mess?

Critchley looked bored and watchful at the same moment. He often raised his eyes from the chattering child to flick his beady gaze all about them. Madeleine had the horrifying suspicion that he already knew too much.

The park was too sparsely occupied today to hope for any help from strangers. Madeleine looked about her for some kind of weapon and spied a ring of fist-sized stones circling the base of the tree. Kneeling, she quickly stood with one in each trembling fist.

The first stone went into the canal, creating a satisfying splash and putting a dozen ducks to startled, quacking flight. Both Critchley and Melody turned to look at the commotion.

No, Melody, look at me!

Madeleine sent the second stone rolling and bouncing across the grass like a bowling ball, directly to Melody's feet.

Melody gazed down at the stone, then looked up curiously. When Melody made eye contact with her, Madeleine put her finger to her lips and grinned mischievously. *Come here*, she signaled to Melody with her hands.

Knowing that Melody was always ready for a game, Madeleine ducked back behind the tree and watched. In a matter of seconds, Melody calmly walked around the tree, humming a little tune.

Madeleine pulled her down into her lap and squeezed her hard in relief. "Does the bad man know where you went?"

Melody wrinkled her nose. "The bad man smells."

"He certainly does." Madeleine twisted about to risk a look around the edge of the tree. Critchley stood blinking in confusion and kicking at some of the ducks who had come to rest near his feet.

She turned back around to gaze into Melody's eyes. "We're going to play Hide from the Bad Man, mousie. We're going to run from tree to tree, making sure he can't see us. Then, when we're far away from him, we're going to run straight home to Brown's. How does that sound?"

"Can we make the ducks fly again first?"

Madeleine gave her another squeeze. "Not today, my love. Uncle Aidan will bring you to the park soon and you can show him how to make the ducks fly, all right?" She stood and picked Melody up, settling her on one hip. "Are you hanging on?" She hitched up her skirts a bit with the other hand.

Melody wrapped her little monkey fists into Madeleine's spencer and nodded. "Ready, steady, go!"

Madeleine ran.

* * *

Aidan and Colin set out at once, striding through the West End streets, splitting up as necessary, joining again at the corner, setting out once more to scan the crowds, to accost many a slender woman in black, to follow the high piping of a childish voice for several minutes before realizing that it was someone's little boy squealing for a sweet. They hunted through every shop, every tearoom, every cluster of people surrounding a street hawker.

Then there was St. James Park. It was one of the first places Aidan looked, but as he stood in the center, having inspected every tree, every shrub, every cobble in the walkway for signs of them, all he could think was that every time he'd turned a corner, he'd turned the wrong direction, that every time he'd entered a shop, they'd passed by the door outside it. They were the pea in a street thief's shell game and he was the hapless loser who couldn't spot the sleight of hand.

Madeleine held the small grubby hand tightly in hers as they scurried down another strange street. "I know you're tired, mousie, but we must be sure of which way we're going." She wasn't precisely lost. When they had fled the park, she had mistakenly run in the wrong direction. She had the vague notion that she was a bit east of St. James Street. Being lost wasn't what made the fear swirl through her.

Perhaps she traced this London maze for nothing. Perhaps they were not being followed and there was no danger of leading danger back to Brown's. Perhaps Critchley hadn't even seen her—perhaps his seeming interest in Melody had been random and unrelated.

The very thought of Melody within a yard of Critchley left her cold. Some people in this world were bad, some were weak.

And some were evil.

Even so, she fought to believe that it was a coincidence—or even that Critchley knew her general location but not her precise one. After all, she was useless as a source of money, and he must know that she would only run again the moment she had the chance.

Melody whined and stomped her little feet but kept going nonetheless. Madeleine paused to pick her up. She suspected that she hadn't been nearly as successful at hiding her terror as she'd hoped. She'd managed to make the child think that slipping away from the fat man was a game, and Melody, clever little minx that she was, had caught on quickly. But now the game had gone on too long.

Then they rounded a corner and found themselves on St. James Street once more, not two establishments away from Brown's.

Slipping into the servants' entrance wasn't too difficult. She told Melody they were playing the secret game again and that she should walk on her toes and whisper. The staff was busy in the kitchen preparing dinner, with their backs to the door and their minds on their work. Only that one moment of danger and then they were on the back stair, heading up as quickly and quietly as they could.

Once they'd safely reached the third floor, Madeline had to stop and breathe. There was a small window high on the outer wall to provide light for the stair and on impulse she stood on her toes to peer out of it. She promised herself that if she saw him, she would tell Aidan everything. If Critchley wasn't in sight, she would consider herself safe and free. Not logical, but the fizzing panic within her wasn't a rational emotion.

The street was plainly visible. She took her time, squinting to make out every gentleman's face and form. Relief began to coil through her. She braced one hand on the wall, keeping the other firmly clutching Melody's while she stretched as tall as she was able in order to see.

He was there, a still, solid, bilious green object in the swimming tide of humanity walking in both directions.

And he was looking right at her.

She froze. Surely he couldn't make her out through this high, small, dusty window? Perhaps he couldn't, but he was certainly watching Brown's most intently. Not even her active imagination could convince her he wasn't.

So he suspected she was here.

Suspected? Don't you think it's time to stop lying to yourself?

He knew. He knew and he was waiting out there to pounce upon her the moment she stepped foot from the building.

The sickening chill that he'd brought with him lodged firmly in her stomach now, growing until it pressed up against her throat, stealing her breath away.

Black spots of panic began to spread across her vision and she felt her locked knees go weak. Turning her back on the window, she slid down the wall to sit awkwardly on the stair. Through the roaring in her ears she heard Melody complain.

"Maddie, you hold too tight."

Madeline used everything she had to order her hand

to loosen from Melody's. *Oh, God, Melody!* He knew about her, knew that she had something to do with Madeleine, knew that she had something to do with this refuge at Brown's—

The back of her throat burned but she fought back the sick, tearing fear, forcing down the urge to run far and fast away. All reluctance to tell Aidan the truth was incinerated by the danger she'd put Melody in with her secrets.

There was no time to waste. No fear, no wavering. No more hiding. Aidan must know everything.

CHAPTER 26

At last, there was nowhere left to search. Aidan returned to his rooms to find Colin already there, sitting on the edge of the sofa with his head in his hands, his hair wild from absently running his fingers through it. Colin looked up when he entered, but his hopeful gaze faded quickly into further panic.

"I fell asleep. I shouldn't have fallen asleep."

Aidan fought back the dread freezing solid in his own chest. Tossing his coat down violently, he went to gaze out of the window, his eyes still helplessly searching even though there was nothing to see but the dreary garden fading into the dusk. "Don't be tedious. We simply need more pairs of eyes. I'm calling Wilberforce up. The staff can help us search."

Colin looked up. "You still don't think Madeleine disappeared intentionally?"

Aidan didn't turn away from the window. "She is no liar," he said firmly. "I'd stake my life on it."

"I can see you've already staked your heart." Colin sighed. "Perhaps you're right." He stood. "After all, if she wanted Melody, all she had to do was marry you." He hesitated. "Aidan, you did propose, didn't you?"

Aidan grunted. "More or less."

"Oh, no," Colin groaned. "You buggered it, didn't you? You said something about a reasonable arrangement, or a logical solution, or something else cold and soulless and bound to send any woman running for a fast boat to elsewhere!"

Aidan whirled on him. "I didn't bugger it!"

"Bugger!" · A high childish voice delighted in the forbidden word. The two men spun about to see a pale, ill-looking Madeleine standing in the doorway, holding the hand of a cheerfully dirty Melody. "We went to the park and then we hided from the bad man," Melody informed them enthusiastically. "It was fun!"

Aidan locked gazes with Madeleine, whose eyes were filled with fear and shame. Whatever was wrong, he knew he was about to see a brand-new Madeleine—one he was suddenly quite certain would break his heart for good. Something inside him, something newborn and helpless started to die at that moment. "Colin." Was that his voice? It sounded so far away. "Would you take Melody to your rooms please and give her some supper?"

Colin glanced back and forth between them for a moment. To Aidan it seemed that his friend was tempted to leap to Madeleine's defense. One flat, empty look was all that was needed to prompt Colin to sweep Melody into his arms. "Let's take Gordy Ann down and tell her a story, shall we, my pocket darling?"

"I want carrots," Melody declared as they left the room. "I hided very hard."

CHAPTER 27

Colin took Melody away. Aidan saw Madeleine reach a hand toward Melody as Colin passed, but then she dropped it before touching the child. The gesture filled Aidan with bitter premonition. The door closed on a new high-tension silence.

"You're leaving me."

She flinched. Then she took a deep breath. "Aidan, don't speak for a moment. Please, simply listen to everything I have to tell you. When I'm done, if you want me to leave, I will."

He opened his mouth to protest, but she stopped him with a hand. "Please, Aidan."

He'd never seen her like this. She was deathly pale, and her hands shook with fear. Sickening alarm swept him, for it seemed his worst nightmares might not have been imaginative enough.

With slow deliberate movements she removed her spencer and lay it carefully over the arm of the chair nearest the door. The silence grew until Aidan could scarcely bear it.

Then she raised bleak eyes to meet his gaze. "Aidan, you asked me once how my husband died." She took another deep breath. "He didn't. He is, I believe, alive and well and about to arrive in London."

Shock went through him. "You're *divorced*?" It was scandalous. It made her an impossible match for him, socially. It was also, he realized with a chill, the better of the only two options left.

She met his gaze and crushed his hope. "No," she said simply. "I am quite thoroughly married."

"But—" He could not help it. He had to make it untrue. He stepped forward, his hand out to her. "You wore black. You're still in black." It was a ridiculous thing to say. It was the only thing he could think of.

She looked down, pressing her hands down over her skirts. "Mere protective coloration. A tan dove in a field of straw. So many widows, so many women alone. I knew no one would question me about it." Her lips twisted wryly. "I wasn't prepared for you, of course."

He shook his head disbelievingly. "It was a way to lie?"

She met his gaze, not trying to defend, only explain. "It was a way to *hide*." She stepped forward, lifting her hands urgently to him. "When we met and I defied that thief, it was because what was in my reticule was all that I had in the world—what I stole before I ran away."

He recoiled. "Stole?"

She rushed on. "I'd been taking things, small valuable things and concealing them in a spot in the wood. He kept me locked in my rooms for over a year—"

Aidan's eyes narrowed suspiciously. "A year? Yet you managed to go to the wood?"

She took a breath. "Yes. Once in a while I was able to persuade one of the housemaids to change clothes with me. She felt sorry for me for she knew my lady's maid was aligned with my husband, as were most of the servants. I suppose I cannot blame them—it was not I who paid their salaries. Even so, I never dared be out long. A few brief moments in the outside world was like heaven. It was the only thing that kept me from going mad. Only sometimes I wasn't sure it worked."

Her words tumbled over each other in the rush to tell him everything he'd ever wanted to know—yet he no longer wanted to know any of it. He wanted to rewind the clock, turn back time to when he'd only thought her secretive and mysterious, not full of falsehoods and *married!*

She went on, gazing down at her twisting hands, compulsively talking—she who had been so silent before.

"Then one evening while I was outside, there was a fire. The wing I occupied went up in flames so quickly. I'd hoped Sally got out. It seems she did not.

"I realized that either he knew I was out of my room or he believed me burned inside it. Either way, I could not go back. I found my little cache and ran for my life." Madeleine took a breath at last. She'd thought she would feel unburdened by her confession. She'd thought the truth would be freeing.

Her words seemed to fall upon deaf ears. Aidan seemed unable to fix upon anything but her marital state.

"You were married, all that time we were having an affair? What were you thinking to lead me on so?"

She blinked in surprise at the question. "Oh, Aidan, I wasn't thinking. Neither were you. We lived those days very carefully not thinking, I suspect. It was time out of time, secret and not quite real."

There was little argument he could offer there. "And what of the last few days, what have they been?"

She gazed at him for a moment. "A gift," she said simply.

His eyes narrowed. "A parting gift?"

She flinched then, very slightly. "If you insist."

"Divorce him," he said abruptly. "Cut him loose and marry me."

She shook her head. "You don't want that sort of scandal, Aidan. You and I might somehow survive it, but what of Melody?"

"Yes, what of Melody? Are you saying you would rather be a fugitive from your husband than stay here with your own daughter?" He folded his arms. "I don't believe that for a moment."

Oh, yes. *That.* Madeleine wavered in her determination. God, how could she tell him? What a heinous thing she'd done, to make Melody believe such a foul lie. Sickened by her own actions, Madeleine pressed a palm to her belly, to her tragically unused womb.

"Melody— Melody isn't my daughter. I've never had a child." She shrugged helplessly, her lips twisting in sympathy as he drew back from her. "It must have been another of your lovers."

He flinched as if the blow was physical. "Other lovers . . ." He shook his head slightly. "You lied?"

She spread her hands. "I felt I had to. That horrible little man, Critchley, had come to blackmail me. He wanted—I knew he wasn't going to stop unless I disappeared again."

She trailed off. He was gazing at her like a stranger— a revolting, possibly mad stranger who related a tawdry tale he didn't want to hear.

Oh, my love, would you have helped me if you knew

the truth? If I had reached out to you that day you came to my house, would you have given me shelter? Or would you have assumed some nefarious plot on my part and walked away again?

"You aren't her mother." Aidan stopped, unable to say the words. Clenching his jaw, he swallowed and forced himself to stop—now and forever—stop being such a gullible, fantasizing idiot who didn't want to face the truth. "Therefore I am not her father."

Madeleine's eyes widened. "But I thought surely you—"

He stopped her words with a violent shake of his head. She wasn't Melody's mother. That meant he wasn't Melody's father. Once again he'd trusted her and once again she'd broken his heart. The life of possibilities he'd found had been nothing but another lie.

A ghost of a laugh broke from his lips. "Do you know, when I first saw you I thought you were as fragile as a china doll. I worried that I would break you if I touched you, yet I couldn't bear not to. Now I see that was an illusion. You are steel and stone and pretty paint, and I'm a fool."

He lifted his gaze to meet hers. "There was only you, M—" His throat closed against uttering her name. He gazed at her, unable to hide the starkness of his pain. Father and husband no more, nor would he be, ever. He might as well deliver the killing blow himself.

"From the first moment I saw you fleeing down that street, there has only been you. Ever."

Pulling breath into his aching chest felt like inhaling fire. "You are the only woman I have ever loved or ever will love . . . and I now wish to never set eyes on you again."

"But—" She reached out to him, her dark eyes wide and pleading.

"Go *away,* Madeleine." He turned away, twisting violently from her toward the wall. His voice cracked. "For God's sake, have you no mercy in you at all?"

Madeleine ached all over. So cruel her lies were, however necessary they might have been. And yet she could not give him his wish, not quite yet. "Aidan, as hard as that was for you to hear, there is more. Please let me finish."

More? The only thing more she could do to him would be to kill him.

She took a breath. "This man—"

"Your husband."

She nodded. "I married a monster," she said quickly, desperately. "He imprisoned me in his house, he watched me every moment, he beat me—" She swallowed hard. "He isn't an ordinary sort of bad. He isn't simply brutal or unfair. He is *evil*—" Her breath caught. She pressed a hand to her throat and continued. "And now he knows I have some tie to Melody, and to you. I fear he will retaliate against you for sheltering me!"

The husband did not concern him. The man's very existence had already slain him. "I'm quite sure he could do no more damage than you have done."

She lifted her chin. "No, you're right. I never should have loved you. It was only bound to hurt us both." The breaths she took didn't seem to fill her lungs. "I'll go away. I'll stay away this time, if you promise me one thing."

"I hardly think—"

"Get Melody out of London. Immediately."

He frowned. "Melody needs to wait here for Jack. He is certainly her father."

She shook off his objection. "If you ever believe one thing I say, believe this—anyone connected to me is in danger, especially someone weak and vulnerable."

He stared at her pitilessly. "Is this more of your theatrics?"

She closed her eyes. "Just . . . take her somewhere. To your house. To a hotel. Anywhere not connected to Brown's!"

Deep blue eyes, icy as an arctic sky—God, had she ever seen eyes so cold?—met her anxious ones. "Yes, if that will make you leave. So leave."

Still she hesitated.

"Now."

CHAPTER 28

Madeleine took her spencer and reticule from where she'd deposited them on the chair. "I'll . . . I'll send someone for my other things tomorrow—"

His fist hit the wall with a sickening thud that she felt to her bones. She knew he'd never strike a woman. However, she feared that in a battle between Aidan and the wall, the wall might do him some harm before it came tumbling down.

She gazed at his broad back, regret searing her heart as she watched his shoulders heaving slightly.

Live on, my darling. Love someone worthy someday. Be happy, if you can.

Her eyes filling, she fumbled for the door handle behind her. Letting herself out quietly, she shut the door carefully. He must have heard the click anyway, for another thud resonated though the walls.

A single low sob tore from her throat before she could catch it, but it rose alone in the empty hallway. She had no right to tears. She alone had created this mess with her cowardice.

In penance, she intended to board that ship to Jamaica first thing in the morning. She only hoped it would draw the danger away from Brown's and all who dwelled there.

"Wilhelm isn't going to be pleased," she murmured to herself as she turned automatically to check the street from the window at the end of the hall.

As she approached, a shadow moved in the embrasure. "Oh, no, my dear," said a silky voice. "Quite the contrary."

Madeleine froze. *No. It couldn't be. Not here.*

Wilhelm moved forward into the dim light shining from the hall sconce. He smiled at her fondly. "Wilhelm is going to be very pleased indeed."

With horror, Madeleine realized that in her desperate confession to Aidan, she had neglected a vital bit of information.

She had not spoken the monster's name.

She had not a breath of time to cry out before his fist rose to strike her into darkness.

She was gone. Had she simply walked out the front door? It didn't matter. Let the staff at Brown's apprehend her and throw her out. What did he care?

Aidan clenched his throbbing fist but didn't vent his pain with another blow to the wall. The last thing he had the strength to do at this moment was to explain to his daughter why there was a hole in the wall.

Not your daughter.

He leaned his forehead against the cool plaster but the wall had given him all the solace it was capable of. He was all alone in his grief.

Alone. What a surprise.

Colin was going to crow over this error, Aidan was sure. Then again, even the ever-cynical Colin had fallen under the witch's spell in the end.

It didn't really help to know they had all been fools this time—he, Colin, Melody.

Oh, God, what am I going to tell Melody? Sorry, dear child, it was a nasty trick. No mother, no father. You're just a little foundling after all. Oops.

He who'd been determined to spend his life in bachelorhood had risen to the occasion and become a father and a husband-to-be. And now it was over. She'd left devastation on so many levels that he felt numb from it.

The last time, he'd had Jack to help him regain his sanity. *In that case, madam, I have had my fill of harmless fun. Good-bye.*

The following hour, the following week, the following month—now, those were darkly clear in his memory, as if seen through a smoke-blackened glass. The cost of every continuous breath was so high that he barely spoke. The effort to dress, even with his valet's help, drained him so that he rarely went out. His appetite deserted him until his suits scarcely fit him anyway.

Jack was the one who brought him back. Jack's grief over Blakely's death and his guilt for inheriting had drained what little was left of him after he'd nearly died in battle as well. Colin and Aidan had put their own concerns aside and had shelved their long-lived enmity in order to help Jack survive that black time.

Moreover, Jack had begun to respond somewhat normally again—until the girl whose memory had sustained him in wartime had refused his heartfelt proposal and had him cruelly thrown out of her house.

That had nearly put an end to the Jack they'd known. In the dark months that followed, both Colin and Aidan had been called out to rescue their friend from drunken brawl after drunken brawl. It seemed that if there was a self-destructive bottom to unending misery, then Jack was determined to find it.

Finally, they'd managed to dry him out long enough to remind him of his obligations to the people on his family lands. Serious and distant where he'd once been jovial and animated, Jack had agreed to continue walking and talking and breathing. About anything else, he'd made no promises.

Aidan, by helping Jack, had learned to do the same.

His heart had begun to mend. Mend but never be like new again. He'd tried to flirt, to chase Madeleine from his thoughts with new assignations, but nothing ever came of it in the end. Aidan had no longer seemed to have the ability to adore anyone and he'd refused to inflict himself on any woman heartlessly.

And yet, this time he'd fallen hard and completely. It was not because of Madeleine's charm or beauty, though she possessed those in plenty. It was something new and altogether terrifying and thrilling. A resonance of souls, perhaps. A fitting together of pieces long sundered.

Not only had he let down his guard and let himself love a woman who could tell such horrible lies, but he had fallen in love with a child who would never be his. He had set aside every defense he had to open himself to both Madeleine and Melody and yet, here they were, sundered again.

And to think it wasn't her lies that had ripped them apart—it was her truth.

She'd fought so hard to keep her secrets. Now he knew why. He knew what she would lose if she told him the truth.

She would lose *him*.

Which he'd known, somewhere deep inside. He'd known that whatever it was she had locked away behind those dark, troubled eyes, it would cost him just as much as it would cost her.

Which is why you didn't press her harder, of course. A man doesn't hurry his own execution, does he?

How bitter to realize that some things were, in fact, insurmountable.

Pain—streaks of pain like fire-tipped lances shooting through her head. Through the throbbing Madeleine somehow knew that opening her eyes would only make it worse. Light would pierce her vision like darts. She lay as still as possible, for she knew if she rolled over the severity of the headache might make her vomit.

How did she know that?

Oh, yes. That's right. I've been beaten before.

The comfort of that recognition was almost enough to relax her and send her back into the throbbing fog, until she traced that thought back farther.

Pain. Beating.

Wilhelm.

Wilhelm finding her. Wilhelm in the club, horribly close to Aidan and Melody. No. It was a nightmare, just like before. Just another monstrous dream.

Fear gained supremacy over the pain. Wake up. *Wake up!*

She opened her eyes. That's when she knew that monsters were real. She knew because she was looking at one. Leaning nonchalantly in the doorway with his arms folded, Wilhelm smiled fondly at her. However, his eyes were icy. He was very tall, and lean, and handsome enough if one didn't know him. Madeleine knew him all too well, so the flash of white teeth did nothing to reassure her. He was just as likely to bite as to smile.

He cast a hinting sort of glance about the room, then gave her a what-do-you-think lift of one brow.

Warily pulling herself up to sit, Madeleine blinked away another surge of pain and looked about. She was in a long narrow room with a window on one end wall and the door Wilhelm guarded about halfway down one long wall. The room was mostly empty but for a few odd bits of furniture. The ceiling was slanted and that meant . . . her thoughts came so slow through the pain . . . it meant the room was in an attic. That was slightly better than a cellar, but she couldn't quite think of why.

She looked down to discover that she was awkwardly sprawled upon a nest of blankets piled upon a bare, unpolished wooden floor. Some were rough wool and some were silk coverlets. She blinked at them owlishly for a moment, trying to collect her thoughts.

There was light coming through the window, though the panes were very dirty with soot and city grime. It was day . . .

Hadn't it been nearly evening by the time she'd brought Melody home from the park?

The park. Critchley. Wilhelm . . . in Brown's? She couldn't think.

"I'm going to vomit," she said calmly.

Wilhelm stepped to one side and kicked a heavy copper chamber pot over to her. The harsh clang nearly made her weep. Still, she managed to sweep her hair carefully out of the way before she heaved. Nothing much came of it. When had she last eaten?

Yesterday. Breakfast with Aidan. *Oh, Aidan, my love!* For a moment tears of weakness and loss threatened, but she blinked them back. She might have been groggy but she knew better than to cry in front of the monster. He had dozens of ways to make the tears worse.

And he liked to use them all.

Disliking the feeling of looking up at him, she tried to stand. The room spun and she nearly reached for the chamber pot again, but she managed to keep her feet as long as she pressed her back to the wall.

It was whitewashed stone, cold and rough. She could feel the dry, elderly lime wash flaking off beneath her touch. She let the stone steady her while she tried to collect her thoughts and string them into something resembling sense.

Wilhelm had found her. He'd taken her someplace where comfort was not an important component. He'd thrown her in here on a pile of blankets and had been thoughtful enough to provide her with a chamber pot.

It seemed she was going to be here for a while.

And no one even knew she was missing.

Yet she could not allow panic to overwhelm her. Wilhelm could be managed . . . somewhat.

"How did you gain entrance to Brown's?" Keep him talking. Be reluctantly impressed by his cunning. Let him feel he had the upper hand.

Which, in fact, he did.

He gave her a smile closer to a sneer. "In the classic manner. I, my dearest wife, am a member. Someone in my ancestry must have felt that rathole was worth it. Oh,

I've been a little lax in my dues, but that was easily for-given with a mention of my prospects of marriage."

Oh, Wilberforce, you don't know who you let through your doors.

"I followed Critchley to Brown's after I found your locket in his quarters. I didn't know why he was watching the club but I was willing to linger. I can be very patient when it suits me."

He'd been waiting for her in the hallway outside Aid-an's room. "How did you know where I was hiding? I could have been anywhere in that building."

He dusted at a speck of old plaster on his sleeve. "I knew you were on that floor because I saw you there myself." He casually toyed with his cuff. "Such a pretty little girl. She was hiding in that window for nearly an hour. Whatever were you up to to neglect her for so long?" He shot her an accusing gaze from beneath his brows.

Whatever were you up to? Don't blush. Don't look away in shame. Don't even let a stray moment of memory arise.

And for pity's sake don't let any love for Melody show!

She held his gaze with unconcern. "Children can be troublesome," she agreed distantly. "I've never been ter-ribly interested in them." All true. *I was more interested in survival.*

When lying to Wilhelm, it was best to speak the truth as much as possible. His uncanny sensitivity to others' weaknesses made him a formidable opponent. A twisted sport of flattery and attachment, then cruel betrayal. She knew the game well.

How silly she'd been to believe she could escape it forever.

"You'll understand if I must leave you now?" He tugged his weskit straight. "I'm to be wed soon. Don't you wish to congratulate me?" He tilted his head and smiled slightly. So handsome.

She would kill him where he stood had she a weapon to hand.

"I'd invite you to the wedding, but you'll be far too dead to attend."

Her fate, it seemed, was sealed. Oddly, she was numb to the fear. Perhaps it was a muscle too long overused. Perhaps he'd simply worn that mechanism out.

He spread his hands, encompassing her prison with enthusiasm. "So very grim, isn't it? I must say, I always longed for a dungeon of my very own."

CHAPTER 29

Wilhelm's smile widened and he leaned toward Madeleine confidentially. "When I was a boy, I watched my caged bird die. I stopped feeding it, stopped giving it water. It was fascinating watching it get weaker and weaker, until its tiny feathered chest didn't move again. I've tried it with all sorts of creatures, but nothing has quite had the magic of that first event. Perhaps you will give me that, sweet Madeleine."

He laughed in delight. Always laughing, always smiling, always false Wilhelm—it made her quite long for Aidan's honest severity.

"After all, I can hardly be accused of your murder. You're already dead, if you recall." He gazed at her tenderly. "You're going to die very slowly, and I'm going to watch."

He reached into his waistcoat pocket and withdrew the gold locket resting there. He didn't open it, but only let it spin in the air, glinting in the dim light like a warning. "Won't you die with this token of my affection about your neck?"

Madeleine recoiled from the pretty thing. "I will not don your leash and collar again!" She spat the words at him, unable to contain her revulsion any longer.

He merely laughed again. "Adieu, my pet." He put the

locket back into his waistcoat pocket and chuckled. "Pet. A perfect term for you. Now, I shan't be back—or at least, you won't see me again. But rest assured, I will be watching you." He blew her a kiss. "But then, you knew that already, didn't you, pet?"

As he opened the door, he turned back. "By the way, such a pretty child. Too young to be mine, I'd say. You have been a naughty creature, haven't you, *wife*?"

With that he was gone. She heard the key turn in the lock. It sounded through the empty room like a church bell tolling a death.

She closed her eyes, listening. Nothing.

He was still out there. She could feel him. She gazed at the door where there was a freshly drilled spy hole, not even attempting to hide her fury. If he was watching, let him see that she was no longer the fearful girl she had once been.

She had spent her life trying to be someone who was wanted—the perfect daughter for her parents, the perfect wife for Wilhelm, the perfect mistress for Aidan, even the perfect mother for Melody. All the years she'd spent being what they all desired her to be—and where had that gotten her? Alone in an attic with a madman, that's where!

Well, bugger that.

If she had to claw her way through the bricks using nothing but her fingernails, she was not going to spend her last moments being the perfect prisoner!

Aidan woke with the scent of her in his sheets. Soft and subtle, yet all the more seductive for it.

He smiled sleepily.

Madeleine.

That brief flare of intense happiness was followed by an equally intense shock of truth. She was gone.

Worse yet, in fact, the woman he had wanted for his bride had never truly existed.

Rolling over, he found he'd thrown himself onto the bed fully clothed. His mouth was dry and his head pounded. Unfortunately, he'd not had a thing to drink to earn such a state. Pity.

With an effort, he rose to sit on the edge of the bed he'd so recently shared with her. Her scent clung to him. She was everywhere around him. Her wrapper and gown remained neatly folded on the chair. Her valise still sat against the wall beneath the window. Upon his dresser was a hairbrush and beneath it on the floor glinted a lost pin, the sort that women used to fix their hats to their hair.

He shut his eyes against those reminders, although he knew perfectly well that in his study there were more. Even now he could picture her sewing box on the sofa where she'd been stitching tiny clothes for Melody, who had spent the night in Colin's rooms.

Melody . . . who was not his daughter. A different pain, that. More of a deep ache, like after a terrible blow—though he'd never been struck quite that profoundly before.

He rubbed one hand over his face. There was a great deal to do today, or rather, things to undo. He ought to tell his man of business not to vacate the house—although by the slant of light through his windows, it was a bit late for that.

And precisely how did one "undo" a special license? It wasn't as though he were going to get that bribe back.

Perhaps he ought to hang onto it, in case he found another heartless liar who wished to dupe him.

He was stalling. He didn't want to open his eyes. He didn't want to face the life that now lay before him.

He didn't want to face his life without *her*—and he hated himself for such weakness.

On the other hand, he hated her more.

Madeleine walked the perimeter of the room slowly. Wilhelm would be watching, of course.

At least in this stone attic there could not be more than one spyhole.

The day after the Incident, she had woken to find Wilhelm in her rooms at Whittaker Hall, preparing them for her imprisonment. She had once tried to change the awkward arrangement of the dressing screen only to have him furiously insist that she return the room to exactly as she'd found it.

He'd stopped even pretending to desire her and left her alone every night. Yet he had seemed so ardent when he'd pursued her and proposed.

She had understood when she'd found the spy holes drilled through her walls, carved into the pattern of the ornate woodwork.

What had sprung from Wilhelm's suspicion and mistrust—for he'd been so terribly afraid she would betray him—transmuted into his own personal obsession.

Wilhelm had discovered that he liked to watch.

In her bedroom at Whittaker Hall she'd found the peepholes all over her chamber. She'd eventually hit upon the method of using a smoking bit of wood to find the drafts. They had been everywhere, even positioned behind the screen where she used the chamber pot! Locked in her room, under guard by a burly footman, her only means of defense had been to do nothing personal until after the sun set and she'd blown out all the candles.

Now, however, her intention was not to frustrate Wilhelm's perversion but to defeat him by surviving. Better yet, by escaping.

But how to get out? There was only the one door.

She could feel him out there, could feel the creeping sensation of his gaze upon her. Her stomach turned. She'd been so close to being free forever!

She shivered and pulled her racing thoughts from the abyss of panic. Think!

There wasn't much to the chamber. It wasn't part of any servants quarters. No one would ever tolerate such a place, not even the poorest scullery maid. Nor did it seem to be any sort of storeroom. There was a massive fireplace, long unused. The chill threatened to turn her inward shivering into something entirely more physical. There was no candle or lantern. Fine. Wilhelm would have to be satisfied with the gloomy light filtering through the grimy panes to light his observation.

The window was large with many panes. At some point, someone had wished for large amounts of light in this chamber. The panels of glass had once opened, it seemed, although now they were soldered shut by years of grime. She pushed against the latch with all her might but could not budge it.

Outside the filthy glass—

Her breath caught. Outside the window was a strangely

familiar view. It looked just like the view of the garden through the window in Aidan's chamber, only from a higher elevation!

Good God! Wilhelm had trapped her in the attic of Brown's Club for Distinguished Gentlemen!

Her knees went weak and she almost laughed aloud from relief. Help was only a few yards away!

She threw back her head and screamed. "Help! Aidan! Colin! Wilberfoooorce!" She began to dance about the room, stomping and shouting. "Come and get me, Aidan! I'm up here! Come and find my hiding place! One, five, two, four, nine, six, eleven, *ten*!"

Breathless from her cavorting, she halted in the center of the room and listened eagerly.

The only sound aside from her own panting was the clear sound of Wilhelm on the other side of the door.

Laughing with delight.

Cold fear hit her belly like a dash of icy water.

Are you sure these walls are made of stone?

Oh sweet heaven, *no.*

The same reason that Melody had not needed to be unnaturally silent, the very reason why hers and Aidan's pleasures had not been overheard—the club's sturdy fire-proof construction would be the death of her.

In panic, she ran to the window and struggled once more to open the latch. No use.

She leaned her forehead against the cool panes, nauseous with the sudden, inescapable realization that she might, actually, in fact, *die.*

"Oh, Aidan, I'm so sorry," she murmured. More than anything else, that would tear at her as she slowly died here. What she had done to Aidan's heart—twice!—was the worst thing she had done in her life.

With a shaking hand, she cleared the inside of one pane. She could dimly make out the back garden through the outer filth. She was immediately above Aidan's apartments, then.

She turned her back on the empty garden. No help would be had from that quarter. No one would see her from down there. What had seemed a blessing when she was trying to keep an active child unseen was now a curse, for no one ever ventured into that sodden place.

She shivered, as much from fear as from the chill. The blocky, prisonlike feeling of the room oppressed her. What sort of place was this room? It had not the graceful proportions of the rest of the club. She could not imagine why someone would wall off a portion of an attic thus—unless it were for some nefarious purpose. Was she not the first prisoner to be held here? Was this a piece of Brown's darker history, perhaps from a time of unrest or perversion?

Don't be an idiot! You're just frightening yourself further!

Finally, she spotted the answer. In the wall, higher than her head, she saw the hooks. Heavy iron hooks, spaced evenly in a horizontal line from one side of the room to the other. On the opposite wall there were an equal number of identical hooks. If one tied a cord from a hook on one side to the other, each line would parallel perfectly.

Parallel cords. Of course!

She almost laughed, despite her grim situation. She was in a laundry drying room. The window was to let in light and fresh air. The solid walls and door were merely a reflection of the general building quality of Brown's.

Not quite the sinister origins of her imagination.

Her foolishness subsiding, she began to see the room as it really was. The piled refuse in the shadowy corners suddenly became clearly the odd broken furnishing and detritus of an untidy attic. The club had been popular in an earlier century, Aidan had said. This space was extra, probably for laundry overflow when the rooms were full during Parliament.

There was no overflow now. Brown's few servants had no trouble keeping up with the few gentlemen staying here.

Laundry.

There was something important about laundry . . . something she needed to remember.

CHAPTER 30

Her ship had sailed today. Madeleine had given up her chance of freedom—perhaps of life itself!—to spend these few precious days with Aidan. Yet she could not regret it for her own sake. It was only Aidan's and Melody's fates that made her mind go numb with terror.

She closed her eyes, forcing her anxious thoughts to still. Here she was, trapped but safe, at least for the moment, on the top floor of a gentlemen's club in the middle of St. James Street. Wilhelm might be watching but he wasn't in the room. He couldn't hurt her at this moment.

As her speeding heart stilled and her breathing slowed, an image came into her mind. Aidan's bedchamber.

Aidan's arms about her . . . his hands on her . . . his mouth—

She opened her eyes. Enough of that.

She closed her eyes again. Laundry . . . and Aidan's bedchamber. What did the two have in common?

She turned slowly in a circle. If she was standing in Aidan's bedchamber, the window would be at her right and she would be facing . . .

She opened her eyes. There was nothing before her but an elderly wardrobe, dusty and broken, its doors hanging awry on their hinges. Aidan's wardrobe was on the left. There was nothing on this wall but the washstand.

And the dumbwaiter.

Her heart sped again. Yes! The dumbwaiter was in that wall—a dumbwaiter that would have been used for transporting linens from the rooms to the basement laundry, and then up to the attic for drying and then back down to the rooms!

Slowly, as though she were dully, hopelessly examining her prison, she moved forward to the decrepit wardrobe. If it blocked the dumbwaiter, how could she move it without Wilhelm being aware?

It didn't, quite. The wardrobe stood crookedly, tossed aside as it had been for finer things. It listed to one side, leaning a corner on the wall while the rest of it angled outward into the room. The door that concealed the dumbwaiter hung just behind it!

There wasn't quite room behind the wardrobe to open the door. However, Madeleine could just fit behind it— which would only bring Wilhelm running. Perhaps tonight, in the dark, she could carefully nudge it aside, hopefully masking the noise in the creaks and groans of the old building. It wouldn't much change his view. He might not notice.

She was surprised he'd not already rearranged the room for better viewing. His lack of preparation did illustrate the spontaneity of his plan.

Madeleine only hoped he'd made more serious mistakes as well.

Come and get me, Aidan!

Wilhelm chuckled. What a charming memory. He decided it might be one of his favorite moments so far. Not to mention, silly Madeleine had provided the final clue to her protector's identity.

Critchley had claimed he knew, but Critchley was a liar. Wilhelm never trusted Critchley's word about anything.

He didn't know why he hadn't thought about staying at a club before. He'd scorned them in general for so long, he'd quite forgotten how comfortable they could be. His family belonged to several. Brown's simply had the added value of the enticing floor show.

He leaned back in the deeply padded leather chair and sipped at his rather decent brandy in the main club room and watched with great enjoyment as Madeleine's lover brooded in the most isolated corner of the room.

Aidan de Quincy, fifth Earl of Blankenship—wealthy, respected, and unscarred. He was everything that Wilhelm had once been—or at least, had purported himself to be. His own wealth had been mostly show and credit, which wasn't hard when one knew how.

Blankenship, now . . . there was real money. Rumor had it that the man had actually increased his family's holdings since assuming the title. Unheard of.

Yet, for all his riches and power, didn't old Blankenship look fixed in the doldrums? Wilhelm sneered behind his paper. The blighter had fancied himself *in love,* no doubt.

Hogwash.

Still, such a nasty ailment could have its uses. If one blackmailed a certain lady's lover—or perhaps ransom?

No. He mustn't, tempting though it might be. In the end, it was most important that Madeleine be quite thoroughly and irrevocably dead. A departed wife meant he could marry for the money he so desperately needed.

Besides, he could hardly be expected to pass up such reprisal-free fun!

The little girl, on the other hand . . . ah, yes, the little girl . . .

Wilhelm was fairly certain that the staff knew nothing about her. If she were kept in that room on the top floor, she was probably there alone much of the time. The possibilities . . . ah, the possibilities were endless.

Eagerness made his hands tremble slightly. He couldn't kill her, not if he truly wanted the ransom. Still, there were ways . . .

Despite his plans of prolonged suffering for Madeleine, he almost hoped she would expire quickly, so he could move on to his next delicacy.

Sitting in a secluded corner of the main club room, Aidan toyed with a brandy and indulged in a fine fit of manly brooding. He'd been poorly used and he deserved a righteously dismal gloom, by God!

Madeleine had lied. Madeleine had turned him into an adulterer—which he had vowed never to be! Madeleine had made him love a child who wasn't his!

Though, if he were being entirely honest with himself—which Aidan truly wasn't prepared to be—he would be forced to admit that he'd been entirely smitten with Melody from the first moment anyway.

He scowled. Self-examination had no place in a grand brooding!

He tried to force his thoughts into line, but they tended to wander.

As in, where did Madeleine go after she left him? Oddly enough, when she had disappeared, she'd done so completely. There had been no uproar from the staff at Brown's, no one had appeared to pick up her things, no word of her destination, nothing. Aidan was furious with her and never wanted to see her again, yet he could not help feeling uneasy. Where had she gone?

Perhaps she simply couldn't face him again.

"Then she's a coward as well as a liar," he muttered into the brandy he wasn't drinking.

Then he realized that he was sitting rather close to Lord Bartles and Sir James. He slid a glance in their direction, but they made no sign of noticing his somewhat mad behavior.

They were asleep, he was sure, as always dozing over their eternal game of chess.

Has anyone poked them lately?

He clenched his eyes shut tight. *Damn it, Madeleine! Get out of my mind!*

To hell with those unanswered questions. She was gone. What did any of it matter now? He raised the glass to his lips, determined to drink this time.

An abrupt clash and shattering of glass interrupted the near-dead silence in the room.

Aidan looked up to see young Bailiwick the footman quailing before the fury of a man Aidan didn't remember seeing previously. A tray lay on the floor, surrounded by what looked to be the remains of the brandy decanter and glasses.

That was a terrible shame. Brown's kept such marvelous brandy.

"You sniveling dolt!" the man snarled viciously. "Look

what you've done!" He alternated between dabbing at his surcoat and advancing upon the young man.

"B-but, my lord—you tripped me!"

Aidan blinked. Bailiwick might not be the most talented of servants, but he'd never been known to be anything but earnest and pathetically eager to please. Aidan peered more closely at the man as Wilberforce smoothly moved into action, soothing the furious member and shooing the confused Bailiwick away with the mess.

The tall fellow seemed dimly familiar. Hadn't he once been a fixture in the House of Lords? Not on his own behalf, for he hadn't any real property or power. He'd been acting as proxy for some distant cousin who couldn't make the sessions.

As Aidan recalled, the fellow had been more interested in currying favor and influence than in enacting his real responsibilities. Aidan had had no time for such a useless parasite, so he could hardly claim he knew the man at all.

After berating Wilberforce roundly, which the head of staff tolerated with an expression that could only be interpreted as serene boredom, the fellow stormed out of the club room, presumably to his rooms, to repair the damage.

"Haven't seen him for years," came a rusty voice from near Aidan.

Aidan looked up in surprise to see that, indeed, Lord Bartles was alive and well and peering nearsightedly after the obnoxious new member.

Or, apparently, old member, for Sir James also roused from his somnolence to nod agreement.

Wilberforce faced the two elder members and bowed.

"Yes, my lords. His lordship returned yesterday after many fortunate years apart from us."

Aidan blinked. Was that a cut? From Wilberforce? Then the fellow must indeed be unbearable.

As if he'd heard Aidan, Lord Bartles shook his head. "He's a bad sort, that one."

"Not the right sort at all, no, no, no." Sir James had not stopped nodding. Perhaps, once begun, he found it hard to cease.

Noticing Aidan's interest, Lord Bartles directed his next remarks directly to him. "A blighter, that Lord Wilhelm Whittaker. He hasn't been in here for years . . . not since old Lord Aldrich smacked him in the face and called him a cowardly upstart and a cheat. Caught him with an ace up his sleeve or somewhat, Aldrich did, in his own club yet! Fool! He thought we were all too old to spot the cheat. Aldrich chased him out at a run with a fireplace poker. We were all agog."

His companion nodded shakily but emphatically. *"Agog."*

Aidan lost interest. How was he to get over Madeleine this time—this time when his feelings were so much stronger than before?

Somewhere in his brandy was the answer, so he gazed back down into it, letting the voices about him fade away.

Wilberforce seemed curious, however. "So Lord Wilhelm never came back until now? Why now, my lord?"

Lord Bartles scratched his grizzled head. "Well, it seems to me he was mourning in the country for a while. Lost his wife in a fire, I heard. Must be where he got those scars . . ."

Aidan's thoughts were circling in his own pit of emotions, so he didn't try to comprehend the conversation going on about him. *Why did you do it, Madeleine? Why did you fixate on me to torture?*

Dimly, the words resounded in his mind. *Lost his wife in a fire . . .*

For a moment, he almost knew something, something terribly important. Then a fresh wave of anger and betrayal swept him, drowning out everything else once more.

CHAPTER 31

In the attic, Madeleine tried to remain focused on her task. Somewhere inside she suspected it was a fruitless one, but it was the only thing keeping gibbering panic at bay. She might as well as not, after all.

When she'd finished moving the wardrobe inch by inch—it had taken what seemed like hours—she'd begun to have that feeling again, the knowledge that she was being watched.

Fear snaked through her. She fought it. She needed to stay clear, to remain determined against it. Giving in to Wilhelm's trap would mean being sucked back down into hell—tentacles of the past grabbing, pulling down, down into the darkness as the light faded and grew indistinct above her and the blackness consumed her.

No. She could not rest until she was free. A few drops of water remained in the bottom of the pitcher. She drank it, for she believed Wilhelm's promise to watch her die. There would be no more water or sustenance coming.

Afterward, she began to amble about the room, pausing aimlessly to examine various items in a listless manner. She managed to restrain herself from approaching the dumbwaiter during her first two turns about the room.

Then, as if she were too weary to take another step,

she leaned her back against the far side of the wardrobe, keeping the edge of her body in view of the doorway. He would see only her shoulder and arm and a bit of her hip and, for the moment, her profile as she gazed unseeing and passive into space.

Then she slowly rolled her head until she was looking at the wall behind the wardrobe. The cables and gears and pulleys were not mysterious at all—not when a single lever, clearly labled "Lock," could be moved to "Unlock." She did so with a quick hand, then began to once again listlessly parade about the room.

She dared not stay in one area too long. Wilhelm was clever and suspicious and he knew her well. He would be alert to any odd behavior.

After a while, she lay down across the bed and feigned napping. Her eyes closed, she listened with everything she had. She waited as her mind began to distinguish between natural attic creaks and sounds from that one particular area on the other side of the heavy door.

Her imagination threatened to create noises that weren't there so she suppressed it, willing herself to a passivity she hated. Breathe. Hold. Listen. Breathe. Hold. Listen.

At last she was rewarded by the obvious scrape of a shoe on a gritty, dusty floor. Again, with a step that sounded as though it might be a bit farther away. Then the unmistakable vibration of a door closing in the next room.

In a flash she was up, flattening herself to the door, stretching herself up on her toes, cupping her hands on either side of her face so she could peer through the hole.

There was light there! No shadow blocked it.

She blinked rapidly, forcing her eyes to focus. She could see into the next area. It was a commonplace attic, mounded with stored paraphernalia of days gone by. She could even see the far doorway, a dark rectangle in the dimmest end of the room.

The doorway to freedom, if she could only batter down this prison door! She wanted to hammer it with her fists and scream aloud in frustration, but all that would do would be to anger Wilhelm should he still be in hearing range.

Instead, she raced to duck behind the wardrobe. She took the main cable in her hands and began to pull with all her might. The aged hemp rope felt prickly and brittle in her hands but seemed sturdy enough. Its oily coating had likely protected it from the years of disuse. She pulled heartily and was rewarded by an answering creak rising up the deep, narrow, dark shaft. The rope shifted a few inches, turning the rusting pulleys. A fine reddish dust of rust fell upon her hands. Encouraged, she lowered her grip and pulled again.

This time the rope moved nearly a foot!

In the main club room, Aidan had managed to down half his brandy, but imbibing enough to dull the pain seemed like entirely too much effort.

Colin appeared in his field of vision. "Don't scowl at me. Melody is napping. I'll be back in my rooms in plenty of time."

Aidan ignored him. Perhaps he could will the interfering bastard away.

No such luck. Colin took possession of the opposite chair with the exaggerated nonchalance of a person who knew he wasn't wanted but didn't care.

"You're an ass."

That was true enough, so it didn't bear comment.

"I take it back. You're an incredible ass."

Aidan looked up wearily. "That's going a bit far, don't you think?" He rubbed a hand over his burning eyes. "Then again, I did expose Melody to that woman without fully investigating her claims. I knew perfectly well she was . . ." He trailed off, unable to excavate a vile enough term from his exhausted brain.

Colin snorted. "Beautiful? Exceptional? Charming, if slightly dotty?"

Aidan scowled.

"Over you, that is." Colin shook his head in wonderment. "See here, you idiot, I know you're disappointed that Melody's not yours, but she hasn't gone anywhere. Jack will be back in a matter of days to clear this mess up. I hardly think he'll mind Melody having a couple of besotted uncles hanging about."

"You don't understand," Aidan said, his voice no more than a bitter whisper. "It isn't what I've lost, it's what I never had . . . never will have."

Colin leaned forward to shake his index finger in Aidan's face. "And *that's* why you're an incredible ass! You're mad for her and you're not going to get over her this time any more than you did before. So help her divorce the bounder. And then you marry her, and no one would ever dare to mock Lady Blankenship to her face!"

"It's hardly that simple."

"The hell is isn't. She's the only woman you've ever looked at twice—certainly the only one you've ever mooned over—so you might as well accept that no one is perfect, forgive her for making a mistake and then get down on both knees so you can beg her forgiveness for being *such an incredible ass!*"

Aidan didn't break that admonishing finger. Later he would be extremely proud of himself for such self-control. At the moment, however, he only glared all his fury at Colin for a long tense moment.

"She lied. Why is that so hard for you to comprehend?"

"Yes, she did lie. And for your part, you believed. In fact, you were downright eager to believe, weren't you? Why do you think you were so keen, my friend? So breathlessly, enthusiastically eager to play dupe to her machinations?"

"Shut your bloody mouth."

"Now that I think on it, for all your faults, you've never been especially gullible. I'd even go so far as to call you discerning, if I wasn't too busy believing you to be a right idiot at the moment. So, why would a discerning fellow such as yourself fall prey to a designing female with no conscience?"

"They're called breasts."

"Other women have them. I don't believe that Madeleine has cornered the market on that particular asset."

Not like Madeleine's breasts.

Which was idiocy, of course. There was nothing universally spectacular about any single part of Madeleine's form. "The unique combination of assets, then."

"Which she uses for nefarious ends, no doubt."

"Too bloody right."

"What are those ends, then? Did she clean out your pockets? Did she flaunt other men before you? Or is she operating on some larger scale? Is it Madeleine's lifelong dream to rule the world? Is she Napoleon in lacy knickers? Or perhaps her goal is something more commonplace. Something like . . . survival? Good God, what a monster. You're well rid of her, I say."

I could kill him in his sleep. I could cut the girth of his saddle. I could trap him in a room with Wilberforce and a spoon and see who comes out alive.

Not much sport there. Wilberforce knew his spoons, by gum.

Unable to bear more, Aidan slammed his brandy snifter down on the table, erupted from his chair, and flung himself from the club, out into the noisy, dirty streets that didn't remind him of Madeleine at every turn.

Aidan stood in the cheerful parlor of the house he'd rented just the day before and stared unseeing at the hearth, which only lacked the cherry glow of lighted coals to complete the happy domestic picture. Had it truly only been yesterday when he'd strode through these very rooms, eager to bring Melody and Madeline here?

It seemed a terrible cheat now, that hope, that simmering happiness that he'd finally, sheepishly, begun to allow himself, eager to begin his new life as a family man with his new wife and daughter.

But Melody was not his daughter and Madeline was nothing but a lie. She was a creature of no remorse. To lie with her words, well, she was only human and who hadn't lied in their lifetime, but to lie with her touch and her body and her smile? She was the devil, after all. He'd known it once. Yet mere days spent with her and he'd forgotten.

It was only that she'd seemed so different this time, especially last evening when she was telling him the truth—or rather, her current version of the "truth." She'd twisted her knuckles to white, but she'd met his gaze evenly, without evasion or defiance.

The whole story was mad, of course. Fleeing her husband across the country, hiding out in *London*? One didn't come to London to hide! One went to tiny, out-of-the-way hamlets with few people but farmers and sheepherders and the like.

Where she would stand out like a flamingo among hens.

But London? The largest city in the world, full of people who might know her, full of people who might know her husband—

So full of widows in black that one scarcely saw them anymore.

Perhaps it was rather clever—he'd never accused Madeleine of stupidity—but it was all simply so unlikely! A drama, a bit of theatre enacted to gain sympathy or aid!

Aid which she didn't ask for.

Nonsense. If she'd needed something, she'd have asked him.

When? When you were accusing her of adultery or when you scoffed at her tears?

He rubbed the back of his neck, suddenly not feeling quite as sure of himself. Madeleine had lied, had raised his hopes again only to dash them to the cobbles, had manipulated the heart of a child, had—

Had fled her own home to avoid that fellow, Critchley. He'd witnessed that himself. She'd gone to ground in a gentlemen's club. What could convince a reasonable woman to do such a thing?

What indeed?

I married a monster.

In only a few strides, Aidan was through the door of his new house and heading swiftly down the street.

CHAPTER 32

It wasn't an ideal situation, to be sure. Wilhelm grimaced in frustration as he peered through the hole he'd bored through the heavy wooden door in the attic. He could scarcely see her.

Well, it wasn't to be helped. He'd had to act quickly, after all. He simply would have preferred more time to prepare.

For instance, if he'd had the opportunity, he would have arranged the room so that no area was completely out of his sight. As it was now, large areas of the damned laundry attic were out of his view—a fact that Madeleine seemed to have figured it out.

He would have made more spy holes, but then again he could hardly be expected to pierce stone walls with only a day to prepare. As it was, it had been all he could do to seal the window with gum and drill through three inches of oak! The blankets he'd gathered from some of the empty but readied rooms in the club, just like the pitcher and chamber pot.

If he was going to make a habit of this activity, he was really going to have to put some thought into the details. Perhaps once he married the heiress, he could purchase his own little playhouse in town. A shudder of arousal went through him. Just think of it—rooms and rooms of enjoyment!

Then Madeleine appeared once more. Moving slowly, she made a weary circuit of the room. She seemed to be pacing her prison, but it looked as though she'd already given up on escape.

Poor fleeing lady. Nowhere to fly to now.

She looked half dead already. So listless and pale in her tired black gown, like fine alabaster but for the bruising on her temple and cheek.

She had never been so beautiful. Dying became her.

How delicious.

Madeleine's little row house stood dark and empty. The door was locked, but when Aidan dropped down the small flight of steps to the servant entry, he found that that door had been broken through. Kicked in, he thought, as he examined the splinters in the doorframe where the lock had once nestled.

He moved into a kitchen just large enough for a cook and a maid to work, although he didn't recall that Madeleine had ever had either. She must have done it all herself.

How many meals had she served him upstairs, simply cooked but savory? He'd eaten them thoughtlessly, more intent on their afterdinner entertainments. He doubted he'd ever complimented a single dish. Why would he, when the women of his world planned menus but never actually touched the food?

Feeling uncomfortable and increasingly urgent, he moved up the narrow back stair to the main floor. Nothing seemed amiss in the hall or the entry, although he noticed that things had become much shabbier in the last three years. Still painfully clean, though. He pictured Madeleine in an apron and cap, scrubbing her own floors. In his mind she looked both pathetic and adorable. She ought never to have had to go it alone . . .

You ought never to walk alone.

The parlor was a shambles.

Old pain and new worry clutched at him. The shattered furnishings, the chill that told him no fire had warmed this house in days—

If she wasn't here, where was she?

Fleeing the monster—the one you don't believe in.

He did now.

The next morning, Aidan and Colin were hatching a plan of action over a quick bite of breakfast. Melody sat with them—or rather, stood on her chair with a giant napkin tied about her neck—chasing a bit of sausage around her oily plate with a stabbing fork, the tip of her little tongue stuck out of the corner of her mouth in concentration.

"I know you want to help look for Madeleine," Aidan told Colin, "but we can't leave Melody alone."

"I know that," Colin responded testily. "I simply hate sitting around—"

A knock on the door interrupted them. Melody looked up, eyes wide. Without a word, Colin scooped her up and went into the bedchamber, shutting the door.

Aidan cast quickly about the room, kicking a pair of tiny boots beneath the sofa and tossing a pillow over Gordy Ann, who looked much more like a doll after Madeleine's stitchwork. Then he opened the door, expecting Wilberforce or Bailiwick.

Lord Aldrich stood before him. Aidan blinked in

surprise. "Er, what can I—" Oops. "WHAT CAN I DO FOR YOU, LORD ALDRICH?"

Aldrich drew back with a grimace. "You can stop shouting for one," he said in a perfectly well-modulated tone. "I'm not actually deaf, you know."

Aidan was confused. "You're not?"

"No." Aldrich had the grace to look slightly ashamed. "It's simply that most people are so bloody boring, I can't bear to listen. So I pretend I'm older and more decrepit than I am. It makes my life more peaceful."

"Oh." Then Aidan froze. Oh, *hell*. The building might be made of stone, but the doors were only wood. Aldrich was a scant three rooms away. He'd taken no care to keep Melody quiet. Or, for that matter, *Madeleine*.

Aldrich was peering up at him with a small wrinkled smile. "Precisely, lad."

Trying manfully to ignore the blush creeping over his face, Aidan stepped back. "I suppose you might as well come in, then."

Aldrich toddled in, narrowly missing Aidan's foot with his cane. "At first I was mightily annoyed at having my peaceful decline disturbed, but then I became interested despite myself. You lot are just full of monkeyshines, aren't you?"

Aidan cleared his throat cautiously. Aldrich obviously knew some things, but perhaps not all. "As in . . . ?"

"Oh, don't get your knickers in a twist, boy. I know plenty about you and your young friend in there." Aldrich gestured to the bedchamber door. "I saw you two bring the little one into the club."

"You did?" Aidan frowned. He'd thought the old fellow nearly blind as well.

"Oh, I can't see so well with my spectacles, but I do splendidly with my old spyglass. I see everything that happens on St. James!" He leaned closer to Aidan. *"Everything."*

Nodding emphatically, Aldrich went on. "I saw the old bird bring the child to the steps and leave her there. I saw you two pick her up. I saw you bring that pretty girl in, too."

Colin entered the room. He'd obviously been listening in. Aidan saw Melody peeping around the edge of the door. Her big baby blue eyes went wide when she saw Aldrich.

"You saw Nurse Pruitt?" Colin gazed narrowly at the old man. "You saw—?"

"I've seen *everything*," Aldrich insisted. "I've seen things you two lads don't know a thing about, so shut your disrespectful trap and listen for once in your life."

Colin opened his mouth to object but Aidan waved him silent. "What don't we know, Aldrich?"

He told them. He'd seen a fat man in an ugly waistcoat spying on the club.

"That would be Critchley," Aidan said in an aside to Colin. Aldrich frowned, so Aidan shut his disrespectful trap and let the old fellow carry on.

Aldrich had seen a thin man who watched the fat man. He had watched Madeleine take Melody from the house laughing and he'd watched the fat man follow them to the park. He'd watched the thin man follow them as well—at least to the corner. He'd seen Colin leave the house and he'd seen Aidan leave and come back distracted and worried. He'd seen Madeleine return with Melody at last, looking very frightened indeed.

"Wait—" Aidan held up a hand as something struck him. "If you were watching, you must have seen Mrs. Chandler leave again—you must have seen which way she went, at least!"

"I'm sorry, lad. I didn't see her go." He shrugged. "I do leave the room occasionally, though I wouldn't have if I'd known it was the last I'd see of her. Lovely girl. A charming laugh. How were you brainless enough to lose her?"

Aidan bridled. Aldrich only raised a brow. "What do I have to fear from you? Not even death frightens me now. So don't raise your quills at me, boy. I was brainless once, too. I never got the girl back. Liked my wife well enough, but there is only one girl like that for any man."

"So if the fat man is that Critchley fellow," Colin mused, "then who is the thin man?"

Aidan turned to Aldrich. "Can you describe him?"

Aldrich looked thoughtful. "He was tall. He wore a hat so I never saw his hair or all of his face. He dressed well enough, I suppose. Had an air about him, like he thought everyone on the street should get out of his way." The old fellow shrugged thin shoulders. "Other than that, he looked just like you lot. Young and annoying."

"Are you a grampapa?"

The three men looked down to see Melody amongst them, staring intently up at Aldrich.

Aldrich blinked. "No, child. I don't have any grandchildren."

Melody considered him for a long moment. "I don't have a grampapa." She twisted one foot shyly. "I could be your gramchildren, if you wanted."

Aldrich blinked. Then a slow smile rearranged the wrinkles. "Well, why not?" He bent down, but not as far as Aidan would have had to, and held out his hand. "Shall we shake on that, young miss?"

Melody giggled and stuck her small, breakfast-sticky paw into the old man's hand. Aidan and Colin exchanged a look. Another willing victim.

"Can you imagine her in fifteen years?" Colin muttered. Aidan nodded. Poor Jack. Perhaps doting uncle was an easier position to be in.

Aldrich's visit had been edifying, yet still Aidan knew nothing—except that she had not, in fact, been lying about her danger. Then again, he'd already begun to believe. Aidan rubbed the back of his neck. There were two men involved. An important clue, yet they were no closer to finding Madeleine.

CHAPTER 33

Alone in her attic prison, Madeleine had spent a busy morning. It had rained during the night, waking her with an insistent drizzle onto her nest of blankets. Disconcerted at first, she'd soon laughed and put the pitcher beneath the leak to catch a bit of sooty drinking water. At least in this way Wilhelm held no power—not over nature and elderly roofing!

Now she sat on her "bed" with her back to the door—though Wilhelm was not typically an early riser, she would put nothing past him—and perused her options.

The dumbwaiter, unfortunately, had not proven to be a possible escape route. Even if she trusted the rusted gears and elderly cords to work properly—which she didn't, really—the casebox of the dumbwaiter itself would never hold her weight.

She'd tried cautiously, but the immediate creaks and cracks when she was but halfway in were too alarming. She'd shuddered and backed out again. She might risk it if there were no other choice, but it was a long way to the hard cellar floor at the other end of the shaft.

Then she'd hit upon the idea of using a bit of coal from

the old fireplace to scratch a message on the inside of the casebox. Clumsy, but she believed she'd gotten her point across.

But it would be better if there were some way to get someone to open it once it went down a storey. She couldn't ensure that would happen, but if someone *did* open it, she wanted to be sure to catch their attention.

Madeleine debated sending down her shoes, perhaps one at a time. In the end, she decided not to. Should the opportunity come, she ought to be prepared to run for her life. These were good, sturdy, leather traveling shoes, the ones she'd originally donned to catch her ship, and then again to walk to the park. Picking up her skirts slightly, she looked down at her shoes critically. It was possible that they could do some damage should she ever get close enough to kick Wilhelm. Besides, the attic was cold. Taking a chill would not help her cause.

Everything else in the attic was too large except for her blankets. She didn't think a blanket in a laundry chute would get much attention.

So, that meant that the only items she had to send down the dumbwaiter were the contents of her pockets: her handkerchief, a button from a not-too-strategic place on her gown, the blue ribbon she'd used to tie her hair, and a small, heart-shaped stone she had carried in her pocket for years.

She hesitated over the stone. A silly thing, not valuable except for the memory it evoked. Aidan, smiling, coming to see her on a fine day. He'd walked through Hyde Park, he'd told her, and had handed her the stone he'd found. "There, I've given you my heart." He'd laughed and she had as well, but the silly gift meant more to her than any of the jewels he'd presented her with.

Well, better to lose it now than to be buried with it. Gathering up her meager arsenal, she prepared to get on with her plan.

The slender thread of hope within her could not bear much more.

Please, please let someone notice. Let someone open it and see!

Colin and Aidan prepared to canvass Madeleine's neighborhood for any sign of her. They'd already spoken to every doorman and shopkeeper on St. James Street and none of them remembered a pretty dark-haired woman walking by or hailing a hack that night. She'd simply disappeared like a ghost.

Aidan knocked on the door of the house to the right of Madeleine's. A young housemaid opened the door. Her eyes widened at the sight of Aidan and Colin on the doorstep, but she quickly recovered, licked her lips, and smiled saucily.

"'Ello, sirs. 'Ave ye come to see Himself?"

Since Aidan had no idea who that might be, he shook his head. "Don't disturb your master just yet. Perhaps you can help us."

She sank her teeth into her lower lip and lifted a brow. "What ye got in mind, sir?"

Despite the situation, Colin had an inane grin on his face. Aidan delivered an elbow to his ribs for it. "We're looking for the lady who lived next door. Have you seen her recently?"

The flirtatious maid slid a knowing glance in Colin's

direction, then returned her attention to Aidan. "Ain't seen 'er for days. She's right quiet, that one. Doesn't go about much. I don't know her name, but I do see her going to market sometimes. The house's been dark now since . . ." She folded her arms beneath her considerable bosom while she gazed into the air, thinking. Colin teetered forward as if about to fall into the abyss of her spectacular cleavage. Aidan rescued him with another quick elbow.

"I reckon I ain't seen 'er for near a week," concluded the maid. "Sorry, sirs."

They thanked her and left her staring wistfully after Colin.

The tale at the house on the other side was much the same. "No, sirs. Haven't seen her in days. Never did get her name."

They tried a few more doors, but it seemed that although Madeleine had lived next to them for more than four years, no one in the vicinity knew anything about her or her life.

"That's odd, don't you think?" Colin studied the street before them. "She's a true Original, if you ask me. She ought to have had the city eating out of her hand."

"Protective coloration," Aidan said curtly. He was becoming quite frantic, in truth.

This was all his fault. He hadn't known anything of Madeleine's life during their affair. Then again, he'd never thought to ask her.

Now, it seemed that her life had been nothing—nothing but hiding.

And him.

And he had walked away, leaving her, alas, with nothing once more.

* * *

Wilhelm lingered in the entrance hall of Brown's, torn between the desire to see the defeat etched upon Blankenship's face when he returned without his lady and the pleasure of watching Madeleine weepily struggling to accept her impending demise.

He'd never been so thoroughly entertained. Really, this was such a treat.

Not since the Incident had he tasted the sweetness of pure power. And that had been an accident—a prank really. An irritating young fellow needed taking down a peg. Hardly more than schoolboy tomfoolery. When matters had then gone rather seriously astray . . . well, that was hardly *his* fault.

Yet that moment—the moment when his lovely young wife had screamed and cried and begged him so desperately to do something—that moment, that taste of absolute power in his mouth, flavored sharp and metallic as blood . . . that had been sweet indeed.

And this feat promised to surpass that one by far.

He decided that once Madeleine died, he must find a way to get her body out of the house and down to the Thames. Wouldn't it be delicious to be an innocent bystander when the authorities informed Blankenship that his love had drowned herself in grief at losing him? He snickered nastily.

Oh, my. A note in Madeleine's pocket, declaring her intention to die. Now that would be perfection itself. How to manage that one . . .

Blankenship walked in the door just then. Wilhelm busied himself with tugging his gloves more tightly and settling his hat upon his head. Black of brow and wretched with worry, Blankenship strode past without a word, although that Lambert fellow cast Wilhelm a curious glance. Wilhelm simply gave him a vague toothy grin and a nod and turned toward the door.

Once the two men had turned the corner toward the stairs, Wilhelm stripped off his gloves and tossed his hat to the nearest servant. Then he, too, turned toward the stairs.

The floor show was over. Time to check out the view from the balcony.

In the entrance hall, Wilberforce stood there with Lord Whittaker's hat and gloves in hand, gazing after the odd fellow with a thoughtful eye.

"Bailiwick."

Instantly Bailiwick appeared from nowhere in particular. Wilberforce had trained him well in one respect at least. "Yes, Mr. Wilberforce?"

"Bailiwick, why would a man put on his hat and gloves to go out, then immediately take them off again and go back upstairs?"

Bailiwick's handsome young brow creased. "Sir? Sorry, sir, but that doesn't make sense."

"Hmm." Wilberforce tilted his head, considering the problem. "Precisely my thinking, lad."

CHAPTER 34

Back in his chambers, Aidan threw his hat viciously across the room as he entered. Colin watched him as he sat on the sofa with his elbows on his knees and head in his hands. Discomfited but not willing to leave his mourning friend alone, Colin restlessly paced. As he passed the table with the bowl full of apples, he picked one up to edgily toss it from hand to hand. *Slap. Slap.*

"We could make up printed posters," he suggested to Aidan. "We could plaster London with them."

Aidan made a noise. "And what if she is in hiding? Running for her life? Do you think that will help her disappear?"

The apple stopped its flight for a moment. "Um. No, I suppose not." Then the pacing resumed and the apple continued its rhythmic sound against Colin's palms. *Slap. Slap.*

Aidan leaned back into the sofa, rubbing his hands over his aching eyes. He'd been up all night, watching over Melody as she slept, trying to will Madeleine to return to him.

I wish to never set eyes on you again.

Good God, what an ass he was. What an unbelievable ass!

Stupid words, Maddie. Don't believe them. Come back to me. Come home.

His weary body throbbed. Absently, he reached behind himself to remove something lumpy and uncomfortable. He pulled out a wadded cravat. Gordy Ann.

Colin whistled. "I can't believe Melody agreed to play in Aldrich's room without her."

Aidan held the doll in his hands, distantly wondering at precisely what point a filthy cloth knot had taken on a gender. He stood, taking the doll with him. "I suppose I had better relieve Aldrich. I'm sure he's had quite a morning."

Colin stuck his apple into his pocket and came along.

They entered Aldrich's rooms to find the elder lord incongruously clad in a tiny pink pinafore, draped over the front of his weskit like a bib, seated at the table, lifting a teacup to his lips, with his little finger daintily crooked.

Even the ludicrous tableau of Melody having a tea party with the fierce old lord wasn't enough to cheer Aidan.

Colin tried, however. "Look who we found, Mellie."

Melody brightened. "Maddie?"

"Er, no. Sorry. I meant—" He indicated the doll.

Melody ran to Aidan, who, instead of handing over the doll, picked up the tiny girl and held her close. He didn't know who was comforting whom, for he felt every bit as devastated as Melody.

She tucked her little face into his neck. "I miss Maddie," she said, thereby muffled.

"I miss her too, mousie." He ran his hand over her head, smoothing her wispy braid. The end of the braid was fixed with a bright blue ribbon . . .

It was not the one he'd tied about her hair this morning. In fact, the last time he'd seen this particular blue ribbon—which was so long it was wrapped several times before being tied in an awkward knot—was in Madeleine's hair as she'd walked out of his room and disappeared. He rubbed it between his fingers.

"Mellie," he said, his tone deliberately casual, "this is a very pretty ribbon."

She sniffled into his neck. "Thank you."

He carried her to one of the chairs at the table and sat with her in his lap. Holding her by her chubby midriff, he leaned back a bit to gaze into her eyes. "Mellie, is this ribbon new?"

Melody nodded as she played with the gold buttons on his surcoat.

"Where did you get this pretty ribbon?"

"I founded it," she said clearly. "With the other presents."

"Presents?" Aidan glanced at Aldrich, who was listening intently. Aldrich shrugged away any knowledge of them. Aidan turned back to Melody.

"Can you show me your presents, pet?"

"Sure!" Melody dug her hands into the pockets of her pinafore and then held them out, cupped for him to see.

Aidan gazed down at the little pile of inconsequential items. A crumpled lacy handkercheif, a button, a small commonplace stone—

No. A chord of memory sounded in his mind. Not so commonplace. He remembered spying the oddly shaped stone in the park and later dropping it into Madeleine's cupped palm with some jest about giving her his heart.

Which she'd kept for years, apparently.

She kept my heart.

"Mellie—" His voice was rough, harsh. Melody drew back, her little face clouding. Aidan took a breath, reaching deeply for patience. "Mellie," he asked in a gentler tone, "where did you find those pretty presents?"

She blinked at him for a long moment. Then, apparently reassured that he wasn't upset with her, she stuck her hands back into her pinafore pockets. "In the magic cupboard."

Aidan felt his patience begin to splinter and cast a helpless look at Colin.

Colin knelt quickly beside the chair. "Cap'n Melody, you found the buried treasure!"

She blinked and her little rosebud lips opened in amazement. "I did?"

Colin nodded. "You discovered Captain Jack's secret hoard! Where did you find it?"

Melody giggled. "I told you. The magic cupboard. Like that one." She lifted a chubby little hand and pointed to the wall of Aldrich's room.

Aidan and Colin turned to look at the wall, frowning. Then they stared at each other in consternation. "The dumbwaiter!"

Aidan put Melody down to stand on the floor and followed Colin from the room at a run. They rushed down the hall and back to Aidan's room. He crossed the room in great long strides and yanked at the door to the dumbwaiter.

It was empty. Aidan sagged back in disappointment. "There's nothing here."

Colin leaned forward to peer at some dark scratches on the old wood. "Is that . . . writing?"

Aidan ducked his head into the dumbwaiter, then emerged swearing. Snatching a candleholder off the mantel, he bent to catch the wick on the coals. Then, armed with light, he wedged his wide shoulders back into the dumbwaiter. The black marks rendered themselves into smeared letters.

Please . . . help . . . locked in . . . (smudge)

Locked where?

Danger . . . Lord Whit (smudge) . . . prisoner . . .

Lord Whit—? Lord Whittaker? That blowhard? What the hell did Madeleine have to do with Lord Whittaker?

Madeleine's voice in his mind, urgent and frightened. *I married a monster.*

In the attic outside the drying room, Wilhelm pressed his eye to the spy hole and savored the view as Madeleine wept in despair. She stood on the far side of the rickety, old wardrobe as if she thought herself hidden from him, but he had a clear view of her blotchy, tear-streaked profile. Such pain. Such unbearable anguish.

How very lovely.

Her raw sobs were muffled and distorted by the large stone room, but he treasured them just the same. Where was her valiant bravado now? Where were her high moral standards and her condemnation?

He had read once that a person could die of lack of water within a few days. Should he point that fact out to Madeleine, or did she perhaps already know? He'd wager that if he opened this door right now, she would offer him anything and everything if only he would allow her to go back to Whittaker Hall with him to be his obedient wife once more.

"Sorry, pretty bird," he whispered to the door. "I need the horse-faced heiress more than I need you."

Besides, he was enjoying it all vastly.

Speaking of entertainment, he wondered how the desolate Blankenship was faring. Ah, so many victims, so little time.

"Good-bye for now, my dying darling," he said to the door with a tender caress. "I think it's time to torture your lover a little bit more."

Humming a sprightly tune very quietly to himself, he trotted down the attic stairs. At the bottom, he turned the latch with a slow, practiced hand and peered through the tiny crack he created.

No one was in sight but he could see that Blankenship's door was open and he could hear voices in the rooms—agitated, urgent voices. Hmm. Some new developments, perhaps?

Curious, he opened the door slightly wider, still alert to any sign of occupancy in the hall. No, it was all clear.

With a self-satisfied smile, he slipped through the door and shut it silently behind him. Now he was simply a member idly touring the club. He was not on his own floor, which might be unusual, but certainly broke no rules.

Keeping out of sight of anyone in Blankenship's rooms, he moved to lean against the wall outside the door and listened.

"Colin, get in there and see if you can read where she's being held prisoner!"

What? Read what, where?

"Damn that Whittaker. Why don't we just find him and beat it out of him?"

Bloody hell! How do they know?

"We can thrash him later. I just want to find Madeleine. Where does this dumbwaiter shaft lead?"

"To the cellar I suppose. Perhaps up to the attic?"

That thrice-damned bitch! That lying, twist-tongued whore! Wilhelm's fury overwhelmed him. He was going to beat that beautiful, betraying face into a gory pulp!

He turned to race back into the attic—

Behind him stood the child with one finger in her mouth, watching him with giant blue eyes.

CHAPTER 35

In her prison cell, Madeleine swiped at her eyes with both hands. Another sob lodged in her throat but she dared not give in to it.

She'd sensed Wilhelm at the door just as she'd been leaning into the dumbwaiter shaft, pondering her odds of successfully climbing down it. Worried that he would figure it out, she'd decided to divert him with a few false tears.

Unfortunately, the simmering panic that lived just below the edge of her self-control had stowed away on those tears, shortly making them very real. She'd been unable to stop, unable to quiet the harsh sobs that ripped from her throat, unable to keep her eyes from leaking, no matter how tightly she'd clenched them shut.

By the time the tears had run their course, she'd realized he was gone once more.

I hope you enjoyed that, you warped hyena, may you rot in hell!

As for herself, she felt weakened, not cleansed by the outburst. However, there was no time for weakness. She opened the dumbwaiter doors once again.

At a strange new sound, she whirled to face the door, her heart in her throat. He was on his way back. She heard him climbing the stairs, his footsteps heavy and furious, with no care for secrecy. She knew that angry tread, had heard it in her nightmares both sleeping and waking.

She knew what it meant for her.

He had found her out!

Instinctively, she backed away from the door, though there was nowhere to go. Escape was impossible. The only other exit from this room lay behind her, a window leap that would leave her shattered on the cobbles below. Closing her eyes, she drew in a breath. God help her if she didn't prefer such a quick and cowardly end!

Wilhelm was at the door now, working the key in the lock. The cold glass was at her back, her palms pressed to it. The wave of rage from the other side of the door made her blood run cold as the lock somehow found the temerity to defy Wilhelm's key. A howl of fury and the heavy thud of a fist on the wood made her lurch backward, hard.

With a startling crack, the glass behind her gave way.

Aidan didn't know what made him turn. Had he heard something? A small noise behind him—a scuffling sound, a quiet click? There was no one in sight.

He relaxed and turned back to Colin, who had his head and shoulders packed tightly into the dumbwaiter with a lighted candle. Perhaps not the safest position to be in.

"I can't make it out." Colin withdrew his head, only slightly singed about the eyebrows. "I say we simply search up and down the shaft. She's somewhere in Brown's. It shouldn't take long to find her."

Aidan blinked. "Of course. Let's go."

Colin peered past him. "Wait. Where's Melody?"

"Aldrich has her still."

Colin shook his head. "I thought she was right behind us."

A chill went through Aidan. That noise behind him— it could have come from the hall. "I have a very bad feeling . . ."

Quickly he ran for Aldrich's room, Colin close behind him. They burst in to see the old fellow tottering about, tidying up Melody's tea party. He looked up and blinked at their intrusion. "Did you find your lady already?"

"Is Melody here?"

Aldrich frowned. "Indeed she is not. She left with you."

Colin's brow creased with worry. "Do you think she's hiding again?"

"No. Come with me."

They ran back to just outside Aidan's room. "I heard something just a moment ago—" He bent to pick something off the floor. It was the heart-shaped stone. It had fallen just outside the concealed door to the attic.

"Melody couldn't have opened that," Colin protested. "The catch is far too high."

Aidan felt sick. "*Whittaker!*"

In moments they were in the attic, staring at a strange sort of prison cell they had never realized was there.

One with no prisoner in it. There was only the dumb-waiter shaft gaping wide and an open window, hanging off one broken hinge.

Aidan pushed Colin toward the dumbwaiter without a word, then ran for the window. Colin peered down the shaft but there was nothing to see but the faint gleam of light from where the similar aperture remained open

down in Aidan's room partially blocked by the dumbwaiter cart.

He turned just in time to see Aidan leap out of the
window.

Climbing from the farthest window onto the portion of
the roof where she'd stood with Aidan—was that only
four days ago?—was a more daunting journey than she'd
realized. Unfortunately for her, she had a very good imagination. It supplied her with all sorts of gory images of her
body smashed to the ground far below.

She shut them off with an act of will and grimly made
her way down the ledge. Without Aidan's strong guiding
hand, and somewhat worse for wear after two days without food, the brief stretch of stone ledge lengthened into
what seemed like miles.

*I'm going to fall. I shall fall and I shall die and Aidan
will never know how much I love him.*

It was possible that that was the least of her current
worries, yet the thought repeated itself, a strangely steady-
ing litany that guided her shaky steps and weak knees
along the wall to the place where the sloped mansard roof
met the dormered window which Aidan had showed her
before.

Wilhelm was behind her now. She could hear him curs-
ing bitterly at her. Her slipper slithered on the damp,
pigeon-dirtied stone. For an instant, she felt her weight
shift in the wrong direction, giving in to the pull of ver-
tigo.

Falling!

She wrenched herself back into balance, pressing herself into the eaves of the dormered window.

Right. Her worry for Aidan was a worthwhile subject, but perhaps one better contemplated at another time.

At last she attained the roof. Slithering up over the railing ungracefully onto her belly, she stood on shaky legs and ran across the roof to the next building.

It was impossible. The club next door was so much larger and more imposing that the wall was at least a full storey higher!

Turning, she gazed over the roof at the next building. It was the same. She would never make that climb, even without her current weakened state. Panic began to claw at her throat. He was so close behind her!

Then she heard a childish cry cut the air.

Melody?

Wilhelm appeared over the edge of the roof and he wasn't alone. He had a small, struggling burden under one arm. Within Madeleine, every dormant maternal instinct went on full alert.

No more running. She turned to fight for her child.

CHAPTER 36

Aidan peered over the edge of the roof. "Look! Madeleine's all right!"

Colin had both feet on the ledge, both hands white-knuckled on the vertical gutter pipe and both eyes tightly shut. "No. No looking. Ever."

"Does the bastard have Melody? I can't see her."

Colin looked. "That's quite a woman you have there, Aidan."

Indeed. Madeleine actually had Whittaker on the retreat. White-hot fury made her dark eyes burn in her pale face. Then Whittaker turned, and Aidan saw Melody dangling limply from his grip. Madeleine and Melody—everything he had in the world. Father or not, they were everything to him. His family. He prepared to spring over the edge of the roof. Time to kill the bastard.

Colin held him back. "No!" he hissed. "Look at where he's standing. If you jump him, you might both go over the edge. Melody, too!"

Colin was right. Aidan subsided with a silent snarl. "We need to get him away from the edge and closer to us. We need to signal Madeleine somehow—"

Abruptly he grabbed Colin and pulled roughly at his surcoat.

"Ack!" Colin clutched at the gutter in panic. "Are you trying to kill me?" he whispered in panic.

Aidan looked at the apple in his hand, the one he'd just plucked from Colin's pocket. "I've found a signal."

Madeleine saw the shiny green apple come from nowhere and roll across the roof behind Wilhelm, who faced her with Melody in his grip.

He turned at the rolling sound, but the apple had already tumbled into the gutter, out of sight. It didn't matter. Madeleine knew precisely where it had come from.

Moving quickly, she picked up a fallen tree branch from last night's storm. *I must distract him.* She brandished her wooden weapon and advanced slowly on Wilhelm. "Put her down," she snarled.

He snarled back, his evil eyes hot with rage. "Drop that branch, and I'll think about killing her quickly. Keep making trouble for me, and I'll make her scream for days."

The threat was ugly. Madeleine felt nauseated at the way Melody, pale and limp with terror, hung so helpless and tiny in the monster's grasp.

I'm so sorry, mousie.

Stay focused.

She had a job to do. She took a half-hearted swipe at Wilhelm with the branch. She didn't get anywhere near him, but he stepped back slightly in response.

She waved the branch again. "I'm going to survive this, you madman, and when I do, I'm going to tell the world what you've done! You'll be running for your life and hiding as well. There won't be a cave in all of England where you'll be safe!"

Wilhelm sneered. "What can you tell anyone if you're dead? Poor Lady Madeleine, dead these four years past. I have rank. I have resources. Do you think anyone will believe that you—you scrawny, tatty harpy!—you could be Lord Whittaker's lady wife? Not that you'll get a chance to breathe a word, for your last breath is soon coming." He lifted Melody and shook her harshly. "Say goodbye to your mummy, *mousie*."

Madeleine's breath left her body at the way Melody's head flopped limply back and forth. God, please! Please, don't let it be too late!

"It's me you want, Wilhelm. Put the child down and I'll go with you, anywhere you want."

"Why would I want you, you betraying bitch, after everything you've done to me?" He thrust his arm up to shake back his sleeve to show her the fibrous burn scars that distorted his arm and welded his fingers into a claw. "Look at it!"

Madeleine swallowed at the gruesomeness of it. "I'm very sorry, Wilhelm." She held her hands out, placatingly. "It must have been terribly painful. But I did not set that fire, I swear to you."

He snorted and yanked his sleeve back down. "Of course you didn't. Thrice-damned Critchley did it. He's always had an urge to burn." Then he switched Melody under his scarred arm and pointed his finger at her, Madeleine. "*Nevertheless,* he only set that fire in order to cover his plan to steal you away. He confessed the entire plan to me afterward, blubbering all the while." Wilhelm laughed derisively. "He was so in love with you, and for years now that cretinous maggot thought he'd killed you instead!"

Madeleine scarcely heard him. She was trying very

hard not to let her gaze slip past him to where Aidan and Colin had crept onto the roof during Wilhelm's tirade.

Please, mousie, don't look. Don't see them. Don't make a sound.

"Wilhelm, I know you hate me. I don't blame you. But you can't . . ." Her voice failed her. She let the branch drop. "You can't harm a child, Wilhelm! Not even you!"

He raised a brow and sneered. "Oh really? Haven't you realized yet that it's easy to kill." He held Melody out over the precipice. "All I have to do is let go—"

He was struck from both sides at full force. Aidan swept Melody out of his grasp even as Colin delivered a mighty blow that sent Wilhelm sprawling onto the roof slates.

"Oh, God!" Madeleine rushed forward, stepping over the prone Wilhelm on her way to Melody. "How is she? Is she breathing? Oh, dear lord! Is she—"

Melody, finally safe in the strong arms of her Uncle Aidan, tipped back her head and let out a healthy, ear-splitting wail. "He—he—he—*pinched* me!"

Thank heaven!

A damp sob of laughter left Madeleine's throat. She pressed both trembling hands over her face, dizzy with relief and reaction, the terror of the last half hour catching up to her. Melody was safe. Aidan was safe.

And she was safe, at l—

The arm that came about her throat was rippled with scars. It tightened cruelly, cutting off her warning cry.

Aidan thrust Melody into Colin's arms for safekeeping and lunged after Whittaker. The scarred madman was dragging Madeleine closer to the edge of the roof. Madeleine fought him even as her eyes widened and her mouth opened, gasping for air that could not come.

"Stay back, Blankenship!" Whittaker locked his choke-hold with his other hand. "I'll break her deceitful neck!"

Aidan slowed and held up both hands. "You can't get away with it, Whittaker," he reasoned, even as he desperately searched for an opening. "So far you haven't really hurt anyone—"

He saw Madeleine's eyes bulge at that and faltered. Obviously the lunatic had already hurt someone. Had he killed? God, how was he going to get her away?

"She's my wife, Blankenship. I have every right to punish my own property!" Whittaker was so close to the edge that a broken slate went spinning away to shatter far below with a faint, tinkling sound. Madeleine's struggles weakened and she slumped in his grasp.

He shifted his grip to accommodate her collapse—

She spun upon him, striking wildly and shrieking like a banshee. "Don't touch me, you revolting animal! You filthy, treacherous lunatic! Go away and leave us alone! Better yet, just die! Do you hear me? Die!"

With only one hand to hang onto her and no real way to defend himself against her wild attack, Wilhelm took one step back. Then another. She scratched and clawed and screamed, ripping at his face, his neck, his waistcoat and shirt. Years of suppressed fury and pain came spilling out—

He struck her hard across the face with his scarred hand. She went down onto her knees, one wrist still locked in his grasp.

At that moment, a shot rang out. Whittaker jerked in surprise.

Aidan flinched, then cast a glance over his shoulder to see Wilberforce standing behind him with pistol raised high and sure, and Bailiwick behind him, ferociously wielding one of the ornamental swords that hung over the fire in the main club room.

Turning back quickly, Aidan saw Whittaker look down at himself in confusion.

A bright red stain began to spread from just below his neck down over his chest, darkening his shirt to crimson. He blinked, then staggered.

Then he fell across the decorative railing with a crash, still clutching Madeleine's wrist in his grasp. The elderly iron work separated from the roof with a groan, then broke with a sound like a bell. Aidan lunged forward, but the body started to slide over the edge.

Taking Madeleine with it.

CHAPTER 37

Madeleine screamed in fear and tried to resist the pull over the edge, her free hand scrambling to hold something, anything to break the inexorable slide down the sloping section of roof.

Aidan reached her even as her head and shoulders started to go over. Throwing his body over hers to provide counterweight, he reached for her wrist with both hands, trying to unfix Whittaker's deathgrip.

He managed to peel the madman's fingers back but something was tying them together—

He and Madeleine both began to slither over the edge. Desperately, Aidan tore at Whittaker's fingers, ripping them free of the cord that had wrapped about Madeleine's hands in the struggle.

Whittaker fell, flying down and away from them to spin once, twice—

Then he crashed to the cobbles of St. James Street, a broken, staring mannequin of death.

Gasping, Aidan pulled Madeleine back from the edge, tugging her far from danger before he stopped to breathe. They clung together, sprawled awkwardly on the roof slates, the air harsh and sweet in their lungs.

Wilberforce stepped forward. "Lord Aldrich sent us to aid you, my lords. Are you well?"

Aidan drew back so he could lift Madeleine's face to his. Gently he stroked back the fallen tangle of her dark hair. "Are you all right? Do you need a physician?"

She opened her eyes. Her face was a mess of bruising, old and new, with a few fresh, bloody scrapes to fill out the blank spots.

"My God," he whispered. "I wish he'd survived the bullet *and* the fall so that I could kill him again."

Her eyes blazed. "As do I."

Colin squatted next to them. "Well, resurrection aside, I think someone had better get down there to explain matters to the watch."

"Oh, no need, my lord," Wilberforce said easily. "I'll take care of everything." With the pistol in his hand, he turned and strode back to the easiest access point of the roof, Bailiwick close behind him.

Aidan and Colin stared after them. Madeleine laughed shakily. "Just another example of the excellent service provided by Brown's Club for Distinguished Gentlemen."

Melody scrambled into their laps. "I like Wibbley-force. He gave me a candy stick." She thrust it into her mouth, sucking happily. Then she pulled it out again. "Can we go home now? This is too high."

Madeleine pulled her close and lay her cheek upon the tangled curls. "We can go anywhere you like, mousie. I'm so glad you're not hurt."

"Me, too. I'm glad Wibbley-force killeded the bad man. Now I can play in the park."

Aidan tipped the little chin up with one finger. "Mellie,

I will take you to the park every day for the rest of your life, but right now I think we should all climb down and go back to our rooms." He glanced at Colin. "Take Melody, will you?"

Colin lifted Melody away, but Madeleine's hands wanted to cling. She turned haunted eyes to Aidan. "I never should have—"

He pressed a finger gently over the unswollen half of her lips. "Later."

He helped her stand shakily on her own feet.

"Wait," she said suddenly. "What's that?"

Aidan looked down to see something glinting at his feet. He bent to pick it up. The cord that had entangled Whittaker's hand with Madeleine's wasn't a cord at all— it was a gold chain. At the end of that chain was a gleaming gold locket.

Madeleine drew back. "Destroy that," she said and then turned away from it.

Aidan shrugged and tossed the pretty thing onto the street below them. Then he supported her as she slowly made her way across the roof.

Madeleine had a marvelous vantage point of the scene on the street from the window in Colin's sitting room. With the window opened she could hear nearly every word as well.

She stood just behind the draperies and watched the entire business with great concern. Though she might have every faith in Wilberforce—for the man had certainly helped save her life—she couldn't help but worry how her own role would appear in this drama.

I have every right to punish my own property.

No matter how unfair it might be, Wilhelm had been absolutely correct. Most men in London would view her as an adulterous, ungrateful wretch who had participated in causing her poor, righteous husband's untimely death.

A shiver went through her. Women had been hanged for less!

Astonishingly enough, there was little mention of her at all.

Three men of the watch gathered about Wilhelm's stiffening corpse and gazed at it in various states of confusion.

One looked up at Wilberforce and the members of the club gathered behind him. Colin and Aidan were there, but remained discreetly on the fringes.

"So you say this man killed himself?"

One of the other watchmen squatted next to the body and gave it a poke with his finger. "What would 'e go and do a thing like that for, d'ye think?"

"Do you see those scars there?" Wilberforce pointed. "On his hand, wrist, and arm?"

The three watchmen nodded. Wilberforce continued. "Lord Whittaker's manor house burned to a ruin five years ago. He lost everything."

Lord Bartles chimed in from behind Wilberforce. "Lost his wife, too. I heard she was a pretty little thing."

The other members nodded sadly. "Poor bloke. He's never been the same since," one said.

Wilberforce nodded serenely. "Lord Whittaker hasn't been back to Town in years. I believe he came to London a few days ago expressly for the purpose of trying to forget his pain."

One watchman removed his hat and rubbed at his bald head. "Don't think it worked, did it?"

Lord Bartles shook his head sagely. "Some things a man can't forget."

The others nodded, rather like connected puppets, Madeleine thought. She'd never heard such complete malarkey. They ought to be ashamed.

"So sad."

"Still in his prime, poor fellow."

"What a pity."

One of the watchmen was not as gullible as the others. "You're saying he shot himself and *then* threw himself off the roof?"

Colin cleared his throat. "Perhaps he got to the edge and found he hadn't the nerve to leap?" His tone was mild, almost indifferent.

The liar!

The clever watchman frowned. "Then where is the pistol?"

"I have it." Wilberforce held it up for them to see.

"How did you get it?" asked the clever one suspiciously.

"It was on the roof not far from where he went over. I assumed you'd want to see it so I brought it down to you."

The wrinkled Lord Aldrich came up behind Madeleine and chuckled. "Have you noticed that every single word out of Wilberforce's mouth is the absolute truth? Masterful. What an admirable fellow."

Suddenly there was a commotion below. A fat fellow in a lurid waistcoat pushed to the fore of the crowd. "Wilhelm!"

The watchmen bridled. "You there! Stand back!"

Critchley held up both hands. "Don't believe anything these men tell you," he cried. "His wife killed him! She's in the club!"

The clever watchman frowned at him. "The dead wife?"

Critchley nodded earnestly. "Yes!" Then he grimaced. "I mean, no, she's not dead anymore!"

The watchman folded his arms. "And you say she's in there?" He indicated Brown's with the angle of his head.

"Yes, yes! She's been in there for days!"

All the members of the club broke out in laughter. The watchmen looked askance at Critchley, then one turned to Wilberforce.

"What ye got to say to that, then?"

Wilberforce lifted his chin to stare down his nose at Critchley. "Brown's is for *gentlemen*. The presence of ladies is strictly against the rules." He glanced at the more clever watchman. "I can state that this . . . person . . . has never stepped foot in Brown's. He is not in a position to speak one word about *my* club."

Madeleine shook her head in admiration. "I see what you mean," she said to Aldrich. "Masterful indeed."

Critchley let out a howl of frustration. "It was *him*!" He pointed at Aidan, who had remained on the fringes of the crowd but who also unfortunately towered over most of them.

Aidan did his best to look mystified and insulted. "I beg your pardon?"

Critchley lunged forward a step. "He's the one who took her away from me! I had her in my hands, and he stole her away!"

One of the watchmen snickered. "Weren't hard, I expect, whoever she is."

Critchley whirled, furious spittle wetting his lips. "She's alive, I tell you! She's alive and she belongs to *me* now!" He waved a wild arm toward Aidan. "Make him give her back!"

The intelligent watchman narrowed his eyes and gazed from Critchley to Aidan. It was clear that he was adding up the conflicting stories and felt he was coming out short one truth.

Aidan hid his growing worry behind a disdainful sneer. "I have never had the pleasure of being introduced to this fellow," he said clearly, "but I can assure you, I have no need to steal a woman from the likes of him."

The very idea made the increasing crowd laugh loudly.

Critchley became nearly purple with rage. His face now clashed rather horribly with his bilious waistcoat. With a roar he ripped the baton from the snickering watchman's hand and charged at Aidan, wielding the heavy stick like a club. Alarmed, Aidan watched the fellow come at him like a beer barrel headed downhill. If he struck Critchley down, it might only convince the watch that he had something to hide.

If he didn't, he was definitely going to have to bathe again. Immediately.

Luckily, the quick-witted watchman took Critchley out with a baton to his knee as he passed. Critchley went down with a shriek of pain.

"All right, you," the watchman said impatiently. "You've been too much on the opium pipe it seems. Attacking his lordship in the middle of the street puts you in irons for a good long while." He looked up at Aidan and tipped his cap. "Sorry about the ruckus, milord. We'll clean up all this if your man there—" He indicated Wilberforce with a tilt of his head. "—will loan us some blokes."

Wilberforce inclined his head. "I'd be only too happy, sir."

"Wait."

All turned to stare at the black-gowned woman who had spoken. The crowd parted before her as she moved forward to stand before the watch commander.

"I am Lady Madeleine Whittaker."

No. Aidan started toward her. The watch commander stopped him with a glare.

"I think I'd like to hear what her ladyship has to say."

CHAPTER 38

In Lord Aldrich's chambers, Madeleine gazed at her audience of four: Aidan, Colin, Wilberforce and the watch commander.

For years she'd tried not to think about the Incident. Now, perhaps, she could bring old secrets to light and be free of them forever. It was time for the real Madeleine to speak.

Madeleine folded her shaking hands before her to steady them.

"I was a foolish girl and married the first fellow who offered. Lord Wilhelm Whittaker was a cruel and malicious husband, but that was not why I left him to think I was dead." She stopped to take a breath. So far, no one seemed particularly surprised.

"He beat me often, for very little reason. One evening we were walking to a neighbor's for a supper invitation and he took exception to something I said. We were standing on a river bridge near Whittaker Hall when a neighbor, a young man of twenty-five, rode his horse down the road and spotted him mistreating me.

"Wilhelm was already in a rage and when the fellow dismounted to interfere, Wilhelm pushed him into the river. To my surprise and Wilhelm's as well, the fellow could not swim at all."

Sickening memory made her throat tighten. "The young man fought desperately but he drowned, right there in front of us." She looked down at her hands, then looked back at the four men. "And Wilhelm held my head over the railing and made me watch."

She shuddered. "I begged Wilhelm to save him. I screamed and cried and then I tried to leap in after him myself, but Wilhelm struck me down. I was dizzy but I remember looking up at him as he watched the young man die."

The room was silent with horror now. "I cannot vow that Wilhelm intended to kill him—but he could have easily saved him and he did not. He enjoyed watching a man die. When the young man slipped beneath the surface of the water for the last time, there was a mad glow in Wilhelm's eyes, like a man in love."

No one said anything for a long moment. Then the watch commander shook his head. "This is an incredible tale, my lady."

Aidan's voice was low and harsh. "Madeleine, to live with such a man—"

She interrupted him, for pity would only rob her of the last of her fortitude. "So you see why I fled—why I lied. I was not a cherished wife, kept protected in a castle. I was an imprisoned witness, silenced by stone walls. When he found me here, he vowed to silence me forever and to kill the child he thought was mine. He tried to throw us both from the roof."

The watchman's eyes narrowed. "Is this true?"

Wilberforce stepped forward. "I shot him myself."

"Well done." The watchman eyed them all. "But why not tell me this before?"

"They wished to protect me." Madeleine gazed at her defenders. "That is no longer necessary."

She turned to Wilberforce. "Sir, I realize it is against your rules, but if you could find a bed for me, just for a few hours."

He bowed. "My lady, the entire club is at your disposal."

Aidan moved toward her. "Maddie—"

She held up one hand. She could not bear to hear it now. Leaving him behind with the others, she followed Wilberforce on shaking limbs.

She was so very weary. After all, she had been running for such a very long time.

Night gathered about the club, hiding the stain upon the cobbles where the body had lain and sheltering the secret members of Brown's from scrutiny.

Madeleine had only slept for a few hours. For all her exhaustion, she'd awoken completely alert and anxious. Now she sat in her borrowed room, freshly bathed and wrapped in someone's discarded dressing gown, running a brush carefully through her tangled hair.

She had made such a mistake, not trusting Aidan with her secrets. To lie to such a man—she must have been mad.

The memory of how he came for her, how he fought for her, even when he knew her to be another man's wife, was thrilling and heartbreaking at the same time.

She deserved nothing from that man. He'd been right to

disdain her, for had she not dragged him into a torrid affair against his own scruples? Had she not exposed him to a kind of soiled degradation he could have gone his entire life without experiencing had it not been for her? Hadn't she put Melody in danger with her selfishness?

So she waited for him to come to her, to announce that he was done with her, that his kindness and his charity had run their due course and it was time for her take herself away from him and Brown's and Melody, never to return.

She waited for her sentence and she accepted it. She would simply have to limp along through the rest of her life with half a heart, for she would be leaving the other half here, with them. She only hoped that Melody would forget her soon, for she could not bear to think of the little girl she'd tricked and lied to asking again and again for the woman who'd claimed to be her mother.

Abandoned twice, my dearest. I'm so sorry.

The pain was no more than she deserved, so when Aidan finally entered, she gazed up at him with something that hopefully passed as serenity. She was going to make this as easy as possible on him. He'd done more for her than anyone had ever done. This was the last thing she could do for him.

That and love him forever. Who knew, perhaps it helped to have someone out there who loved you, who wished you well and prayed for you every night.

Yes, that she could and would do. Always.

He didn't look at her, but only turned away to gaze at the fire. With his hands braced upon the mantle, his head bowed, he looked the very picture a man about to pronounce judgment.

Well, he was due a final say, and she was determined to let him have it.

She only wished he'd hurry it up a little.

"Lady Madeleine, I . . ."

She came to attention immediately, but he trailed off. Her title sounded odd coming from him. Not that he owed her deference at all, for he outranked her father and grandfather as well. She realized with a silvery pang that she would never hear him call her "Maddie" again. Loss swept her anew.

There were going to be many such moments in her future, she suspected. She had best get used to it.

He cleared his throat and began again. "Lady Madeleine, I owe you an apology."

She blinked. *Hardly.* She kept still, however. If she said nothing at all, it was entirely possible he might utter another seven words soon.

He went on, his voice slow and deep, as if he dug the words from somewhere cavernous inside him. "When we first met, I had the feeling that you had a secret. At first I was willing to overlook it, for we began our . . . physical encounters so quickly that I felt as though a deeper exploration ought to be allowed more time."

Heavens, he was so proper and reserved. Almost cold. She had really worked him over, hadn't she?

Another sin to pay for.

"I set my reservations aside for the pleasure of your company. I let your secret lie between us. But that only allowed it to grow. Eventually, I felt I had no choice but to force your hand—to compel you to trust me fully with your past."

Ah, but trust cannot be compelled, my love.

He went on. "However, I have come to realize that trust cannot be compelled. I tried to command it—and in the very act of commanding showed I did not deserve it."

She looked down at her hands but her vision was blurred. This was to be her sentence then—his true understanding. Of course, with classic Aidan timing, he chose to become completely and irresistibly perfect right when he was about to throw her out of his life forever. It was both tragic and annoying. She had the overwhelming urge to throw things.

"So you rejected me . . . and I, full of hurt pride, walked away."

I can still see the pain in your beautiful face, my lord, my love.

"I told myself that you were faithless, that you were capricious and icy hearted and I left you behind me."

The words hurt, but was she not guilty enough of different words? Words like selfish, careless, irresponsible? *Repeat that to yourself nine times. Remind yourself of all the damage you might have done.*

She was going to sit here and let him have his say, blast it—no matter how much she wanted to toss her shoe at his head.

"So when I found Melody, I thought you more than capable of abandoning your own child—"

"Oh, that's enough!"

CHAPTER 39

Madeleine jumped her feet. "I know I did any number of terrible things—all of which I am very sorry for, mind you—but if I have to hear how *one more time* how I abandoned a child I *never birthed* I'm going to—"

He turned, a twisted grin on his handsome face. "Damn. I lost the wager. I thought you were going to wallow in martyrdom for at least another quarter of an hour."

She stared at him, her mouth open, her body poised to flounce in indignation—then she straightened, smoothed her oversized dressing gown with her palms and nodded. "Colin?"

He snorted. "Yes, damn it all. I owe him another twenty quid."

"Don't gamble. You aren't good at it." She folded her arms and gazed at him severely. "And it isn't martyrdom! I have a great deal to answer for!"

He folded his own arms mockingly and leaned back against the mantle. "Such as?"

"I lied about my identity!"

"Yes, in order to escape the clutches of a madman. I think allowances can be made."

"I had an affair with you!"

"Yes, although I shall take a shred of responsibility for that one, if you don't mind."

"Ah, but you thought me widowed!"

He pursed his lips and thought for a moment. Then he shook his head. "I do not concede your point. One shouldn't make assumptions. I never actually asked, you know."

She made an exasperated noise. "I lied again, about Melody! I made you bring me back here!"

He looked oddly guilty then. "I must confess . . . I wouldn't have believed you even if you'd denied it. I likely would have brought you back here anyway."

She narrowed her eyes at him. "You might have *tried*."

He held up both hands in self-defense and gave a bark of laughter. "Point taken."

"But I—" She slid her arms down to wrap about her midriff, to warm the hard knot of chill and guilt that remained there. This was the thing of which she was most ashamed. "I led him *here*. To you! To my mousie! If something had happened to either of you—" Her throat spasmed at the very thought and she shrank into herself, swamped with remorse. "He held her so cruelly—"

He jerked upright, his expression desolate. "No! That was not your doing!"

And then she was in his arms, sobbing out her terror and her shame on his broad, warm chest. He held her, only held her, while she cried so hard she could hardly breathe. All the years of watchfulness and caution, all the lonely months of isolation and brokenhearted loss, all the endless hours imprisoned in the dimness poured from her in hoarse, helpless gasps.

At some point he bent to slide his arms beneath her,

lifting her to his chest and taking her to the large chair to settle her in his lap. She curled there like a child, limp with exhaustion, her eyes burning hot, her breath still coming in hiccupping gasps.

Finally spent, she lay draped across his chest, one hand crooked about his neck.

It was possible that she'd never cried so hard, for when in her life had she ever felt so unconditionally accepted— reddened eyes, running nose and all?

She sniffled surreptitiously. His handkerchief appeared before her blurry eyes. She took it, mentally apologizing to the fine lawn in advance, and blew her nose mightily.

"That's yours now," he said with a chuckle in his voice. "Keep it."

She laughed damply. Her midriff ached from the effort. "What of your coat and weskit?" She dabbed at the tearstains. "Are these now mine as well?"

"Entirely."

There was a different note in his voice, all teasing sympathy gone. She lifted her head and blinked at his face. His gaze was dark and somber and a bit . . . shy?

She scrubbed at her face hurriedly then leaned back a bit so she could see him more clearly. "What is it? What has you worried so?"

"I've hurt you badly, I think."

More tears threatened at his tender, worried tone but she blinked them back. She had the feeling this was going to be important and she didn't want to miss it. "I think we've both done our share of damage," she said carefully.

"I left you there, alone and penniless."

"I was no worse off than I was before. Better in fact, for

I had your gifts to tide me over. I sold them, you know," she confided. "Every single one, but for the pearls."

"I'm glad of it. At least my neglect did not kill you— as it nearly did yesterday."

She narrowed her eyes at him. "This is beginning to sound familiar. Are you feeling competitive? For I warn you, I did much worse things than you did so there's no point in trying to match my score."

His lips twitched. "Perhaps I am." He reached out stroke his knuckles very carefully down her cheek, his gaze fixed grimly on the purplish bruises there. "I pray he burns in hell."

She smiled. "That's terribly sweet." Then she took his hand from her face and enclosed it between both of hers. "But he is quite thoroughly dead and we are not, so let us not speak of him again. I'll serve no mourning period. I've spent enough of myself on that monster already."

He spread his fingers and watched her lace hers through his from both sides. Then he closed his, trapping her hands gently inside. "Agreed. We do indeed have many years ahead of us . . . and I know what I would like to do with mine."

She waited, her heart stuttering just a little.

He raised his gaze to meet hers. "I once urged you to become mine forever. I told you I had to have you, that I had to possess you as my very own."

She nodded slowly, her gaze locked on his, and waited. Hope bubbled up inside her but she didn't trust it entirely.

His eyes crinkled slightly as he gazed at her. "You're very patient. That's not like you at all."

She raised a brow but said nothing. His lips twitched. "Right. Out with it, Blankenship."

He released her trapped fingers and brought his other hand forward, curled around something. "I saw your fire and your brightness and just like Whittaker I wanted to own you, to possess you, to pen you up and keep you forever." He tilted his head. "I was an idiot. You, my lady, are no one's chattel." He paused to take a breath.

She was certain she was holding hers. Things were getting just the tiniest bit fuzzy about the edges . . . except for his face, his chiseled, handsome face that looked so very wary and shy at this moment. *Heavens, and I thought I couldn't possibly love him any more than I did five minutes ago.*

"So instead of trying to possess you, I can only . . . offer."

Sliding her off his lap, he settled her in the chair that was still warm from his body. Then he went down on one knee before her. "Lady Madeleine Whittaker, will you consent to wed me and live with me and laugh with me and grow very, very old and wrinkled with me and poke me to make sure I'm still breathing?"

She laughed damply. "I think that's the most romantic proposal I've ever heard. But where's the ring?"

He smiled. "I have something better than a ring." He reached into his pocket and withdrew—

A large, shiny, green apple. He placed it in her hand and closed her fingers over it. "I promise to feed you apples forever."

She smiled and took a large, enthusiastic bite out of the apple. Then she maneuvered the chunk of it into her cheek, looking rather lopsidely beautiful as she did so. "The apple is marvelous, my lord, my love—" Aidan smiled to hear those words from her lips. "—but if I'm getting married, you'd best hand over the bloody ring."

"At your service, milady." He reached into his smallest waistcoat pocket, then opened his closed fist over hers.

Something warm and heavy dropped into her palm. The ring, its gold heated from his adorably nervous palm, lay like a brilliant, burning coal in her hand.

She inhaled sharply. "Read the engraving," he urged, his voice tight.

She tilted the ring into the light. On the inside of the shimmering gold band, where nothing had been inscribed a few days ago, there flowed two words in beautiful script.

I'm Yours.

This time, when they made love on the carpet before the fire, it didn't even occur to Madeleine to blow out the candles first.

CHAPTER 40

Madeleine was unaccountably sad to leave their chambers.

How strange that two rooms in a gentlemen's club had become their little home. Yet it had. There was where she had sewn Gordy Ann together forever. There was where Aidan had knelt while he fixed Melody's braid. There was the closet where—

Her face heated. *Well.* Back to the matter.

And the matter was that the very creaks and cracks of the building were like the voice of a family member.

She was sure that the house Aidan had found was very nice, but it was in this club where she'd become someone new—someone she liked much better than the Madeleine who had prepared to run away just one short week ago. As she folded her things and packed her valise and Melody's little satchel, her hands slowed as she remembered her fear.

She knew that no one was ever done with fear. Fear was part of life. She, however, was forever done with running from it. She had challenged the monster and had survived virtually unscathed.

"I can't say as much for the monster," she murmured to her hairbrush. Then she raised her gaze to meet her own eyes in the mirror. Behind the bruises and scrapes, there was something new there. A certain . . . self-possession? She smiled. She was fair to becoming as serene as Wilberforce!

Melody blew through the room, a whirling dervish of unbraided hair and bare feet. Aidan was close behind her with a pair of tiny boots in one hand and a hair ribbon trailing from the other. He swept Melody into his arms. "Got you now!"

"No!" Melody protested. "Captain Jack doesn't have ribbons! Captain Jack doesn't wear shooooees!"

Aidan swung the protesting toddler under his arm like a parcel. "I'm going to murder Sir Colin Lambert," he informed Madeleine in exasperation.

She smiled and nodded. "Just wait until after the ceremony this morning. We need at least one witness. I think the bishop would prefer that witness be breathing."

When they left the rooms, they found Colin himself lurking outside their door. He took Melody without a word and held her close as they all descended the many stairs to the main floor.

Madeleine knew that Colin was miserable. Yet he'd agreed with them that Melody was better off in the house with temporary parents than left in the club with a bachelor.

At the bottom of the stairs, Colin set Melody on her feet and busied himself fixing her braids. "He mucked it again, didn't he, Cap'n Melody?" he whispered, making her giggle.

He didn't want to let her see his sadness. Eventually he'd get used to not seeing his little partner-in-crime every day. Eventually he'd get used to not having her just up the stairs.

He simply didn't think he was going to get used to the fact that he couldn't dislodge one particular thought in his head. It was not an impossible thought. He'd done the arithmetic a dozen times. There had been a time that might have made it possible.

What if she's mine?

Melody snuggled into Uncle Colin's arms, Gordy Ann tucked under her chin. She didn't understand why she had to go to a stupid house. She loved the club—loved the smell of it, loved the dark wood and the musty carpet and way Wibbly-force always winked at her when no one else could see.

And why couldn't Uncle Colin come too? Why couldn't Grampapa Aldrich come? Why couldn't Billy-wick?

She stuck her little hands into Uncle Colin's waistcoat and held onto his shirt. She heard him breathe really deep and long as his arms tightened about her.

Aidan tried to put a smile on the way he felt at abandoning their cozy little haven. "We'll be able to stretch out at last," he told Madeleine cheerfully as he gathered her things to carry.

She reached up to stroke a gentle hand across his cheek. "Don't try to be jolly, darling." She smiled lovingly. "You haven't any practice."

As they made their way to the front of the club, two of the stuffy old fixtures from the chessboard by the fire blocked them from the door.

"Won't let you go," Sir James declared.

Lord Bartles nodded. "All this sneaking to and fro and hiding." He harrumphed. "Murderers in the attic! Won't allow it."

Sir James agreed, nodding continuously. "You'll stay put."

"I agree," came a raspy voice from behind them. They turned to see that Lord Aldrich had taken up the flank position, his cane held sideways like a guard stick. "You should stay, the lot of you. This club has never been so interesting."

Aidan frowned in confusion. "You want us to stay?"

Madeleine dimpled at Lord Bartles. He huffed and blinked rapidly.

"Of course they do," she informed Aidan. "This place is crying out for a woman's touch."

Aidan's jaw dropped. "But—I rented a house—"

She grinned up at him. "So unrent it." She took her parcels out of his arms. "Change of plan, my love. Really, one must get used to life's unpredictable currents. It makes steering ever so much easier if one does."

Aldrich nodded. "Your lady is a very wise woman, Blankenship."

Lord Bartles huffed again. "Currents, boy, that's the thing."

Aidan stared at Bartles. "You're instructing me about change? You haven't budged a pawn since Waterloo!"

Madeleine shushed him. "Let me translate, my lords. He means, thank you very much, we joyfully accept the invitation."

"I'm for it." Colin swung Melody up to sit on his shoulders. "How about you, Cap'n Mellie?"

Melody gazed at all of them with large blue eyes. "I want to stay here . . ." She bit her lip. "But can I have a kitten?"

"Good for you, mousie," Madeleine murmured.

"I'm sorry, but I cannot allow it."

They all turned to see Wilberforce behind them, followed by several curious footmen.

"What do you mean?" blustered Lord Bartles.

"I must object," Wilberforce said calmly. "I regret to inform you, my lords, my ladies, that the Brown's Club for Distinguished Gentlemen provides hard and fast rules on the matter. No ladies may visit the club for any reason."

There was an outcry from the several members who had gathered in the hall. "Then change the bloody rules!"

Wilberforce cleared his throat. "There is a proviso for changing the original club charter—"

"Then we'll change it!"

Wilberforce went on. "But it requires a unanimous and undisputed vote by the original charter members themselves."

They all gazed at him in horror. "That was a hundred years ago!" Colin protested.

"One hundred and twelve, to be precise, Sir Colin. As per the charter, if a charter member is deceased, the vote may be utilized by their nearest male descendant—"

Lord Bartles stepped forward. "That'd be me, then. My grandfather was a charter member. I so move that we change the bloody rules."

"I believe I qualify as well." Lord Aldrich stepped forward. "I second the motion."

There was a rusty cheer that faded as Wilberforce shook his head. "My lords, I regret that you do not form a unanimous ballot. There is one other descendant of a charter member . . ."

"Well, man, who is it? We'll get him down here and *make* him vote yes."

"Why, the third member is—"

Colin snorted. "It's Jack, isn't it?"

Wilberforce continued, not dignifying Colin's rudeness with any notice at all. "—is Lord John Redgrave, heir to the Marquis of Strickland."

Aidan blew out a breath. "And Jack isn't here."

Colin narrowed his eyes. "Wilberforce, you know perfectly well how Jack would vote here."

Wilberforce actually seemed slightly uncomfortable. "It is not my place to say, Sir Colin. And until such a vote might be cast, I must abide by the rules of the club. No ladies may visit Brown's at any time."

The tide of dissent rose. A few of the footmen, led by Bailiwick, moved to stand behind Wilberforce as he faced the fuming silver-haired mob.

Madeleine stepped forward. "Now, gentlemen, this is getting a bit silly." She beamed a smile at them all. There was a visible thawing and even a bit of abashed foot-shuffling. "The earl has found us a very nice house and it isn't far from here. You'll all be perfectly welcome to vi—"

"Ahem." Wilberforce cut her off. "If you'll pardon the interruption, my lady. It suddenly occured to me that while the charter forbids that any lady be allowed to *visit* the club, nowhere does it provide a ruling on ladies being allowed to *reside* at the club." He eyed them all serenely, as if he hadn't just narrowly avoided being hanged from the flagpole.

"Hurrah!" said Lord Bartles, and Sir James led another croaky cheer.

Melody cheered along. "We're staying! We're staying!"

Wearied by all the unusual activity, most of the members then shuffled back to their normal occupations. Bones creaked as they settled into chairs, papers rustled, and coffee cups clinked.

Madeleine blinked at the immediate, albeit unhurried, desertion. Only Aldrich, Colin, and Wilberforce remained in the entrance hall with them. Bailiwick took up a dignified stance at the door, his proper demeanor marred only by the slightly conspiratorial grin he cast at Melody, who giggled.

Was that a tiny pained grimace crossing Wilberforce's face? Impossible. However, Aidan decided to keep an eye on Melody and Bailiwick. One child in the club was exertion enough!

Madeleine tucked her hand into his arm. "I suppose we ought to go unpack now," she said with a smile. Then she turned to Wilberforce. "I don't suppose we could put a door through to the next chambers? Melody needs a nursery and—"

She was interrupted once again, this time by a vigorous hand at the knocker. Bailiwick jumped to attention and opened the door.

Unfortunately, the young footman wasn't man enough to halt the purple satin storm that was Lady Blankenship. She swept past him like a rustling, perfumed hurricane headed straight for Aidan.

Aidan's grip on Madeleine tightened. "I'm apologizing for my mother in advance," he murmured to her.

Madeleine gazed wide-eyed at the impending storm. "Make it up to me later," she whispered. "Diamonds are nice."

Aidan tried not to laugh as he bowed to the oncoming figure of his matriarchal disaster. "My lady, what a pleasant surprise."

Lady Blankenship came to rest in a whirl of rich fabric and even richer fury. "Blankenship! What is the meaning of *this!*" She thrust out a begloved hand. Resting in her palm was a wadded and crumpled ball of paper.

Aidan gazed down at it. "I see you received my letter," he said, his tone mild.

"Explain yourself at once!"

Aidan smiled. "My lady, I present Lady Madeleine Whittaker, the woman I am going to wed—" He cast a look at the face of the tall standing clock that graced the entrance hall. "—in less than an hour. Maddie, the Countess of Blankenship." He couldn't resist a mischievous smile. "Soon to be the *Dowager* Countess."

Lady Blankenship's eyes narrowed dangerously at that. Her furious gaze locked on Madeleine. "Lady Madeleine."

"Lady Blankenship." Madeleine curtsied properly but without any deep deference. After all, she ranked nearly as high by birth as the countess did by marriage.

When she rose, she had a smile and a bit of armored fortitude prepared. She aimed them both at Lady Blankenship, who was gazing at her with icy but familiar eyes of night-sky blue.

Madeleine's hand tightened on Aidan's arm. *Here it comes.*

"*Esme?*"

With a startled jerk, Lady Blankenship turned her attention from the impending verbal evisceration of

Madeleine and instead fixed it on the small, wrinkled gnome of a man who stood behind them. Her blue eyes widened and she went quite pale.

"Aldie?"

Aidan turned his head to regard Lord Aldrich with surprise. "Aldie?" he murmured.

But Lord Aldrich's gaze was only for Lady Blankenship. "Why, Esme, you look lovely." His face folded into an admiring smile. "I always told you purple was my favorite color."

Lady Blankenship flew toward him. Her path took her directly between Aidan and Madeleine, whom she passed without any notice at all.

They drew together again after her opening and gazed at the odd couple in confusion.

Aidan's brows rose. "My mother has worn purple every day I've known her," he whispered to Madeleine. "I wonder what that means."

Madeleine's eyes widened. "It means that for most of her life, she was waiting to meet him again."

Aidan snorted but even so he regarded his mother strangely.

And Lady Blankenship was behaving very strangely. She curtsied before Aldrich, girlishly offering her hand. He helped her rise. Upon standing, she stood a good four inches taller, but still she gazed upon Aldrich as if he were a tall and handsome knight upon a fiery steed. Aldrich straightened. For a moment they could almost see the dashing hero of Esme's girlhood.

Then Lady Blankenship—the icy mother, the glacial countess, the bane of everyone who mattered in Society—giggled.

Aidan's brow creased. "Is . . . is she *simpering?*"

Madeleine patted his hand. "You'll be just fine without her, Aidan."

He blinked and tore his gaze from the creature who had abruptly replaced his mother to frown at her. "What do you mean? Where is she going?"

She shook her head at his density. "Why, she is going to marry Lord Aldrich, of course." She gazed at the couple, reunited after so many years and still burning with a passion that threatened to scorch the fine rosewood paneling. "Rather soon, I think." She smiled. "Isn't that sweet? They're kissing."

Aidan closed his eyes. "I can't look. Don't make me look."

Madeleine laughed. "Think of it this way. She'll be much too busy to make your life miserable."

He looked oddly discomfited by that thought. "But she's so good at it. Are you sure she'll wish to give that up?"

"I'll show you." Madeleine stepped toward the enamored couple. "Lady Blankenship? Aidan and I are going to go get married now."

Lady Blankenship didn't even bother to raise her dreamy gaze from Aldrich's. She merely waved an inattentive hand. "That's nice, I'm sure you'll be very happy together, it was lovely to meet you." Then she sighed soulfully. "Aldie, I thought you were dead! I've been so unhappy!"

Madeleine turned back to Aidan with a shrug and a laugh. "Shall we go get married now?"

Melody clapped her hands. "Let's go get married!"

Colin grinned. "If you two are going to play house here at Brown's, you might need another doting uncle on hand." He looked about him at the tottering membership. "One who can actually keep up with Melody."

Madeleine leaned her head on Aidan's shoulder. "I know she isn't ours," she whispered. "But I'm glad I get to pretend a little longer."

He stroked her hair, relishing the rich silky feel in his hands—and the fact that he had the rest of his life to touch her—and pressed a kiss to the top of her head. "Me, too," he murmured. "Just until Jack gets back."

Standing nearby with Melody on his shoulders and one hand securely holding her little feet, Colin nodded thoughtfully. "Until Jack gets back."

EPILOGUE

Melody was astonished. "So you didn't even meet Aunt Maddie until after she was married to Uncle Aidan?"

Lementeur smiled in reminiscence. "The day of the wedding, actually. You were all about to step into the bishop's chambers when you objected to her old black mourning gown. You insisted that she was supposed to get married in a happy dress."

Melody smiled. "Aunt Maddie hates black."

"Indeed. Now you know why. So his lordship ordered the carriage to bring you all to me." He shook his head with an impish smile. "I saw that man walk in with his beautiful bride and you, and I knew I was going to make scandalous amounts of money from him."

Melody laughed. "You love us all and you know it."

He nodded with satisfaction. "Money *and* love. Incomparable." He stretched his legs out toward the fire. "So there you have it. Your early days were every bit as complicated as they are today. You ought to be used to those changing currents by this time."

Melody's lady's maid poked her head into the room. "Excuse me, milady, but her ladyship is making the most awful ruckus about the flowers. She wants Lord Aldrich to go out and fetch all new ones."

Melody shuddered. "Oh, no."

Button smiled easily. "Lizzy, tell Lady Blankenship that I personally approved the flowers, and if she doesn't like them, then I'm sure she won't like the fall wardrobe I've designed for her either."

Melody gasped with laughter at such a dire threat and even Lizzy grinned. "That I'll do, Mr. Lementeur, sir, and with pleasure."

Melody stopped her. "And make sure Grampapa Aldrich has a whiskey. He's going to need it. But don't give away his hiding place to Lady Blankenship." Lizzy nodded and left. Melody rested her head on Button's shoulder once again. "Poor Grampapa. He has to tolerate so much."

Button snorted. "He loves every moment of the madness. It keeps him young."

Melody sighed. "But what about my parents? You only told me about Aunt Maddie and Uncle Aidan."

Button stroked her hair. "You're stalling, Lady Melody."

She snuggled closer. "I know. Tell me anyway."

Button leaned back and wriggled a more comfortable place for his rear in the sofa cushion. "Well, that's another story altogether. Did I mention that it was complicated?"

Read on for an excerpt from
Celeste Bradley's next book

ROGUE IN MY ARMS

Coming soon from St. Martin's Paperbacks

Sir Colin Lambert had thought nanny duty would be so simple. After all, perfectly idiotic people raised children every day. He was an intelligent fellow, some might even say a brilliant scholar, and he'd considered that a platoon of younger cousins had granted him some experience with children.

So why couldn't he manage to keep an eye on one tiny little girl?

He'd had it easy before, he realized. When little Melody had been left on the doorstep of Brown's Club for Distinguished Gentlemen, there had been two of them to take care of her. Then Aidan had brought in his former lover, Madeleine, and things had gone quite smoothly from there—if one didn't count the homicidal maniac kidnapper lurking in the attic. Which, to be entirely truthful, hadn't been Melody's fault. Not even a little bit.

This mess, however, was entirely of his own doing. When Aidan and Madeleine had left on their honeymoon, Colin had blithely decided to leave the safety of the club and all its convenient and tolerant staff behind and venture out into the world of fatherhood.

Where he now suffered on his own with dear little Baby Bedlam.

The hell of it was, he was beginning to suspect more and more that—inexplicable mulishness aside—little Mystery Melody was his own child. Being a man of logic and forethought—usually—he'd thrown caution to the wind and set out with a tiny child to Brighton in the hopes of finding his former lover who might be Melody's long-lost mother. What he was not quite willing to admit to was the secret hope that when he found the lovely Chantal again that she would not only confess to being Melody's mother, but she would also accept a proposal of marriage.

First, however, he had to find Melody!

"Mellie! Mellie, I know you're hiding in there! Come out this instant!"

Of course she didn't come. Why should she? He was doing the same thing he'd thought so idiotic when he'd observed other adults dealing with children. Children weren't stupid. Calling them when one was angry was like a dog trying to coax a cat out of a tree.

Fine. Colin took a deep breath and sat down in the shade of the aforementioned tree. He listened for a moment and was rewarded by the slightest scuffling of little boots. Powdered bark sifted down through the moist summer air to ornament his dark green superfine surcoat. He brushed at it in resignation and then tilted his head back and closed his eyes against the leaf-dappled sunlight.

If one had to be stuck on the side of the road, unable to get one's possible offspring back into the carriage after she'd been turned loose on yet another call of nature . . . well, this was most definitely the spot to do it. Even if a one-day journey had turned into nearly three days.

"I was thinking about a bit of lunch, Mellie . . ." He let

the sentence fade away unsaid. "Well, you probably don't want to hear about that." He picked at a bit of grass. "Or do you?"

Silence. She was undoubtedly hungry, but she was too stubborn to admit it.

You'll need better bait than that.

He nearly whimpered. *Not again.* He'd only been traveling with Melody for a few days and already he'd told her more outlandish pirate tales than there had ever been outlandish pirates! If he had to review the gory details of keelhauling one more time, he was definitely going to lose the last of his mind.

"You see . . . I was wondering what pirates had for lunch . . ."

"Fish."

Speaking of fish, his had just taken the bait. He smiled. "Of course, how silly of me. I imagine they ate a great deal of fish." He hummed to himself for a moment. "What about breakfast? Too bad they didn't have any eggs."

"Fish eggs."

He stifled a laugh. "Ah, yes. Why not?"

More bark fell onto his jacket. The scuffling of little boots was closer now. He was tempted to jump up and reach for her, but he'd learned his lesson well over the last hour and a half. Melody might be scarcely three years old, but she showed an early aptitude for altitude.

So he gave in with a sigh and began the litany that he must have repeated forty times over the last days. "Once upon the high seas—" *Damn the high seas!* "—there sailed a mighty pirate ship. Upon the prow were letters etched in the blood of honest men and they read—" He waited.

"Dishonor's Plunder!"

"Dishonor's Plunder," Colin affirmed wearily. And the story was on. Blood ran, gore oozed, and a horridly high body count mounted. At least three keelhaulings later, he realized that Melody had climbed down from the tree and was seated tailor-fashion on the grass beside him.

"Hullo," he said carefully.

"I'm hungry."

"I'm not." He was, in fact, ever so slightly nauseated by his own imagination. If anyone in the Bathgate Society of Scholars were to hear the dreck he spouted sometimes . . .

Well, that would never happen.

He stood and brushed at his clothing. "Right, then. There should be an inn a few miles down the road. Up you go, Cap'n Mellie." With that, he tossed her giggling onto his shoulders and strode back to where their still-harnessed horses were manfully striving to mow the entire roadside, despite the bits in their mouths. Colin put Melody into the curricle and vaulted up into the driver's seat.

The horses reluctantly pulled their heads up and began to walk.

So convenient, really, just the two of them making this journey together. No servants, no nattering companions. No one telling them when to start and when to stop—

"Uncle Coliiiin! I gotta *go!*"

Prudence Filby threw her sewing bag down onto the dressing room floor in frustration. Damn Chantal! She put her hands over her face, trying very hard to quell the panic icing her veins.

"She isn't coming back?" she asked the manager of the Brighton Theater, even though she knew his answer. "Are you sure?"

The stout man behind her made a regretful noise. "She's gone. Took off with that dandy, sayin' she was in love. I wouldn't take her back if she did return. She might be the most beautiful actress in England but she's also a towering b—" He cleared his throat. "She's a right pain in the arse, she is! The last ten performances, she's only done two! Keeps saying she's too weary, too bored, too good for such a horrid play."

He'd left out spiteful. Prudence raised her eyes to see the dressing room's true disarray. It looked as though a tornado equipped with vindictive scissors had torn through it. Everything was ruined.

Damn you, Chantal.

She looked over her shoulder at the manager and tried to smile. The man had managed to perfectly capture Chantal's petulant tones. "You should go on the stage yerself, sir. You've a right knack for playin' a towering b—"

He smiled, but shook his head regretfully. "It'll do ye no good to flatter me, Pru. I can't get ye another job. Ye can't sew a lick and all the cast knows it. The only reason ye lasted so long was that ye were the only one who could put up with Chantal's tantrums."

Pru nodded in resignation. "Not yer fault, sir. Ye've got the right of it." There was no point in denying it. Not that she was a patient person in reality. She'd simply realized that if she could keep her temper through Chantal's rages and abuses and bouts of throwing breakable objects, she'd be able to keep feeding herself and her twelve-year-old brother Evan. The other seamstresses and dressers had helped her with the actual stitching, grateful that they weren't called upon to personally serve the she-devil.

Now it was over. Chantal had left without paying her for her last month's work and there was nothing left in her pockets but bits of snipped thread and extra buttons.

She couldn't even sell the costumes, for Chantal had shredded them in a last fit of malice.

The manager left her to contemplate her short and miserable future. This was the only job she'd ever managed to get here in Brighton. No one wanted a girl without useful skills—no one but the factories.

Her chest felt heavy with the cold undeniable truth. She was going to have to go into the factories. She only hoped she would be one of the lucky few to someday come out.

All the dressers at the theater had horror stories to tell. Factory work was grueling and unhealthy. Girls froze at their machines in winter and fainted from the heat in summer. Cruel foremen made advances and refused to be refused. Machines lopped off fingers and slashed hands and there was no law that told the factory owners nay. Despite the grim conditions, as soon as one girl was abused past her ability to endure, another would be begging for the work.

It was a last resort, but there were many who were forced to take it out of desperation.

Better her than Evan. The children in the factories scarcely ever saw their next birthday once they walked through those doors. She swallowed hard at the thought.

No. She was stronger than her small frame and large eyes led people to believe. She was smart and careful. Besides, she told herself firmly, ignoring the cold ball of dread in her belly, if she could abide Chantal, she could tolerate anything!

When Colin at last drove the curricle into Brighton, he was exhausted and frustrated. Nevertheless, he nearly turned around and drove back to London at the sight of the sticky seaside crowds with their ludicrous swimming costumes and their whining, sunburned children.

"Summer in Brighton. What was I thinking?"

He'd been thinking that he would see the exquisite Chantal again, that's what. Just the thought of her, so lovely, so sweet-tempered, so delicate, so very, very amorous when he had at last managed to worm his way past her modest and righteous morals—

He gave the distracted and weary horses a small stroke of the whip. *Chantal awaits!*

Except, as it turned out, she didn't.

Colin blinked around him at the empty, shabby velvet seats and the peeling gilt of the stage border—not quite as magical during the day, was it?—then turned back to the stout fellow who claimed to be the theater manager. Melody stood between them, one arm wrapped around Colin's shin, gazing about her in awe.

"She isn't coming back?" Colin asked. "Are you sure?"

The man scowled. "Why do people keep saying that? She ain't comin' back, I don't want her back and she ain't welcome in any other theater in the city!" He threw up his hands in an Italianate manner and strode away muttering resentfully.

Colin's knees felt ancient as he slowly lowered himself to sit on the edge of the deserted stage. At least the theater was dim and cool, a welcome respite from the dusty road. Melody promptly deposited herself in his lap and rested her head on his waistcoat.

"Uncle Colin, I'm tired. I wanna go back to Brown's. I wanna see Maddie and Uncle Aidan and my room and the garden and . . ." She went to sleep quickly, as she always did. Melody only had two settings: go and stop.

Colin rather wanted to crawl somewhere and sleep himself. All this for nothing? The hours and hours on the road, the nondescript inns with greasy food that Melody refused to eat, the hundreds of exhaustively detailed decapitations?

For a moment he fervently wished he was scarcely three years old so he could fling himself down upon the stage and kick and scream in frustration.

"*No!* I won't go and ye can't bloody make me!"

Colin looked up at the furious voice, automatically covering Melody's ears from any further profanity. His action was not so much to protect her innocence as to limit her extensive vocabulary. There had already been a few embarrassing moments on their journey so far.

From around the back of the stage came a small figure, stomping angrily in boots too large, swinging fists that were none too clean, and scowling with a face that had apparently had strawberry jam for breakfast. The person saw Colin watching and glared back belligerently.

"What ye starin' at, ye posh bastard?"

Colin blinked at the miniature vulgarian in dismay. He couldn't be more than twelve years of age, and a poorly grown twelve years at that. However, his large gray eyes showed the shadows of too many hardships and too few childish pleasures.

When had he begun to pay so much attention to children?

"I'm looking for Chantal Marchant," he told the boy. *Why did I share that?* Really, to someone who didn't understand the past that Colin and Chantal shared, for him to come looking for her with the road dust still on his clothing . . . well, it might come across as just a tad—

"Pathetic, that's what!" The boy spat. Then he turned to face the direction he'd just come from. "There's another fancy blighter lookin' for Herself!" he yelled.

Colin turned to gaze at the shadows behind the half-drawn curtain. He saw a dark figure bend gracefully, deposit something on the floor of the stage, and then stretch her arms above her head like a dancer. Against the backlight, he could see that she was slightly built, but there was no hiding the fact that her bosom was lush and full. What a lovely figure!

She lowered her arms and planted her hands on her hips. It only served to show off the narrow dimensions of her waist.

Really spectacular. Colin leaned sideways for a better view. *Chantal?*

A low, velvety voice came from that luscious shadow. "Leave the fancy blighter be, Evan. It ain't his fault he's an idiot."

Colin was so distracted by the sensual richness of that voice that it took a long moment for him to realize that he'd been slighted. In addition, the speech patterns were of an uneducated woman of no social stature, i.e., "not for him." He blinked wistfully at that momentary fantasy as it seeped away.

Still, he couldn't help await her entrance into the light. If her face matched that body and that voice—! Well, he simply might have to reassess his standards a bit.

She stepped into the dim daylight streaming in through the great double doors that stood open to the summery sea air. Colin felt a hit of disappointment. She wasn't precisely unattractive . . . more like a bit plain. She had small, pointed features that did not fit his usual idea of beauty— though her large gray eyes were rather attractive.

They matched the boy's eyes, in fact. Ah, her son, obviously. She must be older than he'd first thought.

She gazed back at him for a long moment with one eyebrow raised. He suddenly had the uncomfortable sensation that she somehow knew precisely what he'd been thinking about her.

Then she tossed a bundle to the boy. "Evan, we got no choice. Go ask the coach driver if he'll let us sit on top for a shilling."

Evan smirked. "We don't got a shilling."

She turned back to gaze speculatively at Colin. "We will."

Evan, defeated at last, stomped his way from the theater, but not without a last resentful look at Colin.

The woman approached him and stood there, looking down at Melody in his lap. "You're lucky," she said, indicating Melody with her chin. "That age is easy."

The very thought of it getting harder made Colin's spine weaken just a bit. "Really?"

The woman gathered her full skirts and sat down next to him, letting her feet in their worn boots dangle next to his costly calfskin ones. "Oh, sure 'tis. Now she thinks ye hung the moon. Yer the champion. When she gets a bit taller, she'll figure out that ye don't know what the hell yer doin' and she'll never respect ye again."

Colin gazed down at the top of Melody's head in alarm. "But what if I do know what I'm doing?"

"Won't matter. Ye'll never convince 'er of it." She shrugged. It did interesting things to the supple burden within her bodice. Not that he was interested in her—but he breathed, didn't he?

She swung her feet idly for a moment. "So . . ." Her tone was conversational. "Ye know Chantal."

She was a bit too familiar for Colin's taste. "Don't you mean 'Miss Marchant'? She was your employer, was she not?"

Her fingers tightened on the edge of the stage but her response was respectful. "Sorry, guv'nor. I just thought ye'd be wantin' to know where *Miss Marchant* took off to."

Ah. The gambit, at last. Well, he had shillings to spare if she had information. "What'll it cost me?"

She slid him a sideways glance. "Five quid."

He snorted. "Nice try."

"Three, then."

"Shillings or pounds?"

Her lips twisted in reluctant respect. "Shillings, then."

Colin shrugged. It was only money and she looked like she needed it. "You have a bargain. Where is she?"

"Not 'till ye fork over."

He reached into his waistcoat pocket and withdrew three shillings. He laid them out in his palm and showed them to her. "You can see I have them. I can see you have something to tell me. So tell me."

Her eyebrows rose and she scoffed. "What, an' ye walk away leavin' me empty-handed?"

"Fine. I get three questions, then. I pay as you answer."

She examined his face closely, then shrugged resentfully. "Right. May as well start cheating me then."

Colin nodded, amused. She was a quirky little thing. "Why should I pay you for information? What makes you privy to Chantal's business?"

"Prudence Filby, seamstress and dresser to Miss Chantal Marchant, at yer service." She smiled and dipped her head elegantly. Damn, she was graceful. Too bad she was so plain. And common. And had the boy . . . well, he was here for Chantal, anyway.

He dropped one shilling into her outstretched palm. "See, I am a gentleman. I pay my debts." She snorted at that. He went on. "Second question . . ." An image of the boy crossed his mind. He looked so much like his mother, it was hard to see the patrilineal contribution. "Who is Evan's father?"

Wait, that wasn't what he'd meant to ask!

She paled slightly and drew back. "Why'd ye want to know?"

He cleared his throat and forced himself not to redden. "I'm asking the questions here. Who fathered your son?"

Her eyes narrowed. "'E's dead."

"You're a widow, then?" Why couldn't he let this go? Perhaps it was Melody and how she'd been abandoned . . .

She gazed down at her very clean, very elderly boots. "I ain't never been wed."

An awkward silence stretched. "Right. None of my business."

She held out her hand without looking at him. He dropped the shilling into it, feeling like a heel.

"Third question . . . where is Chantal now?"

She shrugged. "Can't tell ye that. But I know who she run off with."

"She ran away with some . . . man?" Colin felt a trickle of jealously. "Who?"

"Bertram Ardmore. Him with the pink weskits."

The trickle became tidal wave. *"Bertie Ardmore?"* Melody shifted in his lap so he dropped his tone to an outraged whisper. "That sniveling pup?"

She shrugged and held out her hand. "Chantal said they looked beau'iful together."

No longer interested in correcting her familiar manner, Colin seethed as he dropped the last shilling in her hand. " 'Purty Bertie.' My God."

The clever miss climbed lightly to her feet and grinned down at him. "Don't take it so 'ard, guv'nor. I 'appen to know Chantal ain't really Purty Bertie's sort. Too womanly, if ye take my meaning."

"I know." He dropped his face into his hands. "That's what makes it so mortifying!" Then he lifted his head. "She must not know. That's wonderful. She'll figure him out and be so disappointed—and there I shall be, on one knee—"

Her gaze turned cold. "Right. Off ye go, then." She turned away to pick up her other bundle. "I've a coach to catch. There's no work for me in Brighton. Evan and me are going to London."

He blinked, remembering what she'd told her son. "You're going to ride all the way to London on top of a mail coach? In the summer? You'll roast!"

Gazing at the poor, small woman before him—a

woman experienced with children—a woman who could help him find Chantal—Colin had a wonderful, marvelous, outstanding idea!

"Melody and I have to keep traveling in order to find Chantal, but we'll end up in London. Why don't you and your son come with us?"